Boris Romanovsky

The One Who Changes the Future

Welcome to the tribe!

Book Three

Magic Dome Books

This book is entirely a work of fiction.
Any correlation with real people or events is
coincidental.

Also by
Boris Romanovsky:

A Student Wants to Live

(a LitRPG Apocalypse Series):

The Onset

The Architects

Sangis

The War of the Clans

Level Run

Blood Emperor

The Goldenblood Heir

(a Portal Progression Fantasy Series):

Books 1-7

Table of Contents:

Chapter 1

An Army of Evolvers

"WANG BOLAI, LET'S GO," I commanded, hovering over the mini-army.

"Squad A, follow me!" the burly man bellowed, marching down the slope.

Twenty-two Evolvers followed him, all clad in protective suits and helmets, resembling motorcyclists. All except one — Selena. She walked just behind Wang Bolai, dressed in a white fabric uniform. The tall woman caught the eyes of the men — having become a Weakling, she had grown more striking and more confident. In a short time, she had earned considerable authority among the army's Evolvers and had already gathered her own team.

One of the squad members stepped closer to Wang Bolai. He was the only one whose helmet left his ears exposed — a Listener.

Ten Evolvers trailed directly behind the leader. Some wielded blades, others clutched canisters, and a few bore massive backpacks on their shoulders.

The rear was held by another group of ten, each armed with a hefty metal crossbow that gleamed menacingly under the invisible sun's rays.

"Hey, monsters!" Wang Bolai shouted. "Come to Daddy!"

But nothing answered him. The squad had covered about two hundred feet, and the tension was mounting. I could physically feel the nerves tightening.

"Dumisa, get ready."

"Yes, Boss!"

The African stepped to the edge of the slope, clad entirely in dark leather — thick trousers, boots, and a jacket.Massive bone gauntlets were protecting his hands. Every piece of his armor had been crafted from the hide of an Alpha — specifically, the Black Monitor. Grandfather had it commissioned specifically for Dumisa, the head of the army's combat unit, which numbered fifty-six soldiers. Among them were Liang and Mayor Hansh. Dumisa's gauntlets were special, too — made from the bones of a Rock Tortoise and reinforced by Jiao. At our level, they were virtually indestructible.

Wang Bolai had reached the three-hundred-foot mark when, at last, the first monsters emerged. From the same crevice where the Slithering Wolves had crawled out last time, brown hedgehogs began scrambling forth, while sparrows shot out into the air.

"Magic Sparrows and Rock Hedgehogs. Air units, forward. Dumisa, hold at one hundred feet. Wang Bolai, fall back. Wall."

My voice was calm, but I knew it would carry perfectly. The wind spread my words across the army.

Wang Bolai's group dropped their backpacks packed with dirt and stones. Three Earth Gravitei immediately set to work, raising a defensive wall.

From the camp, a unit of eleven Air Fielders advanced to join Dumisa's squad, led by Officer Ulysses — my mother's man.

A whistle rang out — crossbowmen loosed bolts at the Magic Sparrows. Not a single shot landed. The nimble monsters had a remarkable ability — they could create illusory copies indistinguishable from the original. There were only six of them, but thanks to their trick, it seemed like dozens of Alphas were descending on Wang Bolai.

My heart clenched at the sight of the wasted bolts. Every tip had been reinforced by Jiao. She had spent all her Neutrinos over the past days preparing for the event. Grandfather and I had to work hard to suppress the Johnsons' complaints.

Dumisa's group halted at the hundred-foot mark as the Earth Gravitei hastily erected walls. According to plan, they needed to fortify a temporary base with a thick wall ten or fifteen feet high, forming a square that would enclose a patch of ground where we would later build a few simple stone structures.

Ulysses kept running to join Wang Bolai's squad.

"Selena, stop the sparrows," I ordered. Unfortunately, I had to use this trump card earlier than I'd planned. But Magic Sparrows were Alphas, nearly on par with Space-Time Gravitei. Underestimating them was dangerous.

Selena tilted her head back and exhaled a cloud of Frost Breath — a pale bluish mist. The sparrows caught in it slowed. The Evolvers intensified their barrage, and the first Alpha fell, its tiny body pierced clean through by a bolt.

At last, Ulysses reached Wang Bolai, and the Air Fielders entered the fray. They manipulated the wind to pinpoint the real sparrows and called out their locations to the crossbowmen.

Less than a minute later, all the sparrows lay dead, their bodies swiftly collected and stashed in satchels.

Another whistle — one of the Rock Hedgehogs launched its quills. Around twenty of the creatures scuttled forward, each capable of firing off their spines — a trait common to all hedgehog-type monsters. On top of that, Rock Hedgehogs could make razor-sharp spikes rise from the ground, forming a palisade of sorts around themselves. But the terrain here was far from ideal for them — the slope was covered in yellow and green vines. I wasn't too worried. If this had been a stone-covered descent, we'd be in real trouble — on a terrain like that the Hedgehogs were lethal.

The Rock Hedgehog's quills struck the wall and lodged into it. The rest followed suit, launching volleys as they crept toward Wang Bolai's squad.

More monsters began appearing. At the five-hundred-feet mark, a swarm of hornets, each the size of a kitten, buzzed to life — no fewer than fifty. A little farther to the right, greenish sheep bleated as they clambered out of a cave one after another. From the fifteen-hundred-feet line, massive pelicans with bucket-like beaks took flight. Then an enormous moss-covered tortoise the size of a tank crawled into view out of nowhere and started lumbering toward the squads.

"Fall back to Dumisa. Burn everything down. Lightning, Magnet, move in," I said, tracking the battlefield.

Wang Bolai and Ulysses issued orders, and the Evolvers began their retreat. Two men with canisters stepped forward, aimed their weapons at the hedgehogs, and fired a reddish spray. A second later, it ignited, bursting into greenish flames that spread across the vines and monsters. The liquid in the canisters turned the fire emerald green, while the smoke from the burning vines thickened into a tarry black haze.

Meanwhile, the Magnet Fielders, led by Miroslava, and the Electricity Fielders, commanded by Grandfather's Evolver Irene, reached Dumisa.

"Lightning, the Hedgehogs are yours," I issued my next command.

Irene led her group of eighteen Evolvers into battle.

I watched everything silently from above, not planning to engage anytime soon. The scene below made one thing clear — it was incredibly difficult to find Evolvers with rare abilities.

Two hundred and thirty-seven people had gathered under my command, not counting the Syndicate's core group. Among those two hundred and thirty-seven, not a single one possessed a remotely rare skill. Eighty-three Atomei, ninety-five Gravitei, and fifty-nine Fielders. The latter were the easiest to organize — I split them into three groups and put reliable leaders in charge. The others posed more of a challenge.

Among the Atomei, twenty-seven were Nuclear, and every single one had the same ability — Fire Manipulation. Not a single one had reached five percent. What was I supposed to do with these wimps?

I had to use one of my secrets. If a Synthesis Atomeus with Matter Fusion combined Earth-sourced propane with the blood of monsters close to Nuclear Atomei, the result was a fascinating fine-particle suspension that burned brilliantly in the Primordial World. Strangely, pure propane lost its properties and wouldn't ignite.

Matter Fusion wasn't a rare skill. Eight in my mini-army had it. Until now, everyone had considered it useless.

Every Fire Manipulator Atomeus received a canister of blood-infused propane, instantly turning them into a potent combat unit — the way those vines twisted under the greenish flames was the perfect testimony to their efficiency. And while the Rock Hedgehogs weren't dying yet, they certainly weren't having a good time — the beasts were rolling, sneezing, and crashing into each other as they scrambled to escape the fire and smoke.

Irene and the Electric Fielders reached the hedgehogs. A few of them pulled aluminum rods from their pouches and hurled them toward the monsters. Sparks arced — lightning cascaded over the area, turning the battlefield into a storm. The Alphas couldn't withstand it. One after another, they died, freezing into petrified husks.

"Miroslava, send in the collectors. Dumisa, prepare for the Frost Wasps. Natsuko, get ready to receive."

A few Fielders with backpacks broke off from the squad. Inside those packs were metal nets, which the Evolvers would use to haul the Rock Hedgehogs back to base.

The Magic Sparrows' bodies had already been gutted. All Liquid Cores were sealed in cubes and sent up to Natsuko. She commanded the largest group, nearly a hundred strong. They were the reserves. When the soldiers below ran out of Neutrinos, they would retreat, and Natsuko would send another Evolver in their place — one who, in all likelihood, had the same abilities.

Or, if reinforcements were needed, the reserves would charge down to help. But hopefully, it wouldn't come to that.

Among the two hundred and thirty-seven people under my command, fifty-seven were Earth Gravitei. Only ten of them had combat skills. Five could manipulate mass, like Dumisa. The other five wielded stone spikes and boulders. The rest were only good for raising walls and digging trenches. That was their job — setting up temporary bases.

Still, the Earth Gravitei were useful. But what the hell was I supposed to do with Gravity Gravitei? Out of thirty-eight, fifteen had the most worthless ability — Jump, like Robert, Selena's nephew. Another twelve had Attraction, and eleven had Repulsion. That was it. In the end, I armed them all with crossbows — at least that way, they served some purpose. In certain situations, those with Attraction and Repulsion could put their abilities to use. As for the Jumpers... well, at least they'd be the first to bail if things went south.

"Vladislav, there's something underneath the Frost Wasps," came the calm voice of Andrei, one of Grandfather's officers.

He stood on a special platform that functioned as a makeshift command post. Five people occupied it, including Xiao Jin, who had no idea why she was even there. Anish was sitting off to the side, watching the descent with a bored expression.

Besides them, there was a guy with Enhanced Vision. Another sharp mind — unlike Xiao Jin, he had given some solid strategic input while we were planning. There was also an Air Fielder relaying reports via wind. And, of course, Andrei himself — a Weakling Evolver and a Nuclear Atomeus with the ability known as Explosion, now part of a new organization — Golden Lions. No prizes for guessing the identity of its founder.

I pulled a spyglass from my pouch and focused

on the Frost Wasps. Nasty creatures. Their stingers shot out freezing beams. If one of those hit your bare hand, you might as well chop it off. On top of that, they radiated cold — a weak frost aura.

It didn't take me long to see what Andrei meant. The vines beneath the wasp swarm bulged, as if something was crawling underneath. Not good. The swarm was sixty feet from the temporary base and closing in fast. Evolvers stood on the freshly built walls, canisters at the ready, prepared to meet the insects with a wave of fire. I had noticed the Frost Wasps after the battle with the Slithering Wolves, so we had already rehearsed how to handle them.

"There are snakes under the swarm! Electricity, they're yours. Hansh, Liang — focus on the snakes. Air, create currents. I'll blow the insects away."

The troops sprang into action. The plan was for all three Fielder squads to combine their power and crush the wasps. Their overlapping fields amplified one another, creating a synergy that would wipe the Frost Wasps out like gnats. The fire wave from the Nuclear Atomei would slow them down first.

But now, the attack wasn't just coming from above — it was coming from below as well. The snakes would slip right through the walls and into the stronghold. If that happened, there would be casualties.

I flew down, hovering over the base. While the army was assembling and preparations were underway, I hadn't been idle. Finally, I'd had time to train and master my control over the wind. Before, I hadn't been using even half my potential.

Currents swirled around me — not ordinary air, but wind saturated with Quarks. I took a deep breath, filling my lungs. Then exhaled.

Whoosh!

A hurricane-force gust erupted from my mouth, slamming into the swarm like a train at full speed, blasting them backward and throwing them into chaos. The attack was so fast the wasps couldn't react. Some crashed into each other, mangling their wings, spiraling helplessly to the ground.

"Boss rocks!" Wang Bolai shouted.

Loud cheering followed.

I just chuckled. If I had used nothing but my Neutrinos, that attack would have drained at least half my reserves. But wind infused with Quarks became malleable and responsive. I could shape it as I pleased. That was why I had asked the Fielders to create currents.

But that wasn't all — I had developed a few new techniques and refined some old ones. The mini-tornado, for example, had become far more dangerous.

There were flashes of lightning, and electric arcs fanned out in front of the base, followed a moment later by a furious hissing. Smoke coiled from beneath the vines as the snakes emerged. One, two... six of them. Each over thirty feet long and as thick as an oak trunk.

I recognized them at once — Devourer Anacondas.

"Metal! Archers!"

Magnet Fielders launched a storm of razor-sharp blades at the snakes. The crossbowmen opened fire, bolts reinforced for extra penetration.

"Air, keep the currents flowing!"

The wasps were already back, and this time, they had learned from their mistake. They spread out, moving in a scattered formation. They'd be much harder to take down now. Behind them, Bile Pelicans loomed, while a herd of Blue Sheep crawled out from their burrows.

"Lightning, Magnet — switch to the wasps. Hansh, Liang, Dumisa — finish off the snakes and back us up."

The Air Fielders had already begun whipping up currents. I stretched out both hands, drawing the wind toward me. It coiled around me, howling. Spirals swirled before my palms. I had used this attack once before, when a beast had me cornered. But afterward, I couldn't replicate it.

Air Bullet.

A soft pop — then the first Frost Wasp exploded.

I took another deep breath. The wind shrieked louder around me.

Pop-pop-pop-pop.

I moved my hands, launching a volley of air bullets that tore through the wasps one after another. Lightning crackled, metal sliced through the air — the Fielders weren't standing idle. Out of the corner of my eye, I saw Hansh lift two anacondas into the air while Liang immobilized a third with Grapple.

Air bullets clapped, lightning arced, and blades whistled. There was a sickening crunch as Dumisa shattered an anaconda's skull. Wang Bo-lai viciously gouged out another's eyes like a rabid cat. Bolts thudded into snake flesh, the wounded beasts writhing as they tried to slither away from the slaughter.

Near the back wall, a group of Evolvers had gathered — those who had exhausted their energy.

And then, suddenly, it was over.

No more Frost Wasps.

For a moment, everything was silent. Then I started barking orders.

"Gather the monster corpses. All the wounded and drained should head uphill to Natsuko. Magnets, retrieve all knives and bolts. Take your positions and get ready — the Bile Pelicans and Blue Sheep will be here in twenty seconds."

I flicked my wrist, using the wind to pull three Frost Wasp corpses toward me. I quickly extracted their Liquid Cores and pressed them to my tattoo, refining the purity of my virtual DNA spiral.

After this battle, I had half my Neutrino count left. I feared it might not suffice.

I tossed the bodies aside, took a deep breath, and braced for the next fight, flexing my fingers, heart pounding with exhilaration.

Something told me this day was far from over.

Chapter 2

Foolishness and Sacrifice

BILE PELICANS AND BLUE SHEEP were Alphas, their abilities akin to those of Synthesis Atomei. The pelicans could spew acid from their throats, sometimes dropping acid bombs stored in their scoop-like beaks.

Blue Sheep looked like ordinary sheep from a distance, aside from their greenish wool. But the resemblance was purely superficial — their mouths were full of sharp teeth, eager to tear into anything soft. Their wool exuded a blue mist — anyone caught in it would feel dizzy, weaken, and start hallucinating. Neither Pelicans nor Sheep could be allowed to get near.

I raised my palms, ready to strike. Magnet Fielders' knives rose into the sky, and the crossbowmen took aim. About twenty pelicans, three or four sheep. That was a lot — we had to go all in.

Pop. Pop. Pop.

As soon as the pelicans entered range, I started firing Air Bullets. But unlike the Frost Wasps, these creatures were tough. I managed to wound a few, but none fatally.

The Fielders and archers attacked as well. Only Miroslava was truly effective — pelicans dropped one after another under her blades.

I conjured a mini-tornado in my palm and compressed it, drawing air from all around. The wind sphere took on an increasingly bright blue hue as it filled with Quarks.

"Air — lift the mist! Fire — get ready below!" I yelled as I hurled the mini-tornado. The pelicans had reached the walls by then, beaks open.

The tiny blue orb shot forward at incredible speed, striking the fastest pelican before expanding and shredding it to pieces — along with six others. For a moment, the tornado looked like a glass ball, crisscrossed with frozen blue threads. Then the threads burst outward, cutting into more pelicans before vanishing.

We heard a loud scream as one of the pelicans drenched an Evolver in acid. The bird died instantly — Liang locked it with Grapple, and Miroslava drove a knife through its skull.

A few pelicans got crushed by Gravity Press and finished off by the archers. Their bolts pierced wings clean through, lodging deep in the monsters' flesh.

The shrieks of beasts, the cries of the wounded, and the whistle of slicing air merged into a frenzied cacophony. Blood soaked the walls and ground of the base. Death was everywhere. Alphas' corpses lay scattered, and the soldiers stood pale-faced and shaken.

Then the wind picked up — the Air Fielders had completed their task. The Blue Sheep had lagged behind the pelicans, arriving ten seconds later. That gave us a massive advantage.

As they neared the base, the Air Fielders swept their mist into the sky, then spun it and hurled it toward the pelicans. The effect was immediate — the mist worked just as well on them.

In my past life, General Xu had used this tactic to wipe out over fifty Alphas without a single casualty. I repeated it, and the results were just as effective — the second wave of pelicans was nearly incapacitated. Some nosedived straight into the ground. Others thrashed wildly, spraying acid in every direction. The rest glided helplessly, making easy targets.

"Fire!" I commanded.

The Nuclear Atomei with canisters sprang into action. Flames erupted — an unnaturally fast-growing wave of fire swept across the ground, consuming seventy percent of the Blue Sheep.

The monsters howled. The air reeked of scorched wool and burning fat.

I slashed forward with my arm. A razor-thin blue streak cut through a pelican's head, slicing off half its skull. The bird dropped like a stone.

Wang Bolai, Dumisa, and Liang charged the sheep, leading a squad of melee fighters — mostly Transformation Atomei with Enhanced Bodies or Partial Transformations.

The pelicans were wiped out almost completely — only a few of the Alphas managed to flee.

"Archers, finish the sheep. Lightning, join in. Magnet and Air — help with the wounded."

I landed on a half-collapsed wall. In front of me, draped over the edge, lay a dead Evolver — his face was melted away by acid.

So far, I counted three dead. The wounded were many more, but the healers would handle them. The priority was keeping morale from collapsing.

Some sheep had escaped, but the rest were dead. The slope was clear — except for one spot. A massive tortoise was slowly crawling toward us. At its pace, it wouldn't reach the base for at least an hour. I figured we'd deal with it long before then.

"Gather the bodies," I projected my voice across the base. "Tonight, we feast on Alpha roast. Trust me, you've never tasted anything like it! Less than an hour, and we've taken down over a hundred Alphas! Rest up. After lunch, we move out."

The tension eased slightly. People got to work, hauling bodies, gutting them, loudly discussing the battle. A few Evolvers discreetly packed the fallen into crates and carried them up to the camp. The fewer knew about the dead, the better.

I spotted a crossbow teetering on the edge of the wall and reached for it.

"Vladislav," Miroslava approached from behind. "Fifteen wounded. Four dead."

Her voice carried sorrow.

"It's pretty damn hard to avoid casualties," I said, staring at the tortoise, trying to recall its name. Its moss-covered shell obscured its markings.

Footsteps. An Evolver rushed toward me.

"Watch out!" Miroslava shouted.

The metal crossbow slammed into my chest, knocking me backward. A black bolt whizzed past my face — just as Andrei's voice rang in my ear.

"The camp is under attack."

*   *   *

Natsuko stood on the command platform, watching the battle unfold, when sudden screams erupted from the camp.

A group of masked figures in green cloaks charged forward from the direction of the forest, bows in hand.

There were twenty of them, or maybe more. They ran straight for the largest tent — the one holding the cubes with Liquid Cores. Firing arrows as they moved, they had already wounded two people.

Natsuko activated her abilities. Her skin turned to metal, her hands extending into long razor-sharp blades.

"Can you handle it?" Andrei asked.

"Yes."

She shot toward the tent at inhuman speed. Two of her squad members — both Earth Gravitei in dense uniforms — rushed up to the group in green and said something to their leader.

Then the group split — half surrounded the tent, and the other half went inside.

The traitors joined those standing guard around the tent.

A sound of shattering glass came from the inside, followed by frenzied screams.

Natsuko landed beside the nearest raider, who flinched at the screams of his comrades. A swift slash, and his head flew off, spraying her with blood.

A portal opened nearby. Anish stepped out, followed by three Golden Lion soldiers. Rigid postures, crossbows in hand — grandpa's guys looked military through and through.

The raiders finally realized their attack had failed. They bolted for the forest. Two Jumped, another used Repulsion to knock down a tent, exposing a pit at its center filled with mangled impaled corpses. Flames flared as some Evolvers' bodies swelled — their Enhanced Bodies activating.

Natsuko lunged at a fleeing raider, aiming to cleave him in half. But the Evolver in green suddenly leaped. Like a frog, he sprang to a nearby tree, kicked off the trunk, and disappeared into the forest.

"Don't kill me, I beg of you!" one of the traitors dropped to his knees — only to crumple dead with a bolt through his temple.

"Three have escaped," one of the Lions reported, wiping his knife. The bodies of the raiders lay strewn around. The soldiers of the Urals Principality worked fast and clean.

Another portal opened ten meters away. Three Evolvers from Rosa Vavilonsky's army dashed out and vanished into the trees.

Natsuko stepped up to the edge of the pit, sniggering as she surveyed the corpses and the shattered crates that had served as bait. She relaxed, deactivating her ability. The danger had passed.

To think those morons had actually thought the Liquid Core cubes were kept in the tent.

They couldn't be blamed, though. The cubes were indeed sent here. But Anish had been tasked with immediately porting them elsewhere.

One of the raiders at the bottom twitched.

He rolled over and raised his arm. His twisted lips murmured something. A silver bolt shot from a mini-crossbow.

There was a flash of lightning as one of the Lions killed him instantly. But the bolt had already been fired.

It struck Natsuko right in the chest.

And vanished inside her.

*   *   *

I jerked my hand up — an Air Bullet tore through the shooter's forehead. A young Asian man, his face contorted with fury.

There was a strange sound behind me. I turned.

Miroslava was sinking to her knees. A crossbow bolt jutted from her stomach.

"Mira!" I lunged, catching her, lifting off, streaking toward the camp.

"You okay?" Miroslava murmured, fingers trembling against my arm. Her eyes fluttered closed. Black liquid seeped from her wound.

I didn't answer. Just flew faster, silently pleading with the wind.

I had to make it in time.

"Natsuko's been hit," Andrei reported grimly. "Requesting authorization to use a Crystallite artifact. The girl might die."

I clenched my teeth. The slope was behind me now, and the tents were in sight.

"Vladislav, give the order. Natsuko's dying. The bolt had hit her heart," Andrei's voice held an edge of irritation.

The Crystal Finger, capable of healing almost any physical wound, was with Nitya. But she could only use it on my direct command.

I landed and burst into Nitya's tent.

Natsuko lay unconscious on a cot, her body convulsing. Her chest was bandaged, but a red stain spread at the center. The bolt had pierced her heart.

"Leader!" Nitya immediately understood. I set Miroslava down on the nearest cot and stepped back. My hands were shaking.

Andrei stormed in, but he stopped short at the sight of Miroslava. We both turned to Nitya, waiting for her verdict.

The artifact had one use left. If Miroslava's wound was fatal, then...

"I can heal her," Nitya exhaled. "But it's serious. The bolt's tip was made from the bone of an Alpha with a Decay Atomeus ability. It shattered inside her. Natsuko is dying. If I start healing her, there's a chance I'll kill her. The artifact is the only option."

"Heal Natsuko," Andrei said immediately.

Nitya looked to me for confirmation.

I gritted my teeth. Decay was unpredictable. It could suddenly intensify and kill Miroslava. I knew this — Adele had suffered because of Decay, and not even Crystallite artifacts could save her.

Miroslava was in mortal danger.

But Natsuko was moments away from death.

"Vladislav," Andrei pressed, irritation creeping into his tone.

"Quiet," I snapped. "Let me think."

Andrei pressed his lips together.

I looked at Natsuko.

Then at Miroslava.

Nitya was already pulling shattered bolt fragments from her stomach.

Blood trickled from Natsuko's mouth. Her body convulsed.

Andrei opened his mouth.

Through clenched teeth, I ordered, "Heal Natsuko. Then move to Miroslava immediately. If the artifact has so much as a drop of energy left — use it."

"Understood."

"Get back to the base," Andrei said coldly. "A general shouldn't leave his army. You need to be there. On the way, tell me how Miroslava got hit."

"Do we know who attacked the camp? How did Natsuko get injured?" I forced down my frustration. Andrei wasn't just the head of the Golden Lions at Xin Shang Peak — he commanded the Urals and Novgorod militaries here. I didn't want to antagonize him.

"Not yet, but we will. The girl's inexperienced. Her own fault for letting herself get hit."

"Keep me updated on the healing." I shot him a glance, then stepped outside.

I rose into the air and streaked toward the slope, relaying my account of the unknown Asian attacker to Andrei as I flew. My mood was foul.

Miroslava had taken the bolt meant for me. She had activated her Magnetic Field, repelling the crossbow into me instead. That shot had been intended for me — but Miroslava had exposed herself.

And now she close to dying.

I had wanted to use the artifact on her. To save her, not Natsuko.

But logic had overruled emotion. I made the right choice.

Miroslava could still be saved.

Natsuko would have died.

Rage flared inside me.

All the frustration of the past weeks boiled together with today's stress, dark and simmering. Something stirred within me. Something that shouldn't exist in a person.

But I had reached my limit.

I landed on the base wall and strode toward the body of the dead Asian. A few Evolvers lingered nearby, speaking in hushed tones. Dumisa and Liang stood over the corpse, grim-faced.

At my approach, everyone stepped back.

I crouched, flipping the body onto its back.

I narrowed my eyes, studying the face.

I knew him.

It was Ono Hanyu — one of Felix Von Belga's henchmen. Almost no one in my past life had known him. But I had studied the Von Belgas thoroughly. They had been my greatest obstacle to a future worth living.

I wouldn't have recognized any other Asian.

But not Ono Hanyu.

He had been one of the handlers.

One of the men who had hunted Adele and me through the forest like animals.

And he had died when Adele had erupted in destructive Decay.

"Dispose of the body," I ordered, rising. "That bastard had attacked me and wounded Miroslava."

"Understood," Dumisa growled.

"Look what we found in his pocket," Liang held out a small, old bronze ring. The insignia on its seal had worn away, but I recognized it instantly.

A Li family ring.

My father had worn one just like it.

I pocketed the find.

Felix had clearly intended to pin this on the Li clan so as to pit me against them.

And he might have succeeded — if he'd sent someone else.

"Miroslava — how is she? And Natsuko? Word is she got injured."

"They'll be fine."

"So, what do we do about the tortoise? Looks strong."

I opened my mouth to answer.

Then Andrei's voice rang in my ear:

"Natsuko is stable. She's sleeping. She'll wake up in a few hours, good as new. Nitya and the others are still with Miroslava. She's burning up."

"As soon as we finish collecting the Liquid Cores and send them up, we'll deal with the tortoise," I told Dumisa and Liang.

"Yes, Boss."

"Got it."

Ono's body was taken away. I was left alone, standing there, watching the tortoise slowly approach our base.

"We interrogated the attackers. One of them gave up the employer. It was August Schmidt from the Order of Steel. The Order of Steel is a group the Millers founded recently. August is considered the deputy leader at Xin Shang Peak."

"August, then," I clenched my fists until my knuckles cracked. "I hear you, Andrei. Thanks."

The tortoise kept moving drawing closer, step by step. Its slow heavy tread sent a dull pulse through my chest. Like the beating of a drum, growing louder with every strike.

"August and Felix," I whispered, barely audible. "You really shouldn't have done this."

CHAPTER 3

DAWN

"GUUUUUUUH!"

The tortoise raised its head and let out a guttural roar.

The sound reverberated through my insides — an unpleasant sensation. It stood a hundred feet from the base, and we were already preparing to strike. I still couldn't tell exactly what kind of monster it was. Most likely a Rock Tortoise. But it could just as easily be a Heavy Tortoise, a Crystal Tortoise, or a Swamp Tortoise.

Crack!

Some of the vines sagged, while others lifted. I narrowed my eyes, sensing something was off.

A crackling noise filled the air, growing louder by the second. The defensive wall was beginning to collapse.

"Everyone off the walls!" I shouted, taking to

the air.

Fat pale-white larvae started crawling out from underground. One of the Evolvers attacked them with fire, accidentally hitting an ally.

"Cancel fire!" I barked. "These are White Larvae, regular beasts! There could be a Gray Larva among them — it's three times the size! Marksmen, Electricity, and Magnet users — move in! Melee fighters, stay back!"

The tortoise let out another deep hum, and the ground in front of it shifted even more.

"It's a Black Tortoise! Dumisa, Wang Bolai, get ready! You can take it down. Anish, get over here and bring three cubes with Alpha Cores."

I sent the last message to Andrei. Then I descended and formed a compressed air sphere in front of me. Under their commanders' orders, the Evolvers had managed to organize a solid defense and were now systematically wiping out the spreading White Larvae. These creatures were weak on their own — the key was to avoid touching them, or they'd pull you inside. But they became a real threat in larger numbers. And the Gray Larvae — Alphas — were dangerous in their own right. They spat acid, moved fast, and if they dragged someone in, it would take mere seconds before nothing but bones remained.

I hurled the air sphere into one of the burrows spewing larvae. I didn't stop to check the results — Andrei had just sent word that Anish had arrived.

The Indian emerged from a portal behind the base, glancing around. A backpack with cubes and gloves lay at his feet. I landed beside him and began increasing my DNA purity using the Cores. The virtual DNA spiral climbed to seven point nine percent. I left my main spiral untouched for now.

"You'll send us to the monster, but you stay here. Keep the portal open — we're coming back that way."

"Got it!"

With my DNA purity raised and my Neutrino count restored, I took off running along the base. Anish followed. I stopped when I spotted the Black Tortoise — White Larvae swarmed around it, and I could make out a few Grays among them. Dumisa and Wang Bolai arrived about thirty seconds later.

"Open a portal near its head. Guys, you need to kill this thing fast. If it retreats into its shell, we're screwed."

"Guuuuuuuh!"

Another roar. Another section of the wall collapsed.

"What the hell is this monster?!"

"I'll explain later. Right now, we move. Anish, begin. I'm going in first. You two, follow after one second."

Anish gave a serious nod, squinting as he gauged the distance, then activated his ability. A black vortex swirled open before us, and I stepped in.

Immediately, I whipped up a storm wind around me, blowing the larvae back. Anish had opened the portal three meters from the tortoise's head, just beside its shell. The Black Tortoise didn't realize it was in danger right away — I was tossing larvae aside, not killing them.

I stepped back as Wang Bolai and Dumisa emerged from the portal. A fraction of a second to assess the situation, and both lunged for the monster's head. The path was clear.

But that wasn't enough — I formed a spherical mini-tornado in my hand.

There was a loud bang.

Dumisa glowed yellow as he shot toward the tortoise's head, bringing his super-heavy fist down. At the same time, Wang Bolai struck as well.

The Black Tortoise's head caved in like a melon. The ground trembled, and something white flickered above the shell. I hurled the mini-tornado at it.

"Fall back through the portal!"

Sweeping my hand, I used the wind to shove back the White Larvae and began my retreat. The mini-tornado expanded above the tortoise's shell, turning the long white appendage into a mess of shredded flesh.

Several Gray Larvae were already crawling out from beneath the tortoise by the time we made it back through the portal.

"What the hell was that?!" Wang Bolai stared at me with wide eyes.

"Its tail. That's how the tortoise was laying White Larvae. The tail had its own brain, which is why it had to be destroyed."

"Holy crap." Wang Bolai shook his head. "The kinds of monsters we run into..."

"Head back to the base — we need to clear out

the remaining Larvae. Soon, the creatures that used to protect the tortoise will show up. Anish, you can return to camp."

"Yes, Boss."

"Got it!"

Alphas, like Weak Evolvers, could be either near the peak of their evolution or far from it. It was like comparing two people — one with ten percent DNA purity and another with five. The difference was massive. It came down to Neutrino or Quark reserves — the more you had, the harder you could hit and the longer you could fight.

The full name of this Black Tortoise was Black Earth Tortoise. There were also Black Swamp Tortoises, Black Frost Tortoises, Black Water Turtles, and several other variants. They all shared two key traits.

The first was their unique ability. The Black Earth Tortoise, for example, could create cracks in the ground.

The second was that every Black Tortoise had a semi-sentient tail that produced worms or larvae.

The fact that this Black Earth Tortoise had been attacking our walls from a hundred feet away showed me it was close to an evolutionary threshold. It had a real chance of becoming a Sentient monster. Normally, creatures like this lived much deeper — five to ten miles down. It seemed the Silkworm hadn't been wasting time and had been gathering a mini-army.

In my past life, this side of the Xin Shang Peak descent had been considered the deadliest for a long time. Even teams of Strong Evolvers couldn't get past the second mile.

And it was all because of the Silkworm.

It had become Sentient and taken over the area completely.

When I returned to the base, most of the larvae had already been wiped out. But no one was letting their guard down — dozens more White Larvae were creeping toward us, along with a handful of Grays.

"Liang, Hansh. Can you handle them?"

"Yes."

"Of course."

"Then they're yours. They're mostly beasts, and you're Weak Evolvers. I'll help with the Alphas. Dumisa, get rid of all the human corpses. Do it discreetly."

The last part was directed at him personally.

The Black Tortoise's unexpected attack, the wall's destruction, and the larvae's appearance had inevitably resulted in casualties. At least fourteen had been killed.

Liang and Hansh went to work — Gravitational Press pinned the larvae down, while Gravity Fists burst them apart like water balloons. Even the Alphas couldn't withstand the blows.

"Listen up! Every fighter who took part in today's fight gets an extra Beast Core! If you were wounded, you get two! In addition to the standard compensation in the contract, the families of the fallen will receive a sum equivalent to three Cores in their preferred currency — including Trigono."

A brief silence followed my words. Then the

Evolvers roared in approval, clapping each other on the shoulders and grinning from ear to ear. Even a single Beast Core in a cube could be sold for tens of thousands of yuans.

"Wang Bolai. Gather a squad and move out. We need the new base built before nightfall."

Forty minutes earlier, after the battle with the Pelicans and the Sheep, I had called for lunch. Everyone had gorged themselves on Alpha roast and rested.

I had originally planned to intercept the Tortoise earlier, but Miroslava and Natsuko's injuries had taken up too much time. I had to adjust my strategy.

I had wanted to kill the monster quickly — without damaging the valuable shell.

And it wasn't just the shell. The lungs of large turtles and tortoises were the key ingredient in a potion known as Turtle Draught.

Drinking it would let a person breathe underwater for several hours.

A useful elixir for certain Evolvers.

The Primordial World was still bathed in daylight, but evening was fast approaching. We needed to secure the new base as soon as possible.

After the announcement about a bonus, people seemed to find a second wind. The work sped up considerably — bodies were cleared away, Cores were extracted and sent up, and the tortoise was butchered and hauled off to the camp. For now, the old man's lab couldn't brew potions, but that was only a matter of time. And once the first elixir was ready, the Syndicate would pull ahead, leaving all the other international organizations far behind. The old man wasn't ready to bring the Lions into the public eye just yet or recruit outsiders. Only those he knew from Earth were allowed into his organization.

Watching Wang Bolai, Selena, and twenty-two Evolvers make their way down the slope, I suddenly thought of my mother. How was she, up in the Great Ridge? It had been nearly twenty days since she left. And Lily? No word on her yet. There were vague rumors, but they sounded ridiculous. Delong had even forwarded me a message from some chat where a guy claimed to have seen a little girl carried in a palanquin by six enormous black apes. Supposedly, this happened on Ape Mountain — the very place my mother was headed. I'd have to ask her to look into it.

"Dumisa, move in behind Wang Bolai," I ordered next.

Everything continued as usual. Wang Bolai had reached the thousandth foot of the descent when his squad ran into monsters. Six Cave Apes burst out of a well-hidden cavern. The scout had picked up on them in advance, so I was able to join the fight.

Cave Apes had thick hides, their main traits being physical strength and an unnaturally high level of defense. But Selena's Frost Breath managed to slow them down, and the marksmen were dispatching them methodically. It took five to six bolts to disable each one. Even when gravely wounded, Cave Apes refused to die.

Once the cloud of Frost Breath dispersed,

Wang Bolai and I finished them off with ease. I ordered a base to be built around the apes' cave, planning to use the monster den as the main facility.

Once construction began, I handed command over to Dumisa and flew back to camp. Before leaving, I warned them I'd be gone for several hours and that they could return to the settlement without me.

I landed outside the tent where Miroslava was being treated and stepped inside.

"How is she?" My eyes locked onto the girl. She lay unconscious on the bed — pale and fragile. Nitya sat beside her, utterly exhausted, while Natsuko sniffled, tears brimming in her eyes.

"Leader!" Nitya flinched.

"Vladislav," Natsuko murmured, her voice trembling as tears spilled down her cheeks. "If I hadn't been injured..."

"How is she?" I repeated, though I could already feel anger rising toward Natsuko. I knew it wasn't her fault. She hadn't been trained to fight, let alone kill. But I still blamed her at some level.

"We removed all the shards, but the wound is refusing to close. We're doing everything we can, but there are too many injured, and everyone needs attention. The healers are overwhelmed. Miroslava won't die, she should..."

The longer Nitya spoke, the quieter her voice became.

"Heal Miroslava. Don't waste Neutrinos on anyone else," I ordered harshly. "Let the other healers handle them."

"But there are only three of us Weaklings, and so many wounded…" Nitya lowered her head.

"Heal Miroslava," I repeated. "Once she's stable, move on to the others."

"Some of them might die if they don't get help in time…"

"I'll increase the bounty for healers. More people will come here in the next day or two. Nitya, I don't care about the rest. Your only priority is Miroslava. Do not spend Neutrinos on anyone else until she's healed. That's an order. Understood?"

Without waiting for an answer, I turned to Natsuko.

"Bring ten Alpha Cores from the Syndicate's share and place them against Miroslava's tattoo. It'll raise her DNA purity past nine percent."

The higher an Evolver's DNA purity, the stronger their health. The new Liquid Cores should help Miroslava recover faster.

"Got it," Natsuko nodded briskly. "I was about to send messengers to Earth to exchange full cubes for empty ones…"

I glanced around the infirmary one last time, lingering on Miroslava before moving to a nearby cot. I picked up a dark knitted blanket, grabbed a pack of bandages from a table, and stepped outside.

Dusk had fallen. The Primordial World was slipping into its most dangerous phase — the night. The time when nowhere was safe. The time when nocturnal monsters, dormant by day, awoke and started hunting.

Shouldering my backpack, I activated my tattoo and entered one of the tents where propane canisters were stored. I draped the blanket over myself, wrapped my face with bandages, then crouched in the corner of the tent. I peeled back a square of sod carefully, revealing a wooden lid covering a small compartment. I lifted it and pulled out a pouch.

Inside, sealed in a special polymer container, lay the Geyser powder taken from the Indian I had killed. Tiny dark granules resembling raw sugar. But with the slightest breeze, each grain would break apart into a myriad of invisible particles. Even the latest gas masks couldn't protect against Geyser. One breath, and a person would drop dead.

Curiously, the powder varied slightly in color from country to country. I'd only seen photographs, but I knew that in Asia, it was pure white, while in Europe, it had a pinkish tint. I had no idea why.

Stowing the pouch, I sealed the compartment and stepped into the translucent pyramid, teleporting to Earth.

Dawn was just beginning to break over Brussels.

The moment I materialized, I shot out of the pyramid and into the sky. Alarms blared, but the military reacted too late — I was already gone, wind roaring around me as I streaked toward the skyscraper.

The pre-dawn night cloaked me like a shroud, and my incredible speed left them no chance of tracking my flight. Had I been in Europica's capital

— New York — this stunt wouldn't have worked. But Brussels was a piece of cake.

I landed on the skyscraper's rooftop and sat at the edge, legs dangling. The last stars twinkled their farewell, while the first rays of the rising sun reached out in greeting.

I squinted a little, savoring the moment. The Primordial World weighed heavily on the mind — it was hard to stay there for too long. With each passing day, the urge to return home, to Earth, grew stronger.

In my past life, I had loved watching the sunrise. It had been my solace — after a month of grueling work, greeting the morning sun felt like a fresh start. In those moments, my mind would clear. I would forget about Adele lying in a coma, about the wars, and about being alone.

Since my rebirth, this was the first time I had watched a sunrise and felt my soul settle, the weight in my chest dissolving, my worries drifting away.

An incredible and indescribable feeling.

Taking a deep breath of the crisp air, I exhaled and pulled my backpack around. I retrieved one of my phones from a side pocket and turned it on.

Once it booted up, I typed out a message:

August Schmidt. Try to keep collateral damage to a minimum. Once the job is done, your wife will be cured.

After sending it, I turned the phone off.

I used to let Oleg handle communications with Muhiddin. But after the old man and I had decided to launch the event, everything changed. Muhiddin became a Weak Atomeus of Decay. I stopped letting Oleg hold onto the phone that connected to Muhiddin. Instead, I kept it in the Primordial World.

I had also ordered the Evolver to change his appearance again and relocate to another city — Nanjing. His task was to make sure a certain felon could break free and bring him into the team. Muhiddin had accepted the mission and hadn't checked in since.

And now, I had given him his next target — August Schmidt.

Muhiddin's wife was already cured.

But he didn't know that yet.

He'd only get the news once the job was done.

Muhiddin wasn't the only one to become a Weakling. With my help, Lilit had also crossed the five percent DNA purity threshold, making her a key member of the Golden Lion on her mountain, where the Lions were now the strongest group. It wasn't just the old man's soldiers anymore — my mother's people had joined as well, along with a few Syndicate members whose abilities were particularly useful.

Peizhi and Kostya had teamed up. The guy had become a Weak Evolver, but Bloody Head was a different story — she'd snapped unexpectedly and outright refused to enter the Primordial World. She wouldn't explain why — just shut everyone down and refused to discuss it. I was assured that she was dealing with waves of depression and that it would pass soon. I didn't interfere.

My sister had joined the Clowns and received

a code name — Blue. I'd only spoken to her once since then. All I heard was excitement and admiration — according to her, every single Clown was an incredible person, especially Black. She'd only seen them once — when the Clowns had gathered to attack a pack of Armored Crushers. Every one of those monsters was an Alpha, and they roamed the descent. Black hadn't even fought — they'd just stood there in silence, watching as the Clowns tore the monsters apart.

The sun had just begun to rise over the horizon when I jumped off the rooftop. The wind caught me, carrying me toward the Brussels Botanical Garden.

My Neutrino gauge had dropped to twelve percent. I'd been using flight too often. But it would be enough to finish what I had planned.

Minutes later, I had the Von Belga estate in sight — a sprawling complex of classical-style buildings. A helipad, a barracks, an underground parking garage, and a vast park bordering the lake that led to the famous Botanical Garden. The Von Belga residence could comfortably house several thousand people, with space to spare.

Hovering above the greenery, I opened my pouch and ran my fingers over the Geyser container.

Half of it would be enough to wipe out the entire Von Belga family, along with all their servants and pets.

As far as I knew, Felix lived in the central building, but he could be anywhere right now. If I wanted to make sure he died, I'd have to turn the entire estate into a graveyard.

People had begun stepping out of the buildings. Some of them would soon be heading into the Primordial World. There was a good chance Solomon's sons would be among them.

I summoned a few grams of Geyser with the wind, let it swirl in my palm.

And then...

I put it away.

Felix would get what was coming to him — but not today.

The black rage inside me had burned away, incinerated by the rays of the rising sun.

Peace and harmony had settled over my soul.

I wouldn't sacrifice so many lives for the sake of one man. My soul hadn't hardened that much. And this world — corrupt as it was — hadn't rotted enough to deserve such a tragedy.

Two little girls came dashing out of the building. One ran ahead, laughing, while the other chased after her, waving her arms in frustration and shouting something.

I watched them for a few seconds, then turned and flew off, heading home.

I had a few hours to finish my business before returning to the Primordial World.

Very soon, I would gain a second virtual DNA spiral.

And then, I'd have far better ways to take Felix down — without needless bloodshed...

Chapter 4

A New Heart

"HAVE YOU READ THE NEWS? Did you hear what's happening on the descent? Damn! The Syndicate's going to get swarmed now. They took down over a hundred Alphas in a single day!"

Adele's excited voice warmed my soul. I lay half-reclined on the roof of her house, smiling. The bandages covering my face kept slipping up or down because of it.

"We're going to have to work even harder," Axel said sternly. "The Brussels branch is falling behind the others. In the United States of Europica, the Syndicate isn't nearly as popular as it is in the Asian Commonwealth or Slavia. The media here keep trying to push their own groups as the strongest — Superhumans, the Lords, Montcreet, Eiffel Tower, the Hird, the Order of Steel, and even the White Squadron founded by our father."

"But they're all weaker than the Syndicate and the Clowns," Adele said stubbornly.

"I agree. From what I heard, when the army base was attacked by dozens of Frost Wasps, Vladislav blew them away like dust."

"And he was sniping Alphas with invisible bullets," Adele added. "I wish I could join them."

I kept smiling, watching the clouds drift by. Lying here and eavesdropping wasn't exactly noble, but... I'd almost wiped out a couple hundred people earlier. My conscience could forgive a small transgression.

"Sounds like you've got a crush, sister."

I froze at Axel's words.

"A crush? I don't think so. I admire him as a person. That's not love. I'm even angry at him."

"Why?"

"He's managed to heal Wang Bolai when even Weak Evolvers couldn't save him. And if the rumors are true, Natsuko was wounded in the heart, and Vladislav saved her, too. So why won't he heal you? Your injuries aren't even that serious—"

"Sis..."

"No, really! We've been saving up to hire a Weak Evolver, and we need at least another six months, maybe more. But Vladislav could send one to you at any time! And you said he liked me. He probably sensed my ability, and that's why he acted the way he did. He needs me as a fighter."

"You're wrong," Axel replied coolly. "You don't understand that we're only able to save money because of him. That we live in this house because of him. That you became an Evolver because of him. That we don't have to hide from our family, that you can live a normal life. Think back to our original plan. How much hardship would we have gone through?"

"You're right... I'm sorry. I get it, I really do, but there's just this feeling inside. This hunger for more and more. But it's not like I'd ever tell him I'm unhappy. I'm confiding in you, the closest person in my life. Or am I not even allowed to tell you what's on my mind?"

I lay on the rooftop, staring at the slow-moving clouds.

The world had lost its color, dulled to shades of gray.

I wasn't thinking about anything. But this wasn't the kind of emptiness that felt light, that made worries fade away. No. This was a crushing apathy.

I didn't want to move. I just wanted to lie there, motionless.

Axel and Adele's conversation faded into background noise, the meaning of their words lost on me.

Eventually, they left. But I remained where I was.

"Mrrrrow."

I flinched and turned my head.

A black cat was creeping toward me, a white patch on its forehead — probably an old scar. It leaped up and swiped at the bandages on my face. Instinctively, I pushed it back with the wind.

The cat tumbled toward the edge of the roof but landed gracefully on all fours, arching its back and hissing at me.

"My apologies," I muttered, sitting up. Then, with effort, I stood.

It felt as though I had no energy left in me. My legs barely obeyed.

The wind carried me upward, and I turned toward the central square, flying in that direction.

Still no thoughts.

From a distance, I saw helicopters hovering over the pyramid. That usually only happened in Brussels when Evolvers had escaped or when the Von Belgas were about to enter the pyramid. Deciding to wait, I landed in the park just before the square, by a small round fountain at the center of an alley.

Normally, soldiers patrolled this area, but they'd probably been pulled toward the pyramid.

I removed my gloves and dipped my hands into the water.

Only then did I realize I wasn't alone.

A woman sat on the fountain's edge — about thirty years old, dressed entirely in black. A delicate black boater hat perched atop her head, a black parasol resting on her lap.

For a few seconds, we simply looked at each other.

"Are you unwell?" she asked in an unexpectedly husky voice — it sounded like it had been ruined by years of smoking.

"No," I admitted.

"Did you lose someone?"

"I've lost my heart."

"But you're alive. That means the loss wasn't

critical.”

“It was all an illusion. I lost her a long time ago.”

I hadn’t even noticed the tears rolling down my face.

“I lost her when I came back. I left her there, in the future. Left her alone against the entire world.”

“She’s alive?”

“No... Yes. No. I don’t know.”

“But you’re alive. Do you have people you care about? People you want to protect?”

Images flashed through my mind — my mother, the old man, Meili, Miroslava, the others from the Syndicate.

“Yes.”

“Then live for them, if you can’t live for yourself. Find a new heart.”

I studied her more closely. Not particularly beautiful, but magnetic. Mysterious.

Gray eyes. Dark hair, neatly styled.

A tattoo of a spider on the left side of her neck — large, almost lifelike.

A silver ring on her finger, set with a black diamond. She kept glancing at it, stroking it. And in those moments, a flicker of uncertainty passed through her eyes.

“And you?” I asked. “Who are you? What’s troubling you?”

She looked sad. Almost heartbroken.

“I have no one. I’m alone in this world. But sometimes, I feel like I lost someone. And I’m searching for them. Searching to bring them back.

Sounds strange, doesn't it?"

"No stranger than my confession."

"That's true. How could you have left someone in the future?"

"It's a metaphor," I muttered, realizing I'd said too much.

"And what does it mean?"

"Does it matter? What are you doing here?"

"I wanted to see the Von Belgas enter the pyramid."

"Why?"

"Does it matter?" She gave a small smile.

She stepped off the fountain's edge, raising her right hand behind her, the parasol tilted back, her left hand resting lightly against her chest as she gave a graceful bow.

"It was a pleasure meeting you, stranger in a blanket. Thank you for easing my boredom. And fix your bandages — they've slipped a little."

"What's your name?" I asked, still seated.

"I have many names. But for you, I'll create a special one, just for you. Hmm... Let's go with Charlotte. Yes, remember me as Charlotte."

She walked toward the park's exit, where a sleek, black, tinted car had silently pulled up.

I watched her go.

She hadn't even asked for my name.

Adjusting my bandages, I realized something.

I felt lighter.

Today, I had lost Adele. Forever.

I had left her behind in that future, in the recovery capsule. I had fled like a coward, abandoning the woman I loved.

And I would never get her back.

Everything else was an illusion.

The Adele in this timeline was a different person. She hadn't endured the same trials, hadn't suffered the same hardships.

And I was different, too.

No longer the young man who had longed for love and understanding, who had found a kindred spirit in Adele. We would never again go through what we had survived together in the Pit of Bo. I had begun to realize it the moment I first saw her again. But I hadn't wanted to admit it. That conversation... There was nothing special about it. Just ordinary sibling concern.

Adele had every right to be upset with me. She had no idea that in my past life, several Weak Evolvers had examined her brother and found him beyond saving. And I couldn't have used a Crystallite artifact on him.

The old man wouldn't have understood.

That wasn't why he had risked his life boarding the Crystallite ship.

Even so, Adele and Axel's conversation was the final straw, the one that broke the camel's back.

I finally understood how wrong I'd been in my thinking.

The Adele from my past life and the Adele from this one were not the same person.

No matter what the old man said, people could change. They weren't carved from stone, destined to remain the same forever.

Adele would never become the woman I had loved. And I would never be the man she had once fallen for in that past life.

This had been meaningless from the very start.

But... should I give up? Run away again?

Charlotte had told me to find a new heart.

But I didn't need to search for one — I had already found it long ago.

Our fates were entwined. No matter who we became, Adele and I would always be connected. That bond could never be severed.

As the tinted car drove off, carrying the enigmatic woman away, I pulled my phone from my backpack and called Oleg.

I told him to send a Weak Evolver to Axel to examine his legs.

Then I put the phone away, took to the sky, and flew toward the pyramid.

It was time to return to the Primordial World.

*　*　*

I arrived late at night and immediately set out for Hansh's settlement. The journey wasn't quick — I had to push myself to make it by morning. Twice, I was attacked by winged Alphas. Dozens of times, by beasts.

I took the Liquid Alpha Cores, using them to refine my virtual DNA, but I didn't have time to harvest the beasts. Three times, I had to stop and rest when my Neutrino count ran too low. But eventually, I made it to the settlement.

Surprisingly, the place was buzzing with activity. Even this early in the morning, dozens of people scurried through the streets, and from the marketplace came the shouts of heated bargaining.

I headed for the infirmary first — it was a long wooden building, painted green for some reason. All the wounded had been transferred here under heavy guard after yesterday's battle.

Outside, three healers stood smoking and chatting. I landed beside them and asked,

"Where's Miroslava?"

"She's in there," the shortest of the three answered first, gesturing to the adjacent building. "She's with Nitya — no one else is allowed in."

The other two just stared at me, mouths slightly open, as if they'd seen a ghost.

"Thanks," I nodded to the man and headed toward the building.

On the way, I nearly bumped into three men deep in discussion — about me.

"I'm telling you, Delta could clear the entire descent alone, but he's running this event to train his people! If they let us fight, we'll not only make a fortune but gain experience!"

"Maybe we should set up our own raid?"

"Who the hell do you think you are? You'd be going in alone..."

The three wandered off, but only now did I fully grasp why the settlement was so lively. People were pouring in, eager to join our army. When we first announced we were clearing two miles of the descent, the reaction had been skeptical. People came, but not in droves.

Forty percent of our forces were Indians, drawn in by the promise that their idol would be part of the raid. Many Evolvers were Syndicate fans — or admirers of its key figures.

Dumisa, the First Evolver.

Miroslava, the Magnetic Princess.

Natsuko, the Steel Kunoichi.

Maybe Liang had his fans, too, but I hadn't seen them.

Now, after just one day, the whole world was buzzing about the Syndicate's raid and its incredible success. The exact number of Alpha kills hadn't been disclosed yet, but it was over a hundred.

In a single day.

Two guards stood at the building's entrance. At the sight of me, they bowed and stepped aside. Inside was a clean room. A table, a chair, and two beds — nothing more. On one bed, Nitya lay fast asleep from exhaustion. On the other, Miroslava. Hansh must have arranged this space for them. I'd have to thank him.

I walked up to Miroslava. She looked as if she were just sleeping. If not for her deathly pale skin and near-white lips, I might have thought she was. She looked like a wax doll, sculpted by a master — delicate, exquisite, almost unreal.

I touched her forehead — cold and clammy. I stroked her hair.

Her lips parted slightly, whispering a silent word. I adjusted her blanket and left. I regretted that I could read lips so well.

Because I had read my name upon hers.

* * *

"One hundred and twelve Alphas were killed. You took six Cores, ten went to Miroslava. Seventy were sent to Earth through messengers, the rest are in the secure storage," Natsuko reported.

She was fully recovered now, brimming with energy.

But there was a stiffness in her movements — remnants of guilt for having had a rare Crystallite artifact used on her.

I sat in a chair inside the mayor's house, listening. With me were Dumisa, Liang, and Wang Bolai, representing the Syndicate. Andrei, Irene, and Ulysses represented the old man and my mother.

"We've received over a thousand requests. People want to join the raid. Two hundred and eighty of them are ready to deploy today. They've agreed to all terms and are prepared to sign contracts."

"What terms?" I asked.

The first wave of participants had gotten the best deals. An Evolver could earn between twenty and a hundred thousand yuan per day, depending on how long they stayed in the descent. Some had spent the whole day in the camp on standby and still walked away with a hefty sum. In addition to money, each Evolver could receive one to three empty helium-3 cubes per day. But these were regular Evolvers with weak abilities — Jump, Fire Manipulation, and so on.

Fielders and healers had higher wages — they

were paid in Beast Cores and cubes. Right now, unless you were part of the military or a major house, getting helium-3 — let alone specialized cubes — was impossible.

The best contracts went to Weak Evolvers and commanders. We promised them Alpha Cores on top of money and cubes.

"I've lowered the price. The minimum is now ten thousand yuan and one empty helium-3 cube. I didn't cut rates for the healers."

I nodded in approval.

"I've also lowered the Weak Evolvers' rate slightly — three hundred thousand, one cube with a Liquid Alpha Core, and three empty cubes. But some want more."

"How many Weak Evolvers will join us today?"

"If all goes smoothly, six. One is a healer. The rest have standard abilities. Two more require your attention — they have rare abilities and are asking for more. If you approve their terms, it'll be eight Weak Evolvers. Here — this is what they want."

Natsuko handed me a piece of paper.

I skimmed the text.

Weak Evolver Hu Xuan Jian — Atomeus of Synthesis. Abilities: Oil and Dispersion. Requests 300,000 yuan per day and 15 Alpha Cores for the entire raid, however long it lasts. Needs five up front to improve himself and maximize his abilities.

Weak Evolver Theodor Kellerman — Graviteus of Space-Time. Abilities: Blink and Long Blink. Requests 500,000 yuan and five Alpha Cores per day.

"Accept Hu Xuan Jian. Reject Theodor. If he

agrees to the standard contract, he can join. His ability is useful for tossing propane bombs, nothing more."

"We're really going to give Hu Xuan Jian fifteen Alpha Cores?" Natsuko asked skeptically. "Isn't that too much?"

"Oil and Dispersion... No, it's not. I want to talk to him."

"Understood. I'll summon him after the meeting. We have a problem with Jiao. She can't supply as many bolt tips anymore — the Johnsons are pressuring her. You know how bad things are for the Lunarians right now. Every day, fewer and fewer of them want to enter the Primordial World."

I nodded.

For the first two days after the Moon and Mars declared their independence, nothing happened. Then, one by one, countries announced that they did not recognize the secession of the satellite and the Red Planet. Yet at the same time they all signed contracts to purchase helium-3.

But on the third day, things took a terrifying turn. Unknown factions began ruthlessly exterminating Lunarians and Martians in the Primordial World. It happened on nearly every mountain.

By the sixth day, the Moon had declared a complete severance of ties with the United States of Europica and the Asian Commonwealth. But that only made things worse — the massacres intensified. Previously, only a handful of families from the Asian Commonwealth had conspired with the Europicans. But after the Moon cut off all contact with the entire nation, many other families joined in the extermination.

Grandfather insisted that it would be wrong to blame only those two states. The entire Earth had suffered from the Moon's and Mars's decision, and there were enough outraged parties in every country. All of them eagerly took part in the slaughter of the Lunarians. Where once it had been normal to see a Lunarian or Martian fighting alongside an Earthborn team, now such instances had almost vanished. No one wanted to become a target because of their teammate. Of course, the Moon and Mars fought back. But they were too few, and they were losing. People from the satellite and the Red Planet had started hiding — using makeup, covering their faces, dressing in loose robes with hoods.

I didn't like how this was unfolding. In just a few days, the death toll among Evolvers had nearly doubled. Now, people weren't only being killed by monsters — they were being slaughtered by other humans. But there was nothing I could do. The Moon and Mars had fully understood the ramifications of their choice.

"We can equip ten more archers right now," one of my officers reported. "Thanks to the durability of the arrowheads, they hardly deform on impact, so we reuse them. If we start crafting bolts with Alpha-class tips, we could increase that number to fifty."

"Not yet," I shook my head. "Anything else?"

"No. We're ready to move. By the end of the day, our forces should reach five hundred strong. We might even push as far as the first mile and establish a base there."

"Excellent. Then let's begin."

I stepped outside and looked up at the sky, strategizing for the coming battles. With Oil and Dispersion, our tactical flexibility would increase dramatically. There was a high chance we would indeed push beyond the first mile by nightfall.

Chapter 5

The Nest

I STOOD AT THE EDGE of the descent, staring into the forest where the monster I needed lived, when a short man approached me.

"Sir, you wanted to see me?" He looked at me warily, tilting his head up and rubbing his hands together.

"Hu Xuan Jian?" I turned toward him.

The guy was short — about five foot three. Thin, hunched, with a complexion that left a lot to be desired. For some reason, I immediately pictured a block of cheese. The short dark hair on top looked like a rind. And his face was just like a hole-riddled cross-section. I even imagined I caught the scent of cheese — or was that just my imagination?

"Yes, sir." Hu Xuan Jian bowed. "It is an honor to meet you!"

"Ahem. Right. You have Oil and Dispersion, correct?"

"Of course, I would never lie to such a respected man, sir."

"Good. Stay on standby and wait for my orders."

"As you wish, sir." Hu Xuan Jian bowed again and left.

I watched him go with some doubt.

Was my subconscious trying to tell me I was craving cheese? It had been a while since I'd had any.

"We're ready," Natsuko approached, scowling, a folder in hand. "It's a mess. Too many people, hard to keep track of them all. I assigned 'veterans' from the first day of the raid as commanders, but the still screw up a lot..."

"We're setting up camp on the descent this time," I cut her off. "The base the Earth Gravitei built yesterday is already in ruins. No idea what kind of monsters tore through it, but it's a wreck."

"No big deal. They'll rebuild it."

"Yeah, I know," Natsuko turned to leave, but paused when I called after her. "Huh? Something else?"

"Don't you think Hu Xuan Jian looks like cheese?"

"What?" Natsuko stared at me blankly. "Cheese?"

"Never mind. You can go."

She gave me a strange look before walking off.

I turned my attention back to the descent. Natsuko and the old man's people were handling all the organizational work. I had no desire to get involved. Even in my past life, my subordinates had disliked me for this — I only ever focused on what personally interested me. Everything else — the mundane and tedious — I delegated.

Nothing had changed since then.

While everyone else was busy, I kept thinking about my meeting with Charlotte. It felt like I knew her, even though I was certain that I didn't. The thought kept slipping away like a mischievous child reaching for me only to giggle and scamper off the moment I tried to touch their hands — before teasingly coming close again, fingers wiggling playfully...

Something familiar lurked at the edge of my consciousness. Who was Charlotte? The most obvious answer was that I had somehow recognized her tattoo. But no matter how hard I tried, I couldn't recall anyone with a similar mark.

"Follow me!" Wang Bolai's voice rang out to my right.

He jogged ahead, leading a squad of fifty. All of them, except Selena, wore specialized suits that resembled motorcycle gear.

"Sir," Hu Xuan Jian approached me again. "I thought it was important to tell you more about my abilities."

I stared at him silently. The longer I looked, the more his head reminded me of cheese. My hand nearly reached out to poke his face before I caught myself, folding my arms behind my back, inwardly embarrassed.

"My ability is abdominal," Hu Xuan Jian continued, oblivious. "The oil forms in my stomach, and I expel it through my mouth. Once it leaves my mouth, I can exert partial control over it. With Dispersion, I segment the liquid and spread it over a large area — anywhere between a hundred and two hundred meters. If I burn all my Neutrinos, I can cover up to five hundred, but recovery would take a long time. Once the oil is on the ground, I can slightly alter its density. I call it partial coagulation — thicker in some spots, thinner in others. But every time I activate my ability, I get a strong urge to drink alcohol. The taste it leaves on my tongue... it's awful. That's why I always carry a flask of baijiu. You don't mind, do you? It's really necessary — if I don't drink, I start feeling nauseous. Sir, are you listening?"

"Yes, of course," I forced myself to look away, trying to recall what he had just said. "If you can follow my orders, I don't care what you drink."

"Oh, don't worry about that," Hu Xuan Jian brightened. "Ever since I became a Weakling, even a barrel of baijiu won't knock me out. I ran a few tests. So, I'll be off then?"

"Sure."

The strange Evolver left, and I took to the sky. I needed to cover Wang Bolai and his team — just in case they were attacked on the way to the base, although I doubted it. Only a day had passed since we'd cleared the area. It would be a while before Alphas resettled here.

As expected, Wang Bolai's squad made it to the two-hundred-and-fiftieth meter without issue. The remains of the old base lay scattered across the ground.

"Dumisa, move in," I commanded. "Natsuko, be ready."

This time, Dumisa's group had over two hundred people. Ten Evolvers per squad, five squads per platoon. Each with its own commander. But most of the army had no military experience, so mistakes were frequent.

"Natsuko, Irene, Ulysses, and Arkhip. Your turn," I ordered as Dumisa reached the base.

The Earth Gravitei immediately got to work rebuilding the base and preparing a new camp.

Irene, Ulysses, and Arkhip were Fielder commanders, military-trained, and Weak Evolvers. Arkhip had replaced Miroslava due to her injury. But even if she'd had recovered by now, she would have had to step down, anyway. Her unit had grown from twenty-three Fielders to fifty-two. She wouldn't have been able to manage a force that size.

It took about an hour to finish preparations. A tent camp sprawled at the thousand-foot-mark where the Cave Apes had once lived. Smoke rose from the center as Alpha meat was cooked. The head chef was a stout Arab who ran a restaurant back on Earth. Wang Bolai was now practically glued to him, bombarding him with questions. Anish had lost his apprentice, but he wasn't the least bit upset. He knew full well that his cooking had only ever tasted good because of the ingredients, not his skill. And Wang Bolai knew it, too — he didn't ask Anish any questions. He just ate.

The Arab, however, was drowning in questions.

After lunch — pilaf made with Blue Sheep meat — Wang Bolai stepped forward. Full and satisfied, he hummed a tune as he strode fearlessly down the descent.

Dumisa's squad prepared to follow, raising a dreadful racket as they did. Squad leaders yelled at their men. Platoon leaders yelled at everyone. And Dumisa just stood there, looking very patient and wisely staying out of it. Beside him, I spotted Liang and Mayor Hansh, engaged in quiet discussion.

"Miroslava woke up," Andrei's voice came through.

He said nothing more, but it was enough. I exhaled in relief. By then, Wang Bolai had reached the fifteen-hundred-foot mark. Only then did the monsters begin to appear. Lone creatures crawled out of burrows and caves, then fled. A bear. Two lynxes. A massive horse with a bone mane. Sensing danger, they all bolted.

"Wang Bolai, slow down," I ordered, eyeing the ravine at the one-mile mark.

Beetles were crawling out in numbers. Some took flight. Others scuttled across the ground. Lightning Rhinoceros Beetles, Metal Stag Beetles, Wood Borer Beetles, Predatory Longhorns, Laser Fireflies, Venomous Darklings, Wind Beetles, and more. It wasn't just Alphas — hundreds of beasts spilled from the ravine alongside them.

I tensed. This was a Nest. A place where monsters of various species congregated. Normally, Nests only appeared below the ten-mile mark —

and were controlled by Sentient monsters.

"Wang Bolai, fall back. Dumisa, prepare for defense. Hu Xuan Jian, burn all your Neutrino and coat the area in oil. We've run into a Beetle Nest. There are over a thousand of them — two hundred Alphas, the rest beasts. Listen closely, I'll break down their strengths and weaknesses. We have five minutes."

The camp burst into motion. Wang Bolai and his squad retreated at full speed. Natsuko dropped the backpack from her shoulder without a word. I grabbed it and flew off to the side, pulling out the Alpha Cores one by one and pressing them to my tattoo.

By the time I opened the eighth cube, the distant sound of crossbows firing rang out. It had begun. I set the last cube aside and quickly checked my status:

Name: Vladislav Li-Vavilonsky
Race: Weak Human
DNA Purity: 9.8%
Evolutionary Branch: Atomeus
Base Skill: Complete Transformation (absolute)
First Virtual DNA Spiral: Bai Hu, Lord of the Wind
Bai Hu's DNA Purity: 8.4%
Second Virtual DNA Spiral: -
Neutrino Count: 97%

I exhaled and took to the sky. The first thing I had done was increase the purity of my primary DNA spiral — the one responsible for my overall

Neutrino reserves. Bai Hu's DNA purity reduced the amount of Neutrino I burned when using wind. It also heightened my sensitivity to airflow and increased my total Neutrino pool, albeit only slightly — just like my primary spiral. A useful upgrade.

The oil was working exactly as planned — dozens of beetles slipped, crashed into each other, and tumbled down. Meanwhile, marksmen on the walls fired bolt after bolt, Fielders of Electricity unleashed lightning, and Fielders of Magnetism hurled razor-sharp blades. Liang was going all in with his Gravity Fists, while Hansh activated Gravity Nullification on command. Selena stood ready with her Frost Breath.

The flying monsters had arrived late. Among the beetles, only the Alphas could take to the air — and not all of them. Most were Wind Beetles, grotesque creatures that spewed high-pressure air blasts capable of puncturing steel. Flitting among them were Laser Fireflies — a species of insects ranking among the deadliest. Their ability was simple, but that only made it more lethal — they fired lasers.

"Air!" I shouted.

The Fielders of Air immediately began generating turbulence, slowing the beetles down. A flash of light — one of the Fireflies fired at me. But my beast instincts kicked in, and I dodged in time. With a flick of my hand, I seized control of the wind currents the Fielders had created. A powerful gust sent a wave of beetles spiraling away.

I bared my teeth, snarling. I had to hurry. I had to make it in time.

Before now, I had avoided using transformation too obviously — I didn't want my ability to be too exposed. But now, I wasn't holding back — my virtual and real DNA spirals began fusing at an accelerated rate. My control over the wind sharpened with every passing moment.

Air Bullets!

I swung my arm, conjuring a dozen high-pressure wind projectiles. They couldn't pierce exoskeletons, but they shredded beetle wings with ease. One by one, the monsters plummeted into the mass of their writhing, oil-soaked kin.

I struck again, summoning a slicing storm. More beetles rained down.

Those I had blown away before returned, launching a barrage — air jets, laser beams, jets of green toxic fluid, bone spines. Every species had its own method of attack, forcing me to dodge an unpredictable array of projectiles.

Mini-Tornado! Vortex, air bullets, wind blades...

I killed few, but I dropped many of them to the ground. From below came screams of pain, Dumisa's clipped commands relayed through a Fielder of Air, and the crunching of shattered exoskeletons. The dying shrieks of beetles filled the air.

"Fire!" Dumisa roared.

And the battlefield went up in flames as if someone had struck a match. The conflagration started consuming beetles and scorching those still on the walls. The oil burned hot and fast, and some of it had splattered onto the fortifications.

I barely avoided getting caught in the blaze myself.

"I'll kill their leader! Hold out a little longer!" I shouted, amplifying my voice.

Thick black smoke engulfed the entire base, rolling upward in dense waves. The walls burned. People abandoned them, shielding their faces with cloth. The noise was deafening — wounded men howling in pain, commanders screaming orders, beetles shrieking, chittering, and cracking apart. The surviving monsters still pressed the attack, and the Evolvers couldn't mount a proper defense. It was an untrained and hastily assembled army — so it was hardly a surprise that it had crumbled under the first serious assault. The soldiers panicked and tried to flee, the commanders failed to rein them in, and the beetles kept killing.

I surged toward the Nest, crushing an Air Beetle with my fist along the way. I forced my way through the acrid, choking smoke, climbing higher. I had to make it. There was no other option.

The moment I burst free of the fumes, I saw it — a horror unfolding before my eyes. Thousands of beetles swarmed toward the base, blanketing hundreds of feet of the descent in a living tide. Some advanced in tight columns, others moved in groups, a few traveled alone.

There were far fewer of them in the air — barely a hundred. Not surprising. Beetles ruled the earth, not the sky. I climbed even higher, winds swirling around me as I flew past them. They had locked onto the base and ignored everything else.

From above, the ravine looked like a gaping black wound riddled with holes. At least eighty percent of the monsters on the descent lived underground — in caves and tunnels. And the beetles were no exception.

I descended toward the ravine, where the swarm continued to pour out. A Nest like this didn't form on its own — monsters would just kill each other without a leader. There had to be one. Either a Sentient monster lurked within, or an Alpha had risen to command — one with a developing brain and astonishing abilities. For example, it could be a White Silkworm, Lord of Monsters — a creature capable of controlling hundreds of monsters with its Mental Threads. It was beast so intelligent that, even as an Alpha, it surpassed many Sentient creatures.

"So that's where you're hiding," I muttered, descending toward a hole in the ravine wall. The floor and walls of the tunnel were coated in white silk.

The White Silkworm couldn't stay hidden in its lair forever. It frequently emerged — to impose its will upon creatures beyond beetles, such as the Black Tortoise or Slippery Wolves, and to search for a mate. Silkworm monsters were insatiable breeders — notoriously lustful. I wouldn't be surprised if I found an entire harem of them inside.

Moreover, the White Silkworm couldn't live long without light. Its den wouldn't be too deep. If things went south, I'd have enough strength to escape. The ideal habitat for a White Silkworm was the forest.

Had I come too early?

The One Who Changes the Future

In my past life, this Nest hadn't existed, and the Lord of Monsters had lived in the forest. But the eastern descent hadn't been attacked until a year after the Eclipse. Anything could have happened in that time.

I shot into the tunnel — and immediately came face to face with two Magnetic Stag Beetles. They lay on their bellies, rubbing against each other lazily. The moment they saw me, they sprang up. I barely dodged as metal spheres shot from their shells, the air ringing with steel. For all its intelligence, the White Silkworm wasn't smart enough. Magnetic Stag Beetles needed open space to be truly effective. In the tunnel, they only got in each other's way. And that was exactly what happened — they accidentally struck one another.

I ignored them, hurtling deeper at breakneck speed.

The farther I flew, the more silk coated the walls. I passed more Alphas but wasted no time on them. My pathetic army could be wiped out at any moment. And with it — Dumisa, Wang Bolai, Natsuko, Liang, and Anish. Although the Indian just might be able to escape through a portal.

I shot into a vast cavern and came to an abrupt halt. Silk. White everywhere. At the far end, against the wall, lay a massive white cocoon. And resting upon it, regal and motionless, was the White Silkworm. Seven feet long and covered in fur.

Its brilliant blue eyes locked onto me.

A buzzing sound rose from all around. I swallowed hard, realizing where I had ended up. There were more than twenty Alphas in this cave — Protector Beetles, considered some of the toughest Alphas in the Primordial World, as well as deadly Devil's Ladybugs, bizarre and incredibly dangerous monsters, and, most importantly, Jumping Beetles, creatures closely related to the Space-Time Gravitei. They were black as night, and their blade-like legs gleamed. They were small, barely bigger than kittens. But despite their size, they were unbelievably deadly.

For a few moments, I stared at the Silkworm, and the Silkworm stared back at me. Its face betrayed nothing, but for some reason, I got the feeling the monster was surprised.

There was a loud screeching sound.

Behind me, the Beetles that had fallen behind in the tunnel burst into the cave, and I sprang into action, propelling myself upward, toward the ceiling. Beams of light pierced through small openings, making the silk-covered cavern gleam.

Aerial Tornado!

I poured nearly every Neutrino I had into it, leaving myself just three percent to stay airborne. A whirlwind of immense power spiraled around me. Surrounded by the raging wind, I shot upward like an arrow. But I reacted too late — four Jumping Beetles teleported right to me, lashing out with their bladed legs.

The wind knocked them back, but two of them still managed to strike me. One sliced off my right foot. The other slashed across my left calf, cutting through skin and muscle as effortlessly as a butcher slicing tender veal.

There was a loud bang as the collapsing ceiling thundered in sync with the explosion of pain. I groaned as I burst out into the open air. Blood gushed from the stump and the gaping wound on my calf. My severed foot, still in its ruined boot, tumbled past, caught in the wind. I reacted on pure instinct — lunging forward, I stretched out my arm and caught the boot.

That action saved my life. A split second later, three Jumping Beetles materialized right where I had been and slashed the air to ribbons. The storm winds swept them away like blades of grass in a hurricane. But inside, I went cold — if I had still been there, they would have struck my head.

Clutching my severed limb tightly, I bolted toward the mountain's summit. In the distance, I saw smoke rising from our base, while the Beetles, panicked, scrambled over each other in a desperate rush back to the Nest. No wonder — someone had attacked their leader. The moment I'd stormed the cave, the White Silkworm must have given the order to retreat. That was exactly why I had to act fast.

Was it just my imagination, or did I hear hissing? Without slowing down, I turned — and saw them. Snakes. A whole sea of them, slithering out from the forest two miles away. All colors, all sizes. All of them heading straight for the Nest.

"Another freaking Nest," I muttered in disbelief.

What kind of descent was this?!

Chapter 6

The Three Armies

KILL. KILL. KILL.

The White Silkworm lay atop its cocoon, wings spread wide. From them radiated tens of thousands of barely visible translucent blue threads. Each one tethered the White Silkworm to an Alpha — Beetle, Snake, Monkey, Tortoise. Each of them was a soldier in its vast army.

Kill. Kill. Kill.

The White Silkworm wanted nothing more than to destroy the biped that had so brazenly trespassed into its inner sanctum. But alongside its fury, there was a lurking fear. The biped smelled dangerous. Lethal.

Fear and rage almost made the White Silkworm lose sight of the real enemy. It was only the warnings of several soldiers at once that helped it regain focus.

From the direction of the Forest, a Snake army was advancing toward the Ravine. And the White Silkworm knew exactly who had given them the order. It forgot all about the biped at once — priorities shifted in an instant. Its entire attention was on the Snake army now. The White Silkworm commanded its soldiers to mass at the Ravine and prepare for defense.

The Pink Silkworm from the Forest had sensed the White's moment of weakness and chose to strike right now. There were indeed two of them. Brother and sister, their eggs had lain in the same clutch. None of the others had survived — only the White and the Pink.

Each instinctively knew that they had to kill the other. Only then could one of them evolve.

The White flinched as its first soldiers clashed with the Pink's. It knew full well that this war would be grueling for both sides. And even if one emerged victorious, they would be left with almost no army and would have to start recruiting soldiers from scratch.

But the White didn't care. After evolution, rebuilding an army would be easy. Moreover, the Silkworm would become even stronger. And it would reign as the rightful ruler, dominating everyone as their only master.

This was where the White and the Pink had differed the most. The sister wanted to evolve and descend — to heed the call that beckoned them both. To return to their birthplace at the foot of the Mountain. But the White wanted an infinite army. It ignored the call, even though it was difficult. It defied its own nature, giving in to greed.

An endless army — this was the White's only obsession. Nothing else mattered. Not even the soft fluffy females, who faded into insignificance whenever it found a new Alpha to subjugate.

*　　*　　*

How the hell could there be a second Nest here?!

I flew, clutching a boot with my severed foot still inside, trying to make sense of it all. How could there be two Nests within the first mile of descent?!

I reached the base and rushed right into the smoke. My lungs seized and my eyes burned at once. But I kept moving — this was the shortest way through.

"KAW!"

A black raven, its glossy feathers shimmering, dove straight at me.

I dodged its attack and hurled a knife with my free hand. Then another. And another. Three blades struck the monster, sinking halfway into its body.

"KAW!"

The deafening screech made my ears bleed. The Black Metal Raven beat its wings and spiraled downward — it couldn't stay airborne with three knives buried in its right wing.

BANG!

A Stork slammed into the Raven, and the two Alphas tumbled from the sky, tearing into each other mid-fall.

I broke free of the smoke and spat out thick saliva.

Ahead, twenty yards away, I spotted my army — less than half remained. But at least they were retreating in some semblance of order.

"Boss!" Wang Bolai called. "Over here!"

I rushed to them. Wounded Natsuko, a pale Dumisa, Liang, Wang Bolai, Mayor Hansh, and a completely unscathed Anish.

"Where's Selena?" I asked.

"She'd gotten injured, so we've sent her up through the portal with the others," Natsuko answered. "By Amaterasu, Vladislav! What the hell is going on?!"

"Did you kill the main monster?" Liang coughed.

"No. Anish, what's your remaining Neutrino count?"

"Not a drop," the Indian said with an apologetic shrug. "All gone."

"Natsuko, get out the Alpha Cores. We need to gather the monster bodies — there are dozens of them."

"In this smoke? We'll suffocate!"

"I'll shield us with wind. If we leave now, we'll lose the bodies forever. Wang Bolai, Dumisa, Hansh, Ulysses, Arkhip..."

I called out names. If I didn't know someone's name but remembered their ability, I simply pointed to them.

Natsuko summoned people, and they brought me several backpacks stuffed with Cores. At least forty, if not more.

"Vladislav, you're pale as a ghost. You've lost a lot of blood. Maybe Nitya should see to you before you do anything else?"

"There's no time. Anish, you're up first. Use the Cores — we need two Large Portal activations. Then you, Ulysses. We need wind to create a tornado. Hansh, you're third. We won't pull this off without Gravity Cancellation. Dumisa, Wang Bolai, you should have enough Neutrinos to shield yourselves and the rest of us."

I was going to use the same tactic that had worked so well after the Iron-Eared Rabbit massacre. Gravity Cancellation would lift the Alpha bodies, and a wind tornado would hurl them into the portal. On the other side, our surviving Evolvers would butcher them quickly and fill the cubes.

The real challenge was time — every monster in the area would swarm this battlefield before too long.

"What's happening down there?" Wang Bolai pointed to the descent.

The smoke obscured most of our view, but we could make out chaotic movement between the first and second mile.

"The Snakes are attacking the Beetles," I scowled. "Another massive army. But that works in our favor — the monsters will be too focused on their war to bother us. We'll have time to gather the bodies. Ready?"

I used five Cores. One went into my native DNA, raising its purity to 9.98. Four more went into the Wind Master DNA, bringing it to 9.4.

Anish took seven Cores — his purity should be

around 8.5, maybe a bit less. Wang Bolai took five, Dumisa needed only three to push his purity close to ten.

Natsuko didn't use any — she was staying here. Hansh, Ulysses, and Arkhip took three each. Three Air Fielders and five Weak Evolvers each got one.

"Anish, open the portal," I ordered once our group was ready. "Natsuko, catch the bodies and start gutting them immediately. I'm leaving my foot in your care — guard it like your own."

"Maybe we should stick it in a helium-3 cube?" Wang Bolai joked.

"It won't fit," Natsuko shook her head regretfully.

Anish opened the portal, and we stepped through.

I never landed — hovering the entire time, enduring excruciating pain, sweat pouring off me. But I couldn't afford to be distracted. If we left the monster corpses here, the entire event would have been a failure.

By my count, we'd killed about a hundred and fifty Alphas and at least four hundred beasts. With that kind of haul, I could clear all our contract debts and boost the Syndicate's core team DNA purity to nearly ten percent.

To my surprise, the operation was fast and casualty-free. A few rats and birds did attack, but we repelled them easily. We swept the battlefield and the base interior with Gravity Cancellation and the wind tornado. As expected, most of the stronger monsters were still locked in battle between the ravine and the forest.

Only those beyond the Silkworm's control had come our way — and there weren't many of them. The rest were off fighting for their furry overlord.

"Well, that was easy," Wang Bolai said, astonished, when we returned. "When the boss suggested gathering the bodies, I thought he'd lost his marbles... I mean, that he was making a mistake. But the boss never makes mistakes!"

"Think you can handle the rest?" I grimaced.

The ground before me was a sea of Beetle corpses — charred, shattered, and leaking ichor. Smoke curled above them, and some still twitched, half-melded into pulp and slime.

The stench was unbearable. I wanted to leave. But the Evolvers were already hard at work dismantling the bodies, unbothered by the smell.

"We've got it under control," came Natsuko's muffled voice.

A sharp whistle, and a dark-skinned old man collapsed with a bolt embedded in his temple.

"Tried to steal a Core," said one of the Evolvers — one of the old man's own kin. His voice was devoid of emotion.

I nodded. It was only natural for people to snatch whatever they could. If someone took a piece of monster — a shard of bone, a bit of carapace — we turned a blind eye. But trying to steal a Liquid Core meant death. No one was surprised. This was the Primordial World, after all, and people died here in droves as it was.

"Make sure to pull out all the bolt tips and knives," I told Arkhip, the commander of the Magnetic Fielders squad.

"I won't forget."

"Leave someone to monitor the descent. Keep me updated on the battle between the Beetles and the Snakes. The smoke will clear soon, and visibility will improve."

"Roger that," Natsuko responded.

Taking the severed foot from Natsuko, I took off toward the upper levels. I needed to get to Nitya as quickly as possible before it was too late to re-attach it. I was lucky I'd caught the boot — if my foot had been destroyed, I'd have been stuck with a prosthetic until the day I became a Strong Human. But I was done with prosthetics. I wanted to be rid of them for good.

The journey back to the settlement turned out to be harder than expected. I was constantly harassed by various creatures — a flock of Rubber Grouse, a pair of Dual Mergansers, and even a Razor-Beaked Owl tried to attack, even though the latter was a nocturnal predator that should have been asleep.

But the Alphas weren't too eager to strike, and the lesser beasts were no match for brute force. I dealt with them without resorting to wind.

I reached the settlement at last and shot straight toward the infirmary. The wounded from our army hadn't returned yet — I hadn't encountered them on the way. I wasn't worried about them since they were accompanied by Andrei and a few soldiers who could handle the escort.

"Leader!" Nitya gasped when I entered the building.

Miroslava was lying on a cot — pale, but awake. She turned her head toward me and whispered something.

"Just heal me, please," I said, placing the severed foot on the table before Nitya. I carefully lowered myself onto a chair and hissed as my injured calf brushed against the leg.

"Are you feeling all right?" Nitya knelt and rolled up my pant leg. "What happened?"

"Beetles. How's Miroslava?"

"A few more days of rest, and she'll fully recover."

"Good. How long will my treatment take?"

"I'm not sure. A few hours, I think. I should have enough Neutrinos."

I closed my eyes, mulling things over. I needed to act. What if the White Silkworm got killed? I couldn't let that happen. I forced myself to recall everything I knew about Silkworms.

"I need to contact the Brittas," I muttered.

"What?"

"Nothing."

The Brittas family was one of the Gold Families. Among the forty-four most powerful families in the United States of Europica, they ranked in the top ten.

I thought of them because, in my past life, the Brittas had been among the first to extract a living monster from the Primordial World. And that monster had been a Silkworm. The Brittas clan were the undisputed kings of silk production. They accounted for forty percent of the world's annual silk output, operating massive silk stations and cutting-edge laboratories dedicated to silkworm research.

If my plan was going to work, I had to get in touch with them. I just hoped I wasn't too late.

The noise outside grew louder. The wounded had finally arrived at the settlement. I flinched as Nitya pressed against my calf, inspecting the wound.

"I'm starting," she said.

A wave of warmth spread from her hands through my entire body.

Regular Atomei of Synthesis with the Matter Regeneration ability weren't much different from one another. They activated their skill, and damaged tissue healed as it should. No medical knowledge required.

But Weak Evolvers had their strengths and weaknesses — small quirks that made them unique. Those quirks became apparent when Weakling healers treated other Weaklings, who were beyond the powers of regular Synthesis Atomei.

"You're really good at making the muscle tissue regenerate," I observed.

"You think so?" Nitya looked surprised. "Babaji Christian says the same."

"Christian?"

"The chief healer of the settlement. He helped when Dumisa, Natsuko, and Wang Bolai were injured."

"Oh, that old geezer..."

The noise outside grew louder, but I ignored it completely. I shut my eyes and tried to make sense of why there were two Nests on the descent.

In my past life, the descent had only been actively cleared about thirteen months after the Eclipse. Back then, there had been no Beetle Nest. And the forest hadn't been crawling with Snakes.

Once the clearing squads had reached the forest, things had gone south pretty quickly. Countless Alphas furiously defended a specific territory. Human casualties skyrocketed, and the mission was aborted.

A few months later, the White Silkworm had appeared for the first time. Back then, no one knew it was a Sentient. But to me, that was obvious from the data I'd studied. Within weeks, the entire forest had become a death zone. Eventually, so had the entire eastern descent.

The only explanation I could think of was that there had been another Sentient monster's Nest in the forest. The White Silkworm must have killed it — but at the cost of nearly its entire army. That was when the eastern descent had been cleared.

But later on, the White Silkworm had digested the other Sentient, becoming a Sentient itself.

So what should I do? I had already decided that I would take the White Silkworm's DNA. That would grant me the ability known as Mental Threads. And not only would it enhance my mind, but it would also unlock countless other possibilities.

Two hours passed as I pondered. I snapped back to awareness when Miroslava sat up, clearly with difficulty.

"Can I return to Earth, Nitya?"

"Yes, you can," she replied, exhausted. "You need to rest — I've healed everything I could. But that arrow with the disintegration power... That was nasty. You have to take it easy. Let the healers check on you morning and night."

"You don't mind?" Miroslava asked me. "It's been so long since I last visited. I want to see the guys at the Institute."

"Of course," I smiled. "Rest as much as you want. The raid is over, and we're not organizing another one anytime soon."

"It's over?" Miroslava looked surprised.

"Yes. There are just too many monsters. We can't handle them."

"And the Silkworm?"

"Don't worry about it. Can you pass a message to the old man?"

"Of course."

"Tell him I want to talk to the Brittas Family. I need their expertise on silkworms."

"Got it. When are you leaving the Primordial World?"

"As soon as I wrap things up here. Three or four hours, I think."

"Need anything else?"

"No."

"Then I'm heading out."

She waited for my nod before stepping forward and vanishing.

"I'm out of Neutrinos," Nitya sighed, wiping her forehead with her sleeve.

I checked my legs. My right foot was back in place — I could even move my toes, albeit sluggishly. The wound on my left calf was fully healed, leaving only a faint white scar.

"Thanks," I said, rolling my pant leg down and standing. A dull pain shot through my leg, making me wince.

"There's still a bit left to do. I'll finish healing it in a couple of hours."

"When Natsuko arrives, take as many Liquid Cores as you need. What's your DNA purity?"

"Eight-point-six."

"We've killed plenty of Beetles with Synthesis Atomeus abilities. Three of those Cores should be enough for you."

"Understood. Thank you." Nitya bowed.

I stepped out of the house and saw a soldier heading toward the infirmary.

"There's news," he began without preamble. "The ravine has been flooded with snakes. The Silkworm and several Beetles escaped into the crevice where the Lurking Wolves used to live."

"How many Beetles are there with Silkworm? And what do they look like?"

"Around twenty. All Alphas. Among them are several species we've never seen before."

The soldier described Defender Beetles, Devil's Ladybugs, and Leaping Beetles. Silkworm had taken his strongest fighters and fled the Nest. He'd lost the battle to that monster living in the forest at the second-mile mark.

"It's a massacre," the soldier's face darkened, his lips twisting slightly. He was clearly shaken by what he'd seen. "Thousands of corpses. More Alphas have swarmed them than I've ever seen in my life. But the worst of it is the snakes…"

"How exactly did they flood the ravine?"

"There was a bunch of these blue snakes — thick and glossy. Several hundred of those creatures opened their jaws and started spewing water."

Water Pythons, I realized. It felt like the monster in the forest had planned this in advance, waiting for the right moment. And we'd given it to him — White Silkworm had sent part of his army to attack our base. He'd gotten distracted by the humans and lost because of it.

"Natsuko and Dumisa are in charge. Handle things here. I'm leaving — I need to go to Earth."

"What about your leg?" Nitya appeared in the doorway behind me.

"I'll finish healing it on Earth. We can't waste time right now," I activated the tattoo.

"And those monsters… Are you sure they won't attack the mountain? There are thousands of them — our settlement won't stand a chance," the soldier nervously adjusted his collar.

"They won't attack. After a feast like that, they'll be resting and digesting for a while. And in that time, we need to finish off White Silkworm."

I stepped into the translucent pyramid and teleported to Earth.

CHAPTER 7

INTERLUDE. MIROSLAVA

MIROSLAVA STEPPED OUT OF THE SHOWER and started dressing, taking her time and moving gingerly. The weakness still clung to her, and sharp pain stabbed through her abdomen from time to time. Sometimes, it felt like parasites had taken root inside her, growing restless and writhing whenever they got bored.

Just now, another wave of pain rolled over her. Clenching her teeth, she gripped the sink for support, breathing heavily.

"Mira, you okay?" Olesya's concerned voice came from the other side of the door.

"I'm fine," Miroslava replied once the pain subsided. "I'll be out in a second."

She lived in a house near the Evolver Institute, sharing it with her friends — Olesya and Darina. They had met while in captivity, and their shared trauma had forged an unbreakable bond between them.

Stepping out of the bathroom, Miroslava found Olesya waiting, her face lined with worry. Olesya looked younger than her age, dressed she was dressed in simple jeans and a sweater, her short dark hair slightly disheveled.

"You're so pale. Are you sure you're alright?"

"Yeah. My stomach just hurts sometimes, but it'll pass."

Miroslava made her way to the living room and sank into her favorite couch. She immediately felt better.

"How did the raid go? I heard there were a lot of casualties," Olesya asked, curling up on the armchair across from her. She brushed an unruly fringe from her forehead, her eyes blazing with curiosity.

"Yes, a lot of people have died," Miroslava admitted somberly. "Vladislav said the raid is over. But I don't know the details."

"The net's full of rumors. Some say Vladislav's army ran into thousands of Beetles. And all of them were Alphas! But Vladislav charged straight into their hive and killed their leader, so his army managed to escape. Or was it an anthill? I don't remember. When is he coming back here? What's he even doing in Brussels? His grandfather lives here, but he's away, and in Brussels, of all the places. If it were Beijing, at least his sister's there — but Brussels?! I bet he's got a sweetheart there."

"You're at it again," Miroslava sighed. Olesya was an incorrigible gossip. She always had to know everything about everyone.

"No, but tell me I'm wrong! When is he coming? I want to see him. I'm sure he'll fall for my charm," Olesya squinted dreamily.

Miroslava snorted.

"What have you all been doing without me? Spill."

"Nothing much. Another ninety-four people joined us. We're out of places to put them."

"Aren't they building new dorms?" Miroslava asked.

"They are. And they're planning more after that. But it'll be a while before they're done. We had to set up a tent city for all the newcomers."

"How many people are at the Institute now?"

"Eight hundred and thirty-nine," Olesya replied without hesitation.

The Evolver Institute only accepted children and teenagers under eighteen, as well as those with nowhere else to go. It had training grounds, dormitories, a school, and a daycare. The fifty-plus staff members were still being paid by the Prince, but Miroslava was determined to make the institute self-sustaining — profitable, even, so it could grow.

"There are only twenty-two Evolvers here, including you," Olesya pointed out. "And just two Weaklings — you and Kostya. Well, Yanling, too, but she's never around. Don't you think it's time to lower the requirements? So many people want to enter the Primordial World. We have beast Cores — twenty-three in storage right now. That's twenty-three new Evolvers!"

"They could die."

"There are always casualties. This is the Primordial World, not a walk in the park. And this is the Evolver Institute, not an orphanage. Let them choose."

"I'll think about it," Miroslava promised reluctantly. "What's happening in the world?"

"Oh, a lot. A whole lot. But don't worry, the Syndicate is still the strongest organization. Right now, the net has divided all the groups into three tiers.

In the first tier, there's the Syndicate and the Clowns. The Syndicate ran the raid that everyone's talking about, and the Clowns recently announced they're going to attack a Sentient monster. Can you believe it? They claim Sentients are the next evolutionary step after Alphas. Also, Black single-handedly killed a Destroyer Elephant a few days ago — the one that had wiped out several human groups and was threatening a settlement. People are spinning wild legends about him, even bigger than the ones about Delta. The Syndicate and the Clowns have a lot in common. Both are headed by highly competent leaders with unique abilities. Both have over ten Weak Evolvers among their ranks, all concentrated on a single mountain. And among them are people with rare and flashy powers — like Red's Laser or Kostya's Bone Manipulation. Have you seen him use it? It's horrifying! Anyway, would you like some tea? My throat's dry."

"Sure," Miroslava agreed. "But Kostya isn't on the same mountain as us, is he? Why bring him up?"

"Let's go to the kitchen," Olesya hopped up, helping Miroslava to her feet. "The second tier is full of groups with more than ten Weak Evolvers. There are tons of them, but the top hundred are the ones that matter. Each country has its own ranking, but the top six are the same everywhere, just in different orders. That's Slavia's Varangians, the Golden Army, Han, the Spirit-Chosen, the Desert Warriors, and the Army of Freedom."

Miroslava nodded. She'd heard of those organizations before. Each was backed by a different national government.

The Varangians hailed from Slavia. Officially, its leader was a man named Vsevolod, but Miroslava knew that the Czar himself made all the real decisions. Vsevolod was just one of his men.

"On Earth, any of those six would wipe the floor with the Syndicate and the Clowns," Olesya continued as she rummaged through a cupboard for tea. "The Golden Army alone has over a hundred Weaklings. But what good are they if they're all spread across different mountains? The same goes for the other groups in the top six. Take The Varangians, for example. Vsevolod is on the Mountain of Eternal Winter. He's only got ten Varangians with him — all Weaklings, but their abilities are unremarkable. His deputy, the one they call the Patrician, is on Mount Shikhan. He has more people — about twenty Varangians, five or six of whom are Weaklings, but again, nothing special ability-wise. Until these organizations manage to consolidate on a single mountain — if that's even possible — nothing will change. The Syndicate and the Clowns will always have the upper hand because Delta's and Black's teams are too strong. And their leaders — if the rumors are true — are far stronger than any ordinary Evolver."

Olesya finally found the tea and put the kettle on. Miroslava had just taken out her smartphone, waiting for it to boot up.

"Virtual currencies crashed fast, by the way. No one uses them anymore — only inside organizations. Why did the Clowns even introduce them? I don't get it. And then everyone else just copied them. Oh, and our Prince's organization, the Golden Lions, is in the top fifty of the second-tier rankings. In our regional ranking, it's in the top ten, but the Asians have shoved it down to eightieth place."

"Asians don't like the Prince. What about the Moon and Mars?"

"They're not even included in the rankings. But they have their own organizations, too, and if you count the total number of Weak Evolvers, they'd definitely make the top ten — especially Mars. Then there's the third tier. That's made up of organizations founded by powerful families — like the Volkovs, Tarasovs, Serovs, Grekovs, Grigoryans, and so on. They all try to hide their involvement, but come on, who are they fooling? Dig a little, and it's obvious. These groups are pretty weak overall, though some are gaining strength fast thanks to charismatic leaders. For example, have you heard of Jessica, the one they call the Ice Queen?"

"No, I don't really follow the news."

"She's only a few years older than us. Her father is the head of a small family, somewhere in Colorado, I think — not even close to a Gold Family. But he sponsors an organization called the Frost Cats. Named it after his daughter — Jessica can create ice and loves cats. There are already seven Weak Evolvers in that group. Seven! And they're not pushovers with five percent DNA purity — they're real fighters. Or take Xu Wei from Hong Kong. He showed up less than a week ago and skyrocketed in influence. He has a real weird ability, and people are calling him Demon Xu..."

Miroslava listened with interest as Olesya rattled on, seemingly able to talk forever. Meanwhile, she was messaging her father. Igor Yerokhin had decided to stay in Yekaterinburg with his daughter.

Miroslava felt both pride and sorrow for him. He had been brutally beaten when he single-handedly defended the young Prince against three powerful Evolvers. But since he hadn't managed to defeat the bandits, he had resigned from his job of his own accord. Miroslava saw it as the act of a true man. The prince hadn't been harmed, but her father couldn't forgive himself for losing to three elite Evolvers.

During that battle, he had also realized something else — he no longer loved his wife. So he had divorced her coldly, despite her begging on her knees for him to stay. As an apology, he left her his apartment and moved to Yekaterinburg to be with his only beloved daughter. In the heat of battle, he had realized how wrong he had been to spend so little time with his own flesh and blood. Miroslava felt a bit sorry for her stepmother, but she didn't blame her father. She was proud of him and had no doubt that a specialist as brave as him would have no trouble finding a well-paid job.

"By the way, did you hear that Meili Li has become a Weakling, too?" Olesya placed two steaming cups of tea on the table. "Delta's sister."

"I didn't," Miroslava admitted, setting her phone aside.

"How many people in the Syndicate do you think will become Weaklings after the raid? I heard they gathered over a thousand Alpha Cores."

"Not nearly that many," Miroslava shook her head again. "Once you factor in all the payouts, I doubt they'll even hit a hundred."

"You think so?" Olesya frowned. "Is the net really lying?"

"Probably."

"That can't be... Whatever. Darina will be back soon. Let's go to Yekaterinburg — you need some fresh air. We'll buy new clothes, see a movie. We'll ask Valentina to drive us. If I ask, he'll definitely say yes."

"Where is Darina, anyway?"

"Outside, handling business," Olesya shrugged. "She's been out all day."

Olesya and Darina — Miroslava's two closest friends — were both Evolvers. The Prince's people were training them to take over the management of the institute in the future.

At first, Miroslava didn't want to go anywhere, but then she thought — why not? It had been so long since she had simply walked through the city...

"Oh, right — what do you know about the Brittas Family?" Miroslava suddenly remembered Vladislav's request. She had passed along his message to the Prince's people as soon as she stepped out of the pyramid.

"The Brittas Family..." Olesya furrowed her brows. "I don't know. Never heard of them having their own organization. Why?"

"Just curious..."

"By the way, did you ever find out who sent the assassin after you? I asked around, but no one's telling me anything."

"No idea," Miroslava shook her head. "Doesn't matter. Let's get ready if we're going."

"Yes! I'll text Darina."

Two hours later, the girls set off for Yekaterinburg.

Darina — a tanned blonde with striking amber eyes — was thrilled to see Miroslava and bombarded her with questions about life in the Primordial World.

For once, Olesya stopped talking and simply listened.

Miroslava gave them a brief recap of the first day of the raid, met with gasps and exclamations of awe from her friends.

"Damn, I'm so jealous," Olesya lit a small flame on her fingertip. "With my weak ability, I'm useless."

"With the right gas tank, you'd be more dangerous than most Evolvers with rare abilities,"

Miroslava reassured her. "You should've seen the fire waves they were unleashing out there. The Rock Hedgehogs looked like they'd been thrown into hell. And that was just regular Evolvers, not Weaklings! The Hedgehogs were Alphas!"

"Yeah, you're right... I used to think Synthesis Atomei with the Matter Fusion ability were useless. But look at what they can create."

"I visited the Prince's new lab today," Darina spoke up in a pleasant husky voice. "About fifty percent of the staff there have that ability. And I ran into Yanling, by the way. She was recently injured in the Primordial World — almost lost an arm."

"What kind of lab?" Olesya's eyes gleamed.

"The Prince is working on some kind of elixir to enhance Evolvers. I only got a glimpse of the main area, but it was filled with shiny equipment, tubes, massive cylinders... And a ton of people in white lab coats. Looked like something out of a sci-fi movie about evil scientists making a zombie virus."

"An elixir? Is that even possible?" Olesya smiled doubtfully.

"Well, they managed to create that fire gas," Darina shrugged. "Who knew that was even possible? Maybe elixirs exist, too. Drink one, and whammo — you grow a pair of hooves and antlers. Nothing would surprise me after the Eclipse."

The car pulled into an underground parking lot beneath Evolver Square — a new plaza built after the Eclipse. All the other city squares were closed off because of the pyramids.

Evolver Square was divided into four sectors, though only two were open for now — the park and the commercial zone. At its center stood a massive three-hundred-foot statue of the Prince, seated on his famous lion throne. In Slavia, the death of Patriarch Heng was still a hot topic online.

Miroslava, Olesya, and Darina arrived at the commercial district. It had boutiques catering every taste, but no vehicles or any form of transport were allowed inside. People strolled along the wide roads, lined with small wooden houses in the style of rustic cabins — the entire shopping district was designed to resemble a settlement from the Primordial World. Occasionally, they passed restaurants and small green islands with benches. Large screens displayed the latest news broadcasts from all across Slavia.

"I heard the third and fourth sectors of the Square will be associated with Evolvers and the Primordial World," Darina said. "Meat from beasts and Alphas, weapons made from their bones, Evolvers selling their services..." She had her cap pulled low over her head, and a cloth mask covered the lower half of her face. The girls had deliberately disguised themselves to avoid being recognized — though, in truth, it was Miroslava who insisted, and her friends had simply followed suit.

"I could perform in a circus," Olesya giggled.

"Where to first? I vote for Señorita — they've got a new collection out."

"That place only sells dresses. Let's go to Jeansies instead. Oh, look! The Fountain of Love!"

Olesya grabbed Miroslava and Darina by the

hands, dragging them toward a green space. In its center stood a towering arch, with streams of pink water cascading along its inner and outer walls. The light within the water shimmered with all the colors of the rainbow, creating a mesmerizing display. The outer part of the arch was designed so that the jets of water collided midair, bursting into a fine heart-shaped mist of droplets. The fountain was humming softly. The arch stood in the middle of a small lake, where mandarin ducks glided across the surface.

The area around the lake buzzed with activity — mostly young women chattering excitedly, admiring the birds, the water, or simply enjoying the fountain's song.

"They say if an Evolver thinks of someone they love and uses their ability on the lake, their wish will come true," Olesya whispered eagerly. "But if you damage the fountain or the arch, it'll have the opposite effect — that person will never love you. I'm going first."

She found an open spot by the lake, crouched by the water, and, after a nervous glance around, released a tiny, barely visible spark.

"It worked! No one's even noticed!" Olesya came bounding back, grinning from ear to ear.

"Who did you think about?" Miroslava asked suspiciously.

"Vladislav, obviously! Have you heard people talking? Half the conversations here are about him. He's a network superstar — Delta. His lineage, his wealth, his youth, his looks... He was the first to come up with the idea of founding an organization, and after that, everyone else just copied him. And his Syndicate? All of them are superstars! Except Liang. The net says he sells shoes at a market."

"Well? Are you two making wishes or not?"

Miroslava strained to catch mentions of Vladislav in the surrounding chatter, but the noise was too overwhelming to make anything out. Darina muttered something disapproving in a grumpy voice before participating in the so-called magic ritual herself.

"I'm not doing it," Miroslava shook her head.

"Oh, come on! What if the fountain really works? Darina, who'd you wish for?"

"None of your business."

Neither Olesya nor Darina noticed as a small coin floated just an inch above the ground before dropping soundlessly into the lake.

Miroslava quickly averted her gaze, her mind still echoing with the name she had just thought of.

"Ouch—"

Pain flared in her stomach again, and she instinctively doubled over.

"Again?!"

"Come on, let's sit down."

Olesya and Darina helped her over to a wooden bench, its edges curling into intricate carvings.

"...updates from the Primordial World. It has been confirmed that the group of Evolvers led by Arseny Samoylov, missing for three days, has been completely wiped out by monsters. Over twenty people are dead. The deputy mayor of Surgut and his squad also disappeared on the same mountain..."

A nearby screen broadcasted the news, the stern-faced anchor delivering the grim report.

Miroslava, Olesya, and Darina turned their attention to the screen.

"...fourteen noble houses from various countries have announced the formation of the Western Alliance, which will encompass seven neighboring mountains in the Primordial World. The Western Alliance promises to establish logistics between the mountains and organize paid transport for civilians. From Slavia, the organizations Crimson Lily and Engineers are joining the Alliance."

"Crimson Lily — that's the Lisyevs from Moscow, right?" Olesya frowned. "And the Engineers — that's the Molodins from Novosibirsk."

"...His Holiness, Patriarch Arsentiy of the Christian Church, addressed the public."

The screen shifted to a tall, elderly man with piercing blue eyes.

"The so-called Primordial World is a road leading straight to HELL!" his voice thundered. "I urge you all — do not sell your souls to the Devil! Do not fall for his sweet lies! Those who bear the mark on their wrist will never be free again!"

Miroslava flinched and instinctively crossed herself, clutching her right wrist.

"...In Australia, an earthquake caused one of the Primordial World's Pyramids to sink underground. Local authorities are in turmoil. The United States of Europica has yet to release an official statement."

"It sank into the ground?" Olesya blinked in surprise. "I didn't even know that was possible."

We interrupt for breaking news! A horrific assassination attempt has been made on Vladislav Vavilonsky! A report has just come in from Brussels, where the flames from the explosions that destroyed Vladislav's and his bodyguards' vehicles haven't even died down yet! Sources confirm that the grandson of Prince Boris has suffered grievous injuries! His whereabouts remain a closely guarded secret! The Prince has already issued a statement..."

Miroslava shot to her feet, pressing her hands to her chest. Her heart pounded violently, and cold fear poured through her veins like syrup.

Chapter 8

Developing the Plan

AS SOON AS I STEPPED OUT of the pyramid, my grandfather's men were waiting. This time, no one tried to stop me — I got into the car without delay. First, I turned on my phone. Only one contact was saved — Muhiddin. His response had come in yesterday.

Understood. It will be done.

I switched to another phone and called my grandfather.

"Did the Beetles chop your damn leg off?!" he barked the moment he picked up. "What the hell are you even doing out there, you little bum?! How the hell do you let Beetles slice you up?!"

"Grandpa, not now," I grimaced. "What's the update on the Brittas?"

"They're already on their way to Brussels."

"That fast?" I chuckled.

"A lot of people want to talk to you after your raid. Everyone's interested in the bloody propane formula and that massive monster horde you ran into. What the hell was that, anyway?! According to the reports, thousands of different creatures were all gathered in one place."

"Yeah… I'll log everything into the database today. These clusters are called Nests. When are the Brittas arriving?"

"You'll meet them in two hours at that restaurant — the Form Archery or whatever the hell it's called."

"Two hours?" I checked the time. "They agreed to meet at five in the morning?"

"Yeah. You got a problem with that?"

"No, it's fine. How are things on the Moon and Mars?"

"Don't even ask," he grumbled. "It's a disaster. I'm bleeding money every damn day! You don't appreciate your grandfather anywhere near enough, you ungrateful little bum."

"What's that got to do with me?"

"Where's Atlantis? Spill it, now."

"No idea."

"Liar."

He hung up.

Seriously? He got mad? But a few seconds later, he called back.

"Got any names? I need fresh recruits — the old ones aren't enough."

"What if they're from other countries?" I asked after a brief pause.

"Write down everyone you know. We'll put

them under surveillance. When the time is right, we'll offer them help. That's why you're holding back, isn't it? Every person on the list you gave me before needed help, and they accepted it gladly. Don't hesitate now — write down everyone, from any country. The more Evolvers with rare abilities we have, the better. They're incredibly scarce, and you know it — each one is worth their weight in gold."

"I don't have that many names, but I'll list everyone I know," I agreed. "What's the status on the elixirs?"

"Still nothing. It's too damn complicated. Some of the equipment doesn't even exist — we're having to invent it from scratch. Where the hell did you even find these formulas?"

"I found them."

"May bums eat you alive."

"Any word from mother?"

"No," his voice darkened.

"That's not surprising. It's still too soon."

"Have you heard about the Western Alliance?" he abruptly changed the subject.

"No."

"A bunch of organizations have joined together to establish a transport network between mountains. You understand what that means?"

I frowned.

"I have intel that the Clowns are somehow involved with the Alliance's leading organizations. I think they've signed some kind of contract."

Now it all made sense.

"Why the silence? What's their angle? I don't

like not knowing things."

"If you relocate to another mountain, your spawn point in the Primordial World changes. When you enter, you'll start appearing on the new mountain," I explained.

People were supposed to discover this when the first group of Evolvers crossed the Great Ridge — in my past life, that had happened about a year after the Eclipse. In this life, my mother was supposed to be the pioneer. But Black had decided to push things forward and start preparing early.

My grandfather went silent for nearly a minute. I braced myself for another explosion of shouting and swearing, but surprisingly, when he spoke, his voice was quiet.

"So that's how it is... Now it all makes sense. Draw up your vision for how this inter-mountain transport system should work. I'm getting in on this business, too."

"Sure thing," I agreed easily. With my experience traveling in caravans, I could save him from a lot of rookie mistakes.

"And it would behoove you to prepare yourself properly," his tone turned serious. "The moment logistics between mountains are established, your Syndicate won't be the strongest organization anymore. Even my Lions — if I gather them all on one mountain — would steamroll your whole group. Never mind the Varangians or the Hanchas."

"That'll take months. By then, I'll have already killed a Sentient and become a Strong Human," I replied without hesitation.

"The moment you kill the Sentient, bring me

the Core first, got it? Give your beloved grandpa a gift before you take one for yourself."

I covered the microphone with my hand and gestured for the driver to stop at a 24-hour store.

"You hear me?" Grandpa's voice turned threatening.

"Yeah, yeah. If that's all, I'll be hanging up now."

"You impertinent bum."

The call cut off.

The car pulled up to the store, but I didn't get out — too many people would recognize me. Instead, I asked the driver to buy several types of cheese. If my body was sending me weird cravings, it was best to listen.

Afterward, the driver took me home, where I found a large, sealed package waiting on the doorstep.

"This was delivered on your grandfather's orders," one of the guards informed me.

I opened the box.

It was filled with colorful spray cans.

I pulled one out, read the label, and grunted.

Beetlebane!

One spray, and the Beetles will never bother you again!

No survivors!

"Toss this somewhere," I threw the can back into the box and headed inside.

I ate, then sat down at my laptop to update the database with everything I knew about the Beetles and Snakes.

The Syndicate's website had changed — work

had sped up, the design was cleaner, and the lay-out of icons and text was way more convenient now.

By the time I finished uploading all the infor-mation, less than an hour remained until my meeting with the Brittas. I started recalling the names and locations of every Evolver with a rare ability I had known in my past life. Unfortunately, there weren't many. I had started gathering intel too late, when everyone had already gone into hid-ing.

I could write something vague along the lines of, "there's a guy called Mbacké somewhere in the African Confederation — he's an insanely strong Evolver."

But what good would that do? There were thousands of Mbackés in the Confederation, and chances were that wasn't even his real name.

Most of the concrete data I had was on Evolv-ers from Slavia. This time, I added Baby Masha, whom I had left out before. Her Matter Creation ability could be incredibly useful in the lab.

When it was time to leave, I headed to the res-taurant my grandfather had named. Even in the car, I kept adding names. By the time we arrived, I had sent my grandfather sixty-three names — forty-one from Slavia, the rest scattered across dif-ferent countries.

I didn't include anyone from powerful families in my list, nor those who had already made a name for themselves — like Curtis or Xiuli. Everyone knew about them. I only wrote down the names of people whose identities had never surfaced anywhere. I checked each one online to make sure. To my surprise, Demon Xu and Ice Queen Jessica had already emerged. Angelina the Magnificent was now the most famous woman in the Arab Coalition, and once Egghead launched his new internet, her influence would spread across every country. Chang the Giant had organized an Evolver Championship, and its ranking numbers had already shattered records — even before the first broadcast.

Almost all the top figures from the New Elite of my past life had begun making a name for themselves. But a few I was interested in were still silent — Mbacké the Angel from Africa, Ganesh the Monk from India, and the Martian Matriarch Agatha had yet to reveal themselves.

This ranking was based on Evocom follower counts. For now, most celebrities were confined to their own countries. Very few had become famous across the entire Solar System. But some already had — namely, yours truly, Black, and Dumisa, the First Evolver. These three names were known in every country, as well as on the Moon and Mars.

Once Egghead launched his Evocom, however, the landscape would shift. A new elite would emerge, worshipped by millions of fans. The names on that list would change. Mine would be on it this time. That, I was sure of. And General Xu's wouldn't be.

Prince Said was another highly influential individual. I had special plans for him. I couldn't get close to the bastard yet, but soon, a day would come that would destroy him completely. And when that happened, I would be there.

The car stopped in front of the restaurant, and I stepped out. Sleepy waiters greeted me at the entrance. The place was empty — clearly, it had been opened this early just for us. Inside the VIP hall, two men were seated at a round white table. The moment they saw me, they stood up.

One looked like an actor — tall, sharp-featured, dressed in an expensive black three-piece suit. White gloves covered his hands, thin elegant glasses rested on his nose. He was composed and focused. The other was his complete opposite — fat, sloppy, and seemingly half-asleep. His hair was unkempt, and a stain dotted the corner of his mouth.

"Oliver Brittas, eldest son of Charlie Brittas," the first introduced himself with a dignified nod, extending his hand.

I shook his dry palm and looked at the fat one. He wiped his hands on his pants before offering one.

"Georgie," he mumbled as I gripped his soft, sweaty, almost boneless hand.

"My brother is here to gain experience," Olivier said apologetically. "Our father has sent him along so he might learn something."

I gave a neutral nod and took my seat.

"La Fromagerie is a restaurant wholly focused on cheese. They have an enormous selection of cheeses, each more exquisite than the last." Oliver picked up the menu with an elegant gesture.

A waiter approached, smiling politely.

"A burrata for me," I said after a moment. "And

a glass of water. Nothing else."

There was no point ordering more — I had already eaten at home. Oliver and Georgie placed their orders. The fat guy rattled off at least eight dishes, if not more. Once the waiter left, I spoke.

"I'm interested in Silkworm monsters. The goal is to draw their attention — through scent or some other method. I need to lure one out of its burrow."

"This is... interesting," Oliver nodded.

But I wasn't paying attention to him. I was watching Georgie. Because he was the real decision-maker here.

The Brittas family was an unusual one. It had multiple heads and an internal ranking system. The higher your rank, the more weight your voice carried. And the only way to climb the ranks was to bring value to the family. Georgie — whose actual name was George — should have already been in charge of the entire Brittas silk production empire at his age. That was the reason he was here. Oliver, though? I had no idea who he was. I had never heard his name before.

Oliver cast a quick glance at his sleepy-looking brother and smiled at me.

"Allow me to make a call."

He stepped out, leaving me alone with Georgie. Neither of us spoke. The door opened, and waiters entered carrying trays. Georgie's eyes lit up. As the waiters set the table, Olivier returned.

"I've passed your request to our family. Our analysts are currently reviewing all possible strategies. Hopefully, by the end of this meal, we'll have an answer for you."

I nodded. This was why I liked the Brittas family — they were creative. Large silk stations existed in the Asian Commonwealth and India, too. But their owners had likely never even thought about studying Silkworm monsters, let alone conducting experiments on them the way the Brittas did.

We ate in silence. Oliver was flawless — etiquette textbook perfect. Georgie, on the other hand, resembled a pig in a wig. I finished my small bag of cheese quickly and simply waited.

"Need to hit the bathroom," Georgie muttered, wiping his mouth with a napkin — then crumpling it and stuffing it into his sleeve for some reason.

"I apologize once again for my brother," Oliver said after he left. "He's a bit... unusual. He's had some issues ever since childhood. When he was little, a pigeon flew over him, and he got so scared he fell and hit his head."

Oliver spoke with great enthusiasm. He clearly enjoyed making up nonsense about his brother when he wasn't around. And Georgie enjoyed playing the role of a clueless slob.

When Georgie returned, Oliver left again. The whole act made me want to bury my face in my hands. While we ate, Georgie had been weighing my words and making a decision. He had stepped out to deliver it to the family. And now, Oliver was listening to whatever Georgie had just decided — and would return shortly with the "official" response. I didn't know why the Brittas family kept Georgie's talent a secret, but I had to admit — if I hadn't known the truth, I might have fallen for the act.

"We are ready to assist you," Oliver returned with a waiter, waiting until the table was cleared before continuing.

"We will set a honey trap. Your task is simple — you must find live female Silkworm monsters. The one you want to lure out — is it male?"

"Is that even the right way to phrase it?" I frowned. "It's an insect. Either way, I don't know. And we have a problem — the Silkworms on my mountain are all in hard-to-reach places. I don't know where exactly they are. And I need a solution today — tomorrow might be too late."

That was true.

I had no idea where to find Silkworms on Xin Shang Peak. Or if there even were any besides the White one.

"Uh..." Oliver wiped his forehead with a handkerchief and adjusted his hair. "I think I should call my family..."

"Enough," I frowned and turned to Georgie. "I've already figured out you're the one in charge. Drop the act."

"What are you talking about?" Oliver feigned shock. "My brother? In charge? This is the same guy who cried for three nights straight as a child, begging our father for a riding pig!"

Georgie shot him a side glance.

"That never happened," he muttered. "How'd you figure it out? Our performance was flawless — we both took an acting course from Master Leonardo Lettiere. He even awarded us medals."

"Can we just get to the point?" My patience was wearing thin.

"All right, all right..." Georgie wiped his hands with a napkin, only for them to immediately start sweating again. "You've set too strict a condition. But... there's a way around it."

He leaned forward with an air of importance.

"Operation Honey Trap remains in play. But instead of using a live Silkworm, we'll use an actor. We'll craft a special costume and give you a unique serum. When the Silkworm smells it, it'll go mad with desire. If it's male, that is. If not, the whole thing won't work."

I stared at Georgie, weighing whether he was serious.

"There's no other option," he placed both hands on the table. "If you gave us more time — at least a week — we could prepare something more elaborate."

"No." I shook my head.

Once the snakes finish digesting the Beetles, they'll start hunting the White Silkworm. And he won't be able to escape...

"Fine. I accept. What do you want in return?"

"The formula for that burning gas," Georgie replied instantly. "And ten Alpha Cores."

I frowned. That was a steep price.

"The formula alone should be enough."

"Five Cores."

"Two."

"Deal," Georgie nodded without hesitation. "Honestly, getting the gas formula alone is already a huge win for us. The ten Cores? That was just me trying my luck. But two is still good — Father will be pleased."

I chuckled and stood up.

Oliver and Georgie immediately followed suit.

Georgie's stomach pressed into the edge of the table, making it look like a hot dog — his fat rolls the bun, the table the sausage.

"You'll be able to deliver everything directly to Xin Shang Peak?" I asked, suppressing a smile.

"Yes. We'll send the name of the settlement and the exact time in about two hours," Georgie said seriously, wiping his hands on his suit. "Within three to four hours, the necessary equipment will be delivered into the Primordial World and handed over to you."

"I'll give the messenger the Liquid Cores."

"Perfect!" Georgie beamed.

After saying goodbye to the Brittas brothers, I stepped out of the restaurant.

Oleg was waiting for me.

"My apologies for not arriving sooner," he bowed his head.

"No problem. Let's go."

"The Li family has contacted me several times. Patriarch Jiahao wants to speak with you personally."

"Get ready. We're about to start blowing up some cars," I said with a nasty grin.

"...Come again?" Oleg frowned in confusion.

* * *

Forty minutes later

I stood by a burning car, watching the wild dance of the flames and the black smoke drifting lazily upward. The crackling of fire filled the air, and the scent of burning metal and rubber stung my nose.

Behind this car, three more were ablaze. A beautiful sight — though an expensive one.

"All set," Oleg approached. "All the evidence points to Felix Von Belga."

"The soldiers who stopped me the previous time — will they testify?"

"Yes. They'll confirm they stopped you on Felix's personal orders. The Von Belga won't be able to deny it."

"The plane?"

"Twenty more minutes."

"Sir!" One of the guards ran up, holding a large bouquet of jet-black roses — exactly ninety-nine of them.

"We found the flowers."

"Excellent," I carefully took the bouquet.

"My grandfather is sulking and won't answer my calls. Does he know what to do?"

"Of course. Once news of the assassination attempt on you spreads and the culprit is confirmed, the Prince will demand Felix's expulsion from the family. Solomon will have no choice but to agree."

"Good."

I reached into my coat pocket and pulled out a

black mask, pressing it to my face.

I used wind to secure it in place so it wouldn't fall off. I couldn't afford to be seen. One of the guards covered the roses with a black cloth, securing it so the flowers remained hidden.

"But... how did you know about this spot?" Oleg looked around. "Anyone could set up an ambush here. It's a blind spot in the city's security."

I didn't answer. Instead, I lifted off the ground and flew toward my home.

Of course, I knew about this place. In my past life, I had meticulously studied the Von Belgas and Brussels. The exact spot where the cars were burning was where I had once planned to kill Nikita Von Belga on his way to visit his aunt. But I had no problem playing that card now. Felix nearly got Miroslava killed. I no longer wanted to just kill him. That was too easy.

Dawn was breaking. I inhaled the crisp morning air, a genuine smile creeping onto my lips. I felt light. Free.

I landed in Adele's courtyard and left the flowers by her door. It was time to deal with the Li family. I couldn't stay here any longer. And I had no idea when I'd see Adele again. But we had plenty of time. No need to rush.

Glancing around the courtyard one last time, I took off into the sky, heading for the airport. In the distance, police sirens howled, shattering the quiet of early morning. Brussels was about to get very, very hot.

CHAPTER 9

BAI HU'S CLAW

DURING THE FLIGHT, Oleg presented me with the full analysis of the event. A total of six hundred and one people had participated, including the Syndicate and the military. There were one hundred and fifty-nine casualties, and another two hundred and twelve had sustained injuries of varying severity. Seventy-five percent of the deaths had resulted from the unexpected attack of the Beetles, which led to the collapse of the army. Eight people had been shot while trying to steal Cores.

Aside from the Cores allotted to the Syndicate's key members, there wouldn't be many left after all the reward payouts — just forty-three. But every single one of them was an Alpha Core. Which meant forty-three new Weak Evolvers. Gramps would distribute them among the Syndicate, his own people, and Mom's subordinates. Good thing I'd insisted on collecting the Beetles' bodies — otherwise, the raid would have left us in debt...

Reactions online were mixed. In the African Confederation and India, the Syndicate was praised, and similar campaigns were encouraged. In the United States of Europica and the Arab Coalition, however, the Syndicate was criticized for the high number of casualties. The exact numbers weren't widely known, but anyone with half a brain could estimate the death toll. Opponents of the event focused on the fact that the dead had been Evolvers — the most valuable people to humanity. In Slavia and the Asian Commonwealth, media coverage emphasized how the raid had brought to light anomalies like the Nest. The name had already caught on, and any gathering of a large number of monsters was being called that now. Journalists expressed amazement that the army had survived at all and were in awe of my bravery — I had entered the Nest alone and taken out the commander-in-chief.

In short, an ambiguous reaction. But those were the opinions of governments. In the chats, it was a different story — ridiculous legends about the raid spread like wildfire. In one major Asian chat, a post had gone viral where some guy claimed to have "insider information." According to him, over the course of two days, the Syndicate had gathered five thousand Alpha Cores.

There was also a lot of discussion about the flaming gas canisters. More and more clans were announcing the creation of their own laboratories.

But I wasn't worried about the blood propane formula getting out. As soon as Gramps brewed his first potion, I'd tell him about a weapon far more effective than blood propane. A weapon with a deceptively harmless name — Music Box. Its creation required an even more sophisticated laboratory than potion-brewing.

The news of my car explosion still hadn't died down. In India, the official media had outright declared me dead. Other countries were more cautious in their reporting, but they all agreed I was seriously injured and that Felix Von Belga was behind it. Gramps' people had done a flawless job.

In a couple of hours, I wrapped up everything that required my attention and decided to get some sleep.

The plane dropped me off in Vladivostok, which was close to the border with the Asian Commonwealth. I had no intention of entering the Primordial World from Commonwealth territory; that was far too risky. In Vladivostok, thanks to Gramps' people, I was able to enter the pyramid without any questions.

All the necessary orders had already been relayed to the Primordial World through Grandfathers' private army. They would also handle the trade with the Brittas family, and by the time I arrived, everything should be ready for the operation.

"Vladislav!"

I saw Miroslava as soon as I stepped into the clearing near the settlement. She was already waiting for me — we had agreed in advance to fly to the descent together.

"Don't use my name," I muttered, adjusting my mask.

"You have no idea how terrified I was when I heard about the attack." She pressed her hands to her chest. "Next time, at least give me a heads-up!"

"Are you recovered?"

"Almost. But I'll manage."

"Let's go. We don't have much time."

"How are we flying? You know I'm slow."

"Get on my back," I decided.

"Uh..." Miroslava hesitated.

"Just do it — it's faster that way."

First, I enhanced my DNA fusion, growing taller and stronger. Then I turned my back to her and crouched down.

"You're huge in this form," she muttered as she climbed onto me, wrapping her legs around my torso and her arms around my neck.I tensed at the feel of her chest pressed against my back, but judging by her sharp inhale, she was even more flustered.

With a slight push, I lifted off the ground, calling the wind to aid me. A while ago, carrying another person would've been impossible for me, but with my current DNA purity, it was effortless.

"Keep an eye on our surroundings."

"Roger."

A couple of minutes later, a flock of Electric Larks locked onto us. There were seven of them, but all were just beasts.

I didn't even have to do anything — spikes shot from Miroslava's shoulder, connected to her suit by thin silver threads. In mere seconds, the larks were dead, their bodies entangled in the threads.

"I see Gramps is still upgrading the suits," I noted.

"Of course. But not as fast as I'd like. And mass production isn't possible yet — the Prince is still ramping up cube manufacturing. That's taking up a lot of resources."

Miroslava adjusted the threads so that the dead larks trailed behind us like a string of beads, curved into the shape of a horseshoe. The gruesome display kept other predators at bay.

After a few hours, we finally reached Mayor Hansh's settlement. I landed at the border, and Miroslava climbed off.

"Make sure the others don't say my name. I'm staying in hiding for now."

She looked me up and down. Dressed entirely in black, I must've looked the part.

"You look like a ninja. I'll just tell them you're my ninja. Sound good?"

"Fine," I agreed easily. I wasn't planning to stick around in the Primordial World for long anyway.

We entered the settlement and headed straight for the mayor's house. The streets were buzzing — people were still talking about the event and what we had encountered there.

"How did they even survive?"

"Delta took down the lead Beetle. The insect army fell apart after that."

"And then the Snakes ate them."

"Is it the same at every descent? The Clowns'

site says Weak Evolver squads can hunt safely within the first ten miles."

"What do the Clowns even know? Did they assemble an army to clear a descent? They're just loudmouths."

"Yeah, they should join some circus."

"Hey, did you hear? Delta's car got blown up in Brussels. They say the Von Belgas were behind it."

I walked on, listening to the chatter. Nothing new — just gossip and speculation. By the time we reached the mayor's house, the courtyard was bustling with activity.

"Miroslava!" Natsuko ran up to us.

"Get the guys together, we need to talk," Miroslava said, briefly glancing my way before giving Natsuko a wink.

"Uh... Okay. Give me a minute." Clearly Natsuko didn't understand, but she didn't press further. "By the way, where's Vladislav? There's talk his car got blown up, but that's BS, right? And should we bring along the gear the Brittas sent?"

"Yeah, absolutely. I'll explain everything later. And have someone take those birds away — I'll keep their Cores for the institute."

It took less than ten minutes for everyone to gather.

"Ah, they patched me up here once," Wang Bo-lai said, surveying the room with a nostalgic look in his eyes. "Those were good times."

He was seated on a chair, hands folded over his belly. Besides him, Miroslava, and me, the room held Natsuko, Dumisa, Liang, Anish, Nitya,

Mayor Hansh, and Andrei. In the corner lay bulging backpacks filled with gear from the Brittas, still unopened.

"Let's begin," I said, removing the mask.

"Great disguise, Boss," Wang Bolai flashed two thumbs up. "But you gotta work on your posture. You sit here just like a boss — anyone can tell it's you."

"Nobody should know I'm alive or that I'm in the settlement," I said pointedly, mostly addressing the mayor, who replied with knowing nod.

"Before we start, there's someone I want you to meet," Natsuko suddenly interjected.

I frowned.

"He's a Lunarian. You can trust him — he's Jiao's personal aide."

"Fine."

Natsuko left the room and soon returned with a tall figure dressed in a black-and-brown hooded robe. He carried a large backpack with a long case protruding from it.

The Lunarian removed the backpack without uttering a single word, extracted the case, and handed it to Natsuko. Grinning like a cat, she approached me.

"It's a gift from Jiao."

I opened the case and withdrew a straight long sword in a leather sheath. Its white bone-carved hilt ended in a tiger's head, each eye a triangle.

I drew the blade slowly — it was extremely light, with matte white finish.

"It's crafted from an Alpha's bone," the Lunarian said hoarsely. "A Storm Buffalo, killed personally by Curtis Johnson."

I raised my brows, inspecting the blade. Jiao had strengthened it completely, sheath included. I couldn't imagine why Johnson would allow such a masterpiece to be made.

"The Moon remembers kindness," the Lunarian said, as though reading my thoughts. "Once, you warned our leader, saving his life. The Earthlings' raid against the Snow Leopard had gotten wiped out completely."

I nodded. So the Snow Leopard, Lord of Silver, had claimed someone else's life this time.

"I'll name this sword... Bai Hu's Claw. Tell your leader I'm grateful. And I'll speak to Jiao personally."

The Lunarian bowed and left.

"Boss, can I touch the sword?" Wang Bolai asked eagerly.

"Natsuko, what's the situation with the Snakes?" I ignored the fat man's request.

"They've started moving. White Silkworm hasn't shown himself yet. Why would he corner himself?"

"With his squad of Beetles, White Silkworm can hold the cave a very long time," I recalled how I'd nearly died in the monster's lair. My leg started aching again.

"You think he's planning to hole up there and defend himself?" Natsuko frowned.

"Yes. Our job is to draw Silkworm out — and we'll do it right now. Anish, Liang, Wang Bolai, and Dumisa are coming with me. Nitya and Miroslava will stay ready. Mayor, will you join them?"

"I suppose so," the Indian smiled. "Working with you is always profitable, Vladislav."

"We'll take Selena along," I decided. "And everyone gets a crossbow with strengthened bolts."

"That's it?" Natsuko said, surprised.

"Yes. But first, I'll need Air Beetle Cores."

"You'll have them," Natsuko nodded. "How many more Cores do you want set aside?"

"As many as you can. Preferably from monsters close to Transformation Atomei."

After acquiring the new DNA spiral, I'd need plenty of Cores to boost purity.

"Give my share to Vladislav," Dumisa spoke up. "I don't need any Cores."

"Mine too," Liang nodded. "I've got almost ten percent purity already. If I bring any Cores back to Earth, I'll have to sell them all to the Li family, anyway."

Seeing doubt in Miroslava's and Natsuko's eyes, I added:

"That'll be enough. All right, let's gear up and move out."

"How exactly are we gonna draw him out?" Wang Bolai asked with curiosity, leaping from his chair and slinging the huge backpack over his shoulder. "What did the Brittas send? Some device that beams cosmic signals straight into Silkworm's ears, making him run right to us?"

"Close enough. We'll figure it out as we get there," I rose and secured the sheath to my side. Later I'd practice to see where it felt best.

We stepped outside the mayor's house.

"Who the hell are you?" came Wang Bolai's

surprised voice.

Sitting atop the fence was a boy about twelve or thirteen years old, staring right at us. He was filthy, dressed in homemade shirt and trousers, sleeves and legs rolled up, barefoot. Dark hair, blue eyes, with a crooked scar across his forehead — he looked like a little thug.

He jumped down nimbly and ran up to Natsuko.

"Let me join the Syndicate!"

Judging by his tattoo, he hadn't become an Evolver yet. And his accent marked him as someone from the United States of Europica.

"How'd you get into the Primeval World?" Natsuko asked in surprise. "Kids aren't allowed in here."

"Let me join the Syndicate!" the boy repeated. "I'm not a kid."

"Prove it," Wang Bolai challenged.

The boy thought for a moment.

"I touched a woman's boob once!"

Miroslava choked. She'd just been receiving another batch of cubes containing Lark Cores.

"And what was it like?" Wang Bolai asked with genuine interest. "I mean, how did it feel?"

"Soft," the boy grinned widely, revealing missing teeth. "Like a really ripe tomato."

"Lucky bastard," Wang Bolai muttered with envy in his voice.

"Well? Are you letting me join?" The boy looked at Natsuko, apparently deciding she was the one in charge.

"We don't let kids join us," she said, shaking

her head.

"I'm not a kid! I've already proved it!" the boy protested. "Where I live, people get killed every day."

"What about the police?" Wang Bolai asked skeptically.

"The coppers know everything, but they don't give a damn," the kid waved him off. "So, what's the verdict? I'm sure I'll have a really rare ability. Just give me a chance, will you?"

Miroslava glanced at me, rolling a cube in her palm. I shrugged, leaving the decision up to her.

"Come here," she said, crouching beside the boy. She placed the cube on the ground and pulled on a glove. "Let's see what your ability is."

The boy's eyes went round — he looked like a deer caught in headlights. He stared at Miroslava in shock, completely transfixed.

"Give me your hand," Miroslava said. "What's your name?"

"A-Allen," he mumbled, stretching out his right hand. "Are you the Magnet Princess, miss? I've only seen pictures of you, but in real life, you're the most beautiful lady I've ever seen. You're..."

He shut up the moment Miroslava pressed a beast's Liquid Core to his tattoo.

"We're leaving," Miroslava said, standing up and ruffling Allen's hair. "Grow up strong."

Natsuko walked over and handed me a cube. I quickly put on my glove, pulled out a Wind Beetle Core, and pressed it to my tattoo. My virtual DNA spiral's purity increased to 9.95%.

"What's the skill?" Wang Bolai blurted out, unable to hold back his curiosity.

Just then, Selena entered, looking grim, accompanied by a Evolver from the military. I gave a signal, and we all started heading out. As we walked, Selena met my eyes and recognized me. Without a word, she joined the group.

"Earth Manipulation. Pit," Allen muttered. The triangle on his wrist turned yellow. "That's a cool skill, right?"

"Even the simplest skill can be powerful," Liang said, giving him a sympathetic look. "So don't lose hope."

We quickly left the settlement, making our way toward the descent. Allen tried to follow, but Natsuko ordered for him to be caught and held back.

"How did he even get into the pyramid?" Miroslava muttered. "Are they letting kids in now?"

"Definitely not," Liang replied. "I think he just got lucky and slipped in unnoticed."

"Poor kid," Wang Bolai sighed. "With Pit, he won't be doing anything exciting. He'll be stuck building structures or setting traps. And I actually believed he'd get a strong ability for a moment."

"Vladislav," Selena said, catching up to me. "Mind explaining where we're going and why you're here instead of in a hospital? And aren't you worried I'll turn you in?"

I smirked. "Go ahead. You'll get a reward for helping with the descent."

I'd read plenty of rumors on the plane. Some claimed I'd been blown up because several of my alleged lovers from the Von Belga clan had found out about each other. Others insisted that Heng had taken revenge on me for killing their Patriarch. A third group swore I'd orchestrated the whole thing myself and even had 'proof' to back it up — likely the work of the Von Belgas. Either way, no one would believe Selena.

"Five Alpha Cores," she said after a moment of thought.

"Three. It'll take ten minutes at most. We're fighting one monster, killing it, and heading back. Your help might not even be needed."

"Oh yeah?" Selena narrowed her eyes. "Fine. Three."

"Vladislav," Liang called to me.

I approached and shot him a questioning look.

"I got a visit from the Li clan," he whispered. "They threatened me and reminded me about my mother. They're demanding I leave the moment I get the chance — Jiahao wants to speak with me personally."

He was clearly scared, and I didn't blame him.

"Don't worry. Stall them for now. As soon as I get the Silkworm Core, I'll deal with the Li clan myself," I promised.

"Thanks." Liang nodded, still looking uneasy.

We reached the descent and started unpacking the gear.

"What the hell is this?" Wang Bolai was holding up a soft gray helmet shaped like a silkworm's head. Dumisa was trying to assemble parts of a wing.

"It's a suit," I said, scanning the descent.

The ravine that had once held the Beetle Nest looked like a pit of mud. The walls had caved in, and pockets of murky water bubbled at the bottom. The Water Pythons weren't spewing ordinary water — it was weak acid. A grayish stain stretched from the ravine toward the forest, streaked with brown, black, and rust-colored patches. Fragments of bone and carapace littered the ground, mixed with bloodstains and mucus. This was where the battle between the Beetles and the Snakes had taken place.

"A suit? I don't get it, Boss," Wang Bolai muttered, eyes darting nervously. He could sense he was in danger.

"What's this?" Selena approached me, holding up a metal canister. I took it from her, unscrewed the lid, and found a spray nozzle inside.

"The plan is called Honey Trap," I explained, sealing the canister. "Wang Bolai, you're going to put on the suit and head over to that crevice. Your job is to seduce the Silkworm. You'll pretend to be a female."

Wang Bolai took a few steps back, mumbling something under his breath. His eyes rolled back, and he collapsed straight onto his back.

Chapter 10

The Honey Trap

"R-RIGHT," I MUTTERED, looking at the fat man who had just fainted. "Anish, wake him up."

"Nuh-uh," the Indian refused immediately. "No way."

"I'll do it." Selena smirked and stepped toward Wang Bolai. She'd caught his sticky gaze on her ass plenty of times, and she was clearly eager to settle the score with the fat man. She wouldn't mind teaching him a lesson.

Liang, Dumisa, and Anish watched her with sympathy.

"Get up!" Selena started slapping Wang Bolai's chubby cheeks. "Hey! Get up!"

She got into it, and her strikes grew stronger, broader. Wang Bolai's face slackened, his eyelids lifted, and his eyes rolled back.

"Get up!" Selena struck him one last time,

straightened up, and dusted off her reddened palms. Then she complained, "He's not waking up."

"He's been awake for a while," Liang chuckled.

"Thanks." Wang Bolai groaned as he got up. His cheeks had turned red and puffed up, and now he looked like a pufferfish. "I'll remember those tender hands of yours. A girl's never caressed me before."

His swollen lips made his speech slurred. Selena wiped her hands on her clothes in disgust.

"I'm ready, Boss!" Wang Bolai looked at me resolutely. "After that, I'm ready for anything!"

Miroslava and Nitya giggled, Liang covered his face with his palm, and Anish and Dumisa had disappeared altogether. I held back my laughter to keep the whole thing from turning into a circus.

"Put the suit on," I ordered once I'd calmed down. "You need to lure out the Silkworm Moth. Then we'll play it by ear. I'm hoping there won't be too many Bugs with him. Now, about them. The Devil Ladybugs — look like oversized ladybugs, but they're purple and black instead of red and white,. They release a hallucinogenic gas that drives both people and monsters insane. The gas is colorless and odorless, making these Bugs far more dangerous than the Blue Sheep. One breath, and we'll slaughter each other. Next — Defender Beetles. You'll recognize them right away — they're crystalline blue. They look like a cross between a mantis and a rhinoceros beetle, with massive armor and long, spear-like legs. And finally — the Jumping Beetles..."

I described the White Silkworm Moth's retinue and spent a couple of minutes answering questions.

"You told me there was only one monster and that it'd take twenty minutes," Selena said, pursing her lips in displeasure.

"No more questions?" I looked at the team and went on, "The crevice is at the five-hundred-foot mark. We'll stop at three hundred and fifty feet and start there."

After a brief prep, we rushed downward. Selena said nothing more — curiosity won out over caution. Miroslava, Hansh, and Nitya stayed above. If we needed backup, Anish could pull them down to us quickly, but for now, they were safer where they were.

We stopped at the three-hundred-and-fifty-foot mark, and Wang Bolai awkwardly squeezed into the female silkworm moth suit. His swollen cheeks kept him from putting the helmet on properly, and Dumisa helped with that struggle. In the end, after much difficulty, they got the helmet on. Despite the suit's elastic material, Wang Bolai had to put in a massive effort just to fit into it.

"Boss, it's hot in here. My blood pressure's up, I can't breathe, Boss."

A massive monster stood before me. It looked nothing like a silkworm moth — legs stuck out from its belly, and its wings dragged weakly along the ground. I started to suspect the suit wasn't necessary at all and that Georgie had just been messing with us. But I wasn't about to take the risk.

"Selena, spray him with the perfume," I handed her the canister.

Selena shot me an annoyed glare but took the can and immediately sprayed Wang Bolai in the face. A thick white stream burst from the nozzle.

I stepped back, grimacing at the stench. Sickly sweet rot mixed with coal and gasoline.

Wang Bolai coughed, and Selena covered her nose as she generously continued dousing him.

"Spread it evenly over the whole body," I called out.

"You do it yourself if you're so smart!" Selena snapped. She circled the fat silkworm, diligently coating him with the reeking substance. The moth choked.

"Boss, I beg you! This is cruel! Boss!"

"Endure it! If you complete the mission, you get a reward!" I egged him on. I did feel a little sorry for him, but someone had to take one for the team. And thanks to his skill, Wang Bolai was the toughest among us — he had the best chance of surviving if things went south.

"What reward, Boss?" Wang Bolai roared, dropping to his knees. "I'll never live down this disgrace! I've dishonored my family, my ancestors, and my country! There's only one path left — I'm going to die by my own hand!"

I winced. The moment he heard "reward," the fat man started driving up his price.

"You'll get five Alpha Cores. You can do whatever you want with them."

"I'll kill myself!"

"Ten Cores."

"Only death can wash away this shame!"

"A custom weapon, reinforced by Jiao."

"I want to live..." Wang Bolai's voice took on a thoughtful note. "But no! I must die!"

"All done." Selena tossed the can aside and walked over to me. I stared at her. An idea took root in my mind. Selena paled.

"Whatever you're thinking — the answer is NO!" Selena started backing away, fear flickering in her eyes.

But considering her personality and weighing the pros and cons, I made my offer.

"Selena will give you a peck on the cheek and a massage," I said. I needed Wang Bolai to perform at his peak. The White Silkworm was too important for me. And Selena... she'd agree to much more than that if the price was right. This I knew from experience.

"In addition to that, you'll get a custom weapon of your choice. And I'll have Jiao reinforce it."

In truth, I was planning to make one for everyone, anyway. Right now, Dumisa, Miroslava, and I were the only ones who had them.

"I said NO!" Selena snapped.

"Boss, I'd lay down my life for the cause!" Wang Bolai lumbered toward the crevice. "Anything for the Syndicate! And let the one who dares call me a coward gouge out their own eyes! I am Wang Bolai — the man who will become the greatest chef in the Solar System!"

Wang Bolai tripped and fell.

"You hear me?! I said NO!" Selena fumed.

"After the event, we had plenty of bolts and crossbows left. I'll give you some. You're planning a caravan, right? Bolts with reinforced tips will come in handy."

"And canisters of that gas," Selena instantly switched to a businesslike tone. "A hundred of each. Bolts and canisters."

"Then you'll kiss Wang Bolai on the lips. Not just a peck — a real kiss. A passionate one even."

"Hah, easy!" Selena grinned triumphantly.

"I'd give my life for the Boss!" the fat man bellowed and shot forward like a bullet.

"Wait, not so fast!"

Wang Bolai had already passed three hundred feet and was rapidly approaching four hundred.

"Get ready!" I drew my sword and took off. "Anish, be prepared at any moment."

"Got it!"

There was a hissing sound, followed by chittering and clacking.

Monsters began emerging from the crevice. Two Defender Beetles were carrying the White Silkworm, which lay atop a cushion of silk threads. They were accompanied by two Jumping Beetles and two Devil Ladybugs. Not enough to attract unnecessary attention, but still a considerable force — this squad was incredibly dangerous.

The moment Wang Bolai came into view, the White Silkworm flapped its wings in excitement, spun its eyes, and started making strange noises.

"Anish, open the portal! Selena, go!"

There was a loud bang.

Wang Bolai tore his suit apart and leapt. Two

Jumping Beetles instantly teleported to him, their blade-like limbs swinging. The fat man dropped, rolled, and let their strikes pass over him.

At that moment, Selena stepped out of the portal and unleashed Frost Breath, enveloping all the Bugs, the Silkworm, and Wang Bolai all at once. Then she jumped back into the portal. The maneuver took only two or three seconds. By then, Dumisa, Liang, and I had emerged from the portal and launched into action.

Dumisa cloaked himself in Mass Armor and charged forward. Liang used Grapple on the Silkworm while I shot upward, whipping up a violent wind. My main targets were the airborne Devil Ladybugs — I couldn't let their gas reach us.

There was a loud crack.

Shivering from the cold, Wang Bolai somehow managed to rip a leg off a Jumping Beetle and began pummeling it with wild fury. The second monster teleported toward Dumisa and tried to slice him to pieces, but Dumisa's multi-ton fist struck first, and the creature literally exploded.

I sent the Devil Ladybugs flying with a blast of wind and pursued them, scattering their gas away from us. Bai Hu's Claw effortlessly sliced the first one in half. At the same moment, an air bullet shredded the second one's wings, sending it plummeting. I dived after it, slashing my sword in a diagonal arc and cleaving it in two. Then I crashed down upon the Defender Beetles.

They were the only ones left alive, along with the Silkworm, which was still restrained by Grapple. The Defender Beetles couldn't move their master, so they assumed a defensive stance. Their long legs extended and crossed over one another, while crystalline growths sprouted from their carapaces and heads. Then the Defender Beetles reared up on their hind legs, forming an uneven blue dome that shielded the White Silkworm. With their remaining spear-like limbs, they lunged at Wang Bolai and Dumisa with lightning-fast blinding strikes.

Dumisa survived only because of his armor. Wang Bolai, on the other hand, somehow managed to dodge three times. On the fourth, he caught one of the legs and threw his entire weight onto it.

There was a loud crack. The limb snapped, and at that exact moment, Bai Hu's Claw drove into the head of the first Defender Beetle.

"Anish, portal!" I shouted, slashing the second Beetle in a sweeping motion and breaking through the gap in their defenses.

More Beetles were starting to emerge from the crevice, Devil Ladybugs taking to the sky. If we didn't hurry, we were dead.

I plunged my clawed hand into the White Silkworm's chest. For a brief second, I thought I saw disbelief and hurt frozen on its face. It had only wanted to find a mate...

Struggling to force my hand deeper, I felt around until I found its heart. Then I squeezed, feeling warm liquid trickling down my palm.

There was a loud bang, and a violent tremor shook me. The last Defender Beetle's shell cracked — Dumisa had reached the insect, and one strike was all it took to finish it off.

"Everyone into the portal!"

Would you like to create a second virtual DNA spiral?

I most certainly would.

The Silkworm withered before our eyes, shrinking into a mummy — something akin to a botched taxidermy specimen.

Virtual DNA spiral created!

Purity of virtual spiral: 3.7%

I bolted backward, tumbling into the portal just as three Jumping Beetles teleported to the Silkworm's corpse. If I'd hesitated even a fraction of a second...

Bursting out on the other side, I soared into the sky. The Defender Beetles' lifeless husks lay stiff at the battle site, their leaderless kin swarming around them in confusion. But beyond them, at the second-mile mark, snakes were slithering out of the forest by the hundreds, racing up the slope. What the hell did they want?!

"We should get back to the settlement as soon as possible."

"They're not stopping," Liang murmured, staring slack-jawed at the tide of snakes. "There are thousands of them!"

The Beetles, finally grasping what had happened, scattered in all directions. The snakes, however, didn't change course — they came straight at us, a relentless flood.

"Feels like the forest's top monster is pissed about the White Silkworm's death and wants revenge," Liang muttered.

"How far do you think they'll go?" Mayor

Hansh frowned, watching the slope.

"In any case, it's best not to let anyone connect us to this. We'll head back to the settlement and see how far the snakes advance. Mayor, you should warn everyone — tell them not to wander off."

Hansh nodded, and we sprinted for the settlement. I didn't try merging the second virtual DNA spiral with my main one just yet. Its purity was below five percent — not much use for now.

"I need Beast Cores. If you spot any creatures, let me know," I said, then fired an air bullet into the canopy of a nearby tree, piercing the head of a Red-Beaked Woodpecker. I dashed over and caught its falling body. With my bare hands, I tore open its chest and extracted its Liquid Core.

Purity of virtual spiral: 4.0%

By the time we reached the settlement, I had raised the DNA purity to 4.9%. Unfortunately, I hadn't come across an Alpha on the way.

Natsuko and Andrei were waiting for us.

"Well?!" Natsuko looked at me eagerly. "Did it work?!"

"Yes. Bring all the Cores to the mayor's house — I'll be there."

"Boss, what about my reward?"

"Until you shower and brush your teeth, I'm not coming anywhere near you," Selena declared flatly.

"What happened between you two?" Natsuko asked, staring wide-eyed at the satisfied fat man and the fuming Selena.

"Love," Wang Bolai winked at Natsuko. "Whatever you say, dear. I'll go wash up right now. It got pretty hot back there — I really did sweat."

Selena grimaced, shooting Wang Bolai a venomous glare. But after seeing his abilities firsthand, her attitude toward the fat man shifted. He had proven himself a fierce fighter, unafraid of risk. I, in turn, once again praised myself for bringing Crazy Wang into my team. His growth was astonishing — at this point, I wasn't sure I could take him in a life-or-death fight.

Natsuko had completely lost track of what was happening. I didn't bother explaining anything and headed for the mayor's house. I covered my face with a mask, and since I wasn't wearing Syndicate gear, no one recognized me.

At the courtyard entrance, I spotted Allen and Hu Xuan Jian. The boy sat by a pit, looking dejected, while Hu Xuan drank baijiu, giving Allen drunken advice.

I needed to decide what to do with Hu Xuan Jian. He was a drunk, but as an Evolver, he was incredibly valuable. If he was telling the truth, he used to be a chemist. Maybe I could lure him to Slavia, to my grandfather's lab? I'd have to ask Andrei.

Inside the mayor's house, I waited for Natsuko to haul in the cubes filled with Alpha Cores and started using them one by one. All the Cores belonged to Alphas closely tied to the Transformation Atomei, so each increased DNA purity by at least 0.6% — sometimes as much as 0.8%.

By the time I had absorbed eight Cores, my status read:

The One Who Changes the Future

Name: Vladislav Li-Vavilonsky
Race: Weak Human
DNA Purity: 9.8%
Evolutionary Branch: Atomeus
Base Skill: Complete Transformation (absolute)
First Virtual DNA Spiral: Bai Hu, Lord of the Wind
Bai Hu DNA Purity: 9.95%
Second Virtual DNA Spiral: White Silkworm, Lord of Monsters
White Silkworm DNA Purity: 9.98%
Neutrino Count: 62%

Looking at my status filled me with genuine satisfaction. This was exactly why I had created the Syndicate — to immediately maximize DNA purity upon acquiring a virtual spiral. Now, all that remained was to test what abilities I'd gained by activating the skill.

The door swung open, and a pale Natsuko entered.

"The snakes are already on the mountain and still climbing, killing every monster and human in their path. If this keeps up, the first ones will reach the settlement in ten minutes. What do we do?!"

She looked completely lost.

"Tell everyone to exit the Primordial World."

"But Anish and Nitya..."

"I'll take them with me. I'll help them reach another settlement. Call them over. This is no joke — there are hundreds of Alphas in that swarm, including monsters like Explosive Snakes, Red-Eyed Snakes, Invisible Snakes, and Jumping Snakes.

Even I might die if one catches me off guard."

"Can't you make the announcement yourself?" Natsuko was visibly shaken by my words. "They'll listen to you. And what about the branded Indians? There are so many of them! Some of them were supposed to join Syndicate Epsilon — they participated in the raid."

"Do we still have canisters of blood propane?" I asked thoughtfully.

"We do."

"Summon everyone with Fire Manipulation and give them the canisters. We'll set the forest ablaze to buy the Indians some time."

"The Evolvers will take the canisters with them when they leave," Natsuko warned. "We won't be able to control them as strictly as before."

"I know. Tell Andrei it's my order. He'll handle the logistics. Get to it."

Natsuko nodded and dashed out of the house. I followed and took to the air, scanning for Mayor Hansh. When I found him, I landed nearby and pulled him aside to explain the situation. The longer I talked, the grimmer his expression became.

"Why don't you announce this yourself?" he asked. "Why me?"

"You already know the answer," I patted his shoulder.

Taking a deep breath, Hansh nodded. Then he spoke:

"Attention!" I amplified his voice to carry across the entire settlement and into the forest beyond. "This is Hansh Khattar, mayor of the settlement! Thousands of snakes have crawled out of the Nest at the base of the slope — they're already on the mountain! The monsters will be here any minute! If you don't want to die, exit the Primordial World! If you can't, run! We'll be setting the forest on fire soon to slow them down!"

The settlement erupted like a powder keg. People scattered in every direction, panicking.

I nodded to the mayor and shot back into the sky.

In the future, every Indian who survived would owe their lives to Hansh Khattar. His popularity in India would skyrocket. A powerful ally like that would be invaluable — the event had only been possible thanks to the Indians who had followed Hansh's lead.

In the mayor's courtyard, a table with a map had already been set up, surrounded by soldiers and Natsuko.

"Can you handle things on your own? I want to get Nitya and Anish out of here."

"Yes, we've got this," Andrei nodded. "But are you sure? The secret of the gas will be exposed to many people — you understand its value."

"This will save the lives of those who are loyal to us."

"Commander!"

A breathless and frightened Nitya burst into the courtyard, with a sullen Anish following behind. Both carried backpacks — ready to flee.

"I'll take you to another settlement."

"What about everyone else?"

"We'll just have to hope the snakes don't reach

the settlement," I said, not believing my own words. Then I flew up to them, grabbing Nitya under my right arm and Anish under my left.

Thanks to my second virtual DNA spiral, my Neutrino count had increased, albeit not by much. Right now, there weren't many people in the entire Solar System with a higher Neutrino count than mine. But with the extra weight, the drain was high.

We had been flying for about two minutes when Nitya spoke:

"There's smoke. The forest is on fire. I pray for them to be safe..."

"We don't even know any of them," Anish grumbled.

"But they're people. Just like us."

Anish snorted but said nothing.

I kept flying, heading for the next settlement. Whenever beasts attacked, I knocked them down into the trees with bursts of wind.

As we got close, I descended.

"Move toward the spot where we appear," I advised. "It'll make it easier to find you."

"You're not coming with us?" Nitya asked.

"No. I need to check on Hansh's settlement."

Inwardly, I added, *"And test the second DNA spiral's ability."*

"Then we'll go."

Once Anish and Nitya disappeared into the trees, I deactivated my ability, losing control over the wind.

Then I activated it again — but this time, I chose the second DNA spiral.

CHAPTER 11

THE SECOND VIRTUAL SPIRAL

Primordial World
Xin Shang Peak

AN INDIAN ARMY SQUAD moved through the forest. Twenty Evolvers in total, seven of them Weaklings, each belonging to India's most powerful organization — the Golden Army, personally commanded by the country's Supreme Commander.

Their mission was clear — eliminate Hansh Khattar quietly. Lately, his influence in Indian political circles had grown too strong. The strangest part was that Hansh Khattar had never left the Primordial World or openly declared any political ambitions, yet the entire nation had been watching his every move.

The squad leader slowed down, frowning. He smelled smoke.

"Snakes are coming," the scout whispered. "A

lot of them — around twenty."

"Yogesh, deal with them," the leader ordered, pressing forward.

Ten men split off from the main group and spread out, preparing to engage the snakes. The leader and the remaining soldiers continued toward Hansh Khattar's settlement. Along the way, they frequently encountered packs of beasts, but so far, no one had suffered even a scratch. Everyone remained calm.

This time, however, was different. Less than a minute later, the scout running beside the leader spoke in alarm.

"I hear screams! Yogesh and his group can't handle them... The snakes are still coming this way!"

The leader halted abruptly and gave a single command:

"Prepare yourselves."

Whoosh!

Flat blade-like snakes slithered out from between the trees, their scales still wet with the blood of Yogesh and his men — forever lost in the forests of Xin Shang Peak. Two soldiers barely had time to react before the razor-edged snakes impaled them right through the torso.

A two-headed cobra emerged behind them, both mouths gaping open as they exhaled thick fog — yellow from the right, pink from the left. From the opposite side, several crimson pythons spat out balls of fire.

"They're all Alphas," the squad leader rasped, his skin turning blue from the cobra's venom.

And in the next instant, the tail of a massive metal snake slammed into him, taking his head clean off.

* * *

Upon activating Absolute Full Transformation, I could select one of my DNA spirals.

A visual appeared before me — my DNA chain spun slowly, with two transparent chains hovering parallel to it, one above, one below. The upper chain was larger, more stable, while the lower one flickered, as if on the verge of vanishing.

I focused on the lower chain. A message appeared:

Merging virtual DNA with the main strand!

The smaller chain rose, touching the primary spiral. Immediately, I felt a searing pain. My blood boiled.

Rigid white bristles sprouted along my arms. The same thing was happening across my entire body. The urge to scratch myself was overwhelming, but I gritted my teeth and endured it. The pain surged from head to toe, stabbing into my eyes, and then my vision changed. Colors took on a deep blue hue, everything became more vivid. My mind expanded, growing colder, more detached. Thoughts surfaced at an astonishing speed — I could analyze problems in an instant.

Remembering how the first Bai Hu merge had ended, I cut off the ability. The bristles vanished, my vision returned to normal. Gasping for breath, I dropped to one knee. Blood trickled from my eyes, my skin burned and itched unbearably.

I slumped against a tree, struggling to catch my breath. My Neutrino count read 13% of its max capacity.

Before, activating my ability had consumed half my Neutrino reserves. But now, after all my upgrades, it only drained about 24%. I'd need another 2% just to fly to the settlement. My Neutrino count regenerated slowly — about 15-16% per hour.

When an Evolver became Weak, they developed unique traits. Some had larger Neutrino or Quark count than others. Some regenerated faster. My stats had always been average in both respects.

I sat there, waiting for my Neutrinos to replenish. I wanted to check on the settlement before returning to Earth. I knew from experience that the second DNA merge would go more smoothly than the first.

Despite the chaos undoubtedly unfolding in Hansh's settlement, I was in high spirits. During the virtual DNA merge, I had felt what I had long craved — the state of cold rationality.

Back when I had the Enhanced Brain ability, I could enter this state whenever I wanted. It allowed me to discard all unnecessary thoughts and emotions, to analyze situations with perfect clarity.

Choosing the White Silkworm, I had known my brain would change during the merge. But I was not the White Silkworm. My mind was wired differently, and I wasn't sure what skills I'd gain from the fusion.

The Silkworm's primary ability was Mental Threads. It could create them by the hundred. I probably wouldn't be able to replicate that, but I was more than satisfied with the cold rationality I had gained. I had missed it terribly in this life. It wasn't quite the same as my old ability, but it was better than nothing.

Once my Neutrino count had sufficiently recovered, I activated the skill again — but this time, I chose the upper DNA strand.

The wind returned to me at once.

The ability consumed no Neutrinos to maintain, which was why I had never deactivated it before. I had grown used to having the wind with me at all times. When I had stopped the ability earlier, it had felt like losing a limb — unfamiliar and deeply unpleasant.

I lifted off and flew toward Hansh's settlement.

Thick columns of smoke rose in the distance, blotting out parts of the sky.

As I approached, I saw that the settlement was gone.

Only ruins remained, swarming with snakes. Here and there, I spotted Indians fleeing. The fire had bought them time — but not much. The only thing saving them was the sheer size of the mountain. The snakes had spread in all directions, fighting not just humans, but also local monsters. No matter how many there were, they couldn't cover the entire mountain.

A scream rang out below — a young Indian woman was sprinting for her life, a Plated Snake slithering after her.

I descended, grabbed her, and took off.

Something purple flashed — a Jumping Snake lunged at me. Not an Alpha, just a beast. Even so, it nearly reached me — on instinct alone, I swung my sword, slicing its head off. Flying a safe distance away, I set the crying girl down.

"Run," I ordered.

"Y-yes! Thank you!"

She bolted, disappearing into the trees.

I ascended once more.

In the distance, a painful shriek echoed — a fellow Evolver had encountered multiple snakes and was quickly devoured.

Trees didn't burn as well in the Primordial World as they did on Earth. More accurately, fire spread much more slowly. That was exactly what was happening now — the patch of forest between the settlement and the slope was smoldering but had nearly burned out. The snakes had abandoned the ruined settlement and were now spreading rapidly through the forest. Had the Sentient Monster from the slope decided to move up the mountain, preparing a new lair? Or had it simply ordered the snakes to kill everything they could reach?

I helped three more Indians. When my Neutrino count dropped to a critical level again, I activated my tattoo.

It was time to return to Earth — it had been a brutal day.

Oleg was waiting for me at the pyramid. He got me through all the security checks without issue, then drove me to the country house, where I collapsed into bed. After using my ability, I had no interest in handling affairs. The past few days had been too overwhelming — I hadn't slept properly in ages.

I woke up very early — five hours was more than enough to feel rested. The first thing I did was stand before the full-length mirror and activate my ability again, choosing the Silkworm's virtual DNA.

Rigid white bristles sprouted all over my body, covering even my face and ears. I looked like an ape. Or, more accurately, like Bigfoot. But the more bristles covered my body, the sharper my mind became.

At a certain stage of the DNA merge, my eyes changed color, turning a brilliant blue. Then a message appeared:

New Skill Acquired: Mental Threads (10).

And I began to understand what that skill was.

Mental Threads could be used in multiple ways — to protect my brain, to attack... and to tame monsters.

I had gained the same ability as the White Silkworm. But whereas it could command hundreds of monsters, I could only control ten. All because of our different physiology. I lacked its wings and special glands.

As the head of the Delta Research Center, I had predicted these complications. Absolute Full Transformation had a weakness — not all abilities integrated equally well into a human body.My fusion with Bai Hu had gone perfectly. But with the Silkworm, I had miscalculated. Just ten measly threads...

I pouted in disappointment and attempted to summon a thread.

A vibrant blue filament slowly emerged from my right eye, visible only to me. It was about three feet long, trembling with micro-vibrations, curling in on itself. When the Thread fully extended, both ends connected, forming an uneven, shifting loop.

This was strange. I had assumed a Mental Thread always had to be anchored to its user's brain. At my mental command, the Thread retracted into my head and I froze, stunned.

I blinked. The Thread was literally inside my mind. I could feel it. It was an indescribable sensation — unlike anything else.

I tried to create another Thread, but failed. To my surprise, my Neutrino gauge had dropped to 10%, despite having been full just moments ago. So creating a single Thread consumed that much energy... Fine. I would generate them as needed. For now...

Still looking like a chimney-swept chimpanzee, I searched my backpack for the right smartphone and turned it on. Then I found the Patriarch's contact and called him.

Old Jiahao Li took his time answering — nearly three minutes.

"I'm listening," came Jiahao Li's heavy voice — a bad sign. "So you finally decided to call me, Vladislav."

"I really do apologize, Patriarch," I replied in an even voice. "First there was my father's death, and then an assassination attempt... All of it had a deep impact on me. And later, my organization's affairs consumed my full attention. But now I am ready to return to the Asian Commonwealth and elevate our family under your guidance and make it the most powerful in the entire country."

Jiahao remained silent. I had to continue.

"I am prepared to take the first step immediately. But I will require a favor from you in return."

"I'm listening," Jiahao said once again.

"I want to become an Elder. In exchange, I will share a portion of the profits we made during the raid."

"An Elder..." Jiahao pondered. "That is possible. How many Alpha Cores are you offering?"

"My entire share. Ten Cores. That's ten Weak Evolvers. And for the next year, I will contribute two Cores per month to the family."

"Make it fifteen Alpha Cores — and two years instead of one. If you agree, I will announce your appointment today, and within a week, the official ceremony will take place."

I paused.

"Fine, Patriarch. The stronger the Li family, the stronger am I as an Elder of the Li family."

"I am pleasantly surprised by your reasoning. You have grown a great deal since we last met."

"It is an honor to receive your praise, Patriarch."

"Well then, I'll leave you to it." Jiahao disconnected.

I lowered the phone. In the mirror, I watched my bristle-covered face — a face that was changing little by little... The eager boy in the reflection was slowly turning into a killer...

Book Three

* * *

United States of Europica, Brussels
The Von Belga family estate

"I didn't blow up his car." Felix Von Belga sat slumped in a chair, gripping his head. "And you know that."

"I do," said Solomon — the head of the Von Belga family, a stocky man with a thick black mustache dressed in an outrageously expensive black suit. He twirled a cigar between his fingers, his gold-rimmed glasses gleaming as he studied his son.

"I know that. And you know that. But that's not enough. I warned you — don't provoke those stronger than us. But you didn't listen. Prince Boris won't stop until you're dead. You understand that, don't you?"

"No one's even got hurt," Felix muttered. "They blew up my hotel!"

"It was *my* hotel," Solomon cut him off sharply. "You've sent an assassin after Vladislav. But that's not even the worst part. You failed, Felix. Your assassin has wounded Miroslava — Prince Boris's right hand. And judging by their response, he gave you up."

"That's impossible!" Felix's bloodshot eyes locked onto his father. "How did they even connect us to Ono Hanyu?! It was impossible to find the link between us!"

"It doesn't matter. You've overestimated yourself — and lost. All the evidence is against you. The Prince is already moving — he's made contact with Bruges, and they've begun squeezing us on all fronts. I recently learned that Antwerp received a visit from the Prince's men. If we don't meet his demands, the others will unite and wipe us out."

"This is the United States of Europica," Felix murmured, his strength failing. "Why is no one coming to our defense? Why are they letting the Prince do whatever he wants?"

"That's my fault," Solomon closed his eyes wearily. "I should never have given you so much freedom."

"Father…"

"You've been erased from the family records. From now on, you're on your own. I'll help you get to Australia — your goal is to survive. I'll try to fix this later. But for now — you need to disappear."

"…I understand, Father."

Felix's eyelids lowered, his eyes narrowing into slits. And deep within those shadowed pupils burned raw, undiluted hatred.

* * *

The United States of Europica
Berlin

Muhiddin silently observed the massive estate enclosed by a steel fence. It was impossible to recognize him now — bald, shirtless, covered head to toe in black tattoos. Behind him stood a jittery young man with a crooked smile. He scratched at the creases of his elbows constantly, glancing around nervously.

"We need to get inside and find a certain bastard," Muhiddin rasped.

"Let's go, let's go," the young man giggled. He was short and dark-skinned, clearly of mixed East Asian and Indian descent.

"We'll try to avoid unnecessary casualties. Take out the guards, get in, kill August Schmidt."

"Yes, yes, I know."

"We'll leave our mark on the walls. We are the Life Devourers. It's time the world knew our name."

Muhiddin took a deep breath, calming his racing heart, and strode toward the gate. His tattoos darkened, emitting a faint mist.

The man beside him giggled even louder. His skin shriveled and paled, the nails on his fingers thickened and extended, transforming into short claws.

The first two — and for now, the only — Life Devourers were about to announce themselves to the world.

* * *

Primordial World
The Great Ridge

Rosa Vavilonsky trudged forward, leading a small squad. Out of forty-four, only thirty-two remained alive, and each one of them was exhausted, both mentally and physically. Many were wounded.

Rosa hadn't expected the journey across the Great Ridge to be easy. But she had underestimated just how dangerous it would be. She had underestimated it badly.

"Your Ladyship, we're close," the man beside Rosa lowered his spyglass. "Three more hours, and we'll be there."

Rosa nodded weakly. Above, a griffon's shrill cry echoed. The bird had been tracking them for hours, hesitating to attack.

Rosa stumbled, nearly falling. Her assistant caught her — and immediately, the griffon whistled and dove. Rosa snapped up her hand, and a beam of light shot from her palm, blinding the griffon. The bird jerked sideways, trying to pull out of the dive. A blade flashed — one of the squad members, a Magnet Fielder, struck the griffon. A second Evolver used Attraction. The griffon never had a chance. Its headless corpse crashed to the ground, the beast never even getting the opportunity to showcase its abilities.

A man and a woman immediately rushed to the body — they were in charge of extracting Liquid Cores.

"Your Ladyship," one of them suddenly called out, surprised. "Look at this."

Rosa took the spyglass, following his pointing finger. And saw something bizarre. A troop of apes was descending the slope. At least fifty of them. It wasn't unusual — after all, Ape Mountain had received its name for a reason. But something was off. In the center of the troop, a golden-furred giant strode majestically. And on his head sat a small girl, pointing forward with her right hand while clutching a ragged stuffed monkey in her left. Her clothes were made of intricately woven branches and leaves, and she wore wooden shoes that dangled loosely from her feet.

"...That's the girl?" Rosa murmured in surprise. The day before she had set foot on the Great Ridge, her people had been given a photograph of the girl. Vladislav had been looking for her. According to him, she had fled to the Primordial World.

"Let's speed up," Rosa lowered the spyglass. "We'll reach the mountain and try to get her attention."

"Yes, Your Ladyship."

* * *

Earth, Beijing
A mansion on the outskirts of the city

I rocked quietly in a chair. If someone had lifted my shirt, they would have been shocked — my entire body was covered in short white bristles.

Four days had passed since I left the Primordial World. Over that time, I had completely mastered the second virtual DNA spiral and created eight out of ten available Threads. Every time I activated my ability and selected the White Silkworm's DNA, the Threads appeared in my mind.

The door opened, and Oleg stepped in.

"It's time. We need to go to the Li estate. The ceremony begins in two hours."

I nodded and rose, taking a few steps toward the mirror to adjust my clothing. My fingers lingered over my right pocket, which bulged ever so slightly.

The last thing I did was deactivate the ability, and then reactivate it. But this time, I selected the virtual DNA of Bai Hu, the Lord of the Wind. Only then did I step out of the house.

CHAPTER 12

THE GRUESOME CEREMONY

AS SOON AS I GOT into the car, Oleg reported,

"An unknown group carried out a massacre at the Schmidts' estate in the United States of Europica. Over twenty people were killed, including August Schmidt. The killers left a message — 'Life Devourers' was written on the wall."

I frowned. That didn't sound like Muhiddin — the execution was too brutal. But he had completed his mission. Later, when Oleg wasn't around, I would send Muhiddin the pre-recorded video of his wife.

"Another piece of news," Oleg added, this time looking elated. "Rosa Vavilonsky has returned from the Primordial World!"

"Excellent." I smiled. "Did she reach Ape Mountain?"

"I don't know. I just got word of her return."

"I hope she made it..."

I had deliberately not told my mother that relocation to another mountain resulted in getting bound to a new point of entry. Knowing her, she wouldn't have left the Primordial World even in the face of serious danger — she would have pushed forward to the end. But I had expected her to at least send one or two of her people back to Earth with news. Not a single one had returned. And lately, dark thoughts about her team's fate had begun haunting me more and more.

As the car sped down the highways, I was already gathering information about my mother. KanOn was buzzing — the media was ablaze with Rosa Vavilonsky's feat. The first to cross to the other side. I also found mentions of the Schmidts — a viral image was circulating in the chats, showing a smoldering black inscription on the wall:

LIFE DEVOURERS.

I didn't like Muhiddin's initiative. I hadn't asked him to be this flashy. And there were far too many casualties — he had wiped out August's entire family, including his two older brothers, his father, and his mother.

"We're arriving," Oleg's voice broke my thoughts.

I put my smartphone away and adjusted my clothes. Today was too important — there could be no mistakes.

The Li estate's parking lot was packed with luxury cars. An event like the appointment of a new Elder had to be witnessed by the entire family.

I stepped out of the car and headed for the entrance. My mind was occupied with the ceremony, so I didn't notice Meili approaching.

"Vladislav," my sister smiled. "Congratulations."

"Thank you." I nodded. "How are you?"

"Not bad. Let's talk later?"

"Of course, Meili. Let's go — I don't want to be late."

Talking casually, we entered the mansion together. Servants led us into a vast hall, already filled with people. As I walked, I nodded politely to some, exchanged greetings with others, mentally noting their faces. In the four days leading up to this, I had studied the Li family's genealogy in detail — I could now recognize almost every person here.

I felt uneasy with so many people staring at me. I wasn't used to this level of attention, especially from women. The young ladies weren't even hiding their stares — some tried to strike up conversations, others "accidentally" brushed against me.

Aside from the Li family, members of other prominent families were present, along with trusted journalists. Drones hovered above the hall — at least six of them were focused solely on me.

"Do you know," Meili whispered, "that you're considered the most eligible bachelor in the Asian Commonwealth? And now that you're about to become an Elder, your popularity will explode."

I winced at her words.

"Milady, you cannot go any further," a servant informed Meili.

"Of course. I'll be waiting here." Meili winked and stepped aside.

I followed the servant toward the back of the hall. The actual ceremony would be conducted in a private circle — only after that would the feast begin, where people would eat, drink, and celebrate the arrival of a new Elder.

I entered a small chamber where seven men sat around an oval table. At the head sat the Patriarch himself. To his right was the head of the family, Zeming Li, Jiahao's eldest son. Everyone present here constituted the core of the Li family — the men who controlled eighty percent of its wealth and held the most power.

"Vladislav," Jiahao nodded curtly. "You may claim your golden card."

He gestured toward a case resting on a rectangular pedestal.

"Thank you, Patriarch," I bowed deeply.

Cough. Cough. The eldest of the seven, the family treasurer, suddenly broke into a fit of coughing. His face flushed red with blotches. The others began coughing immediately afterwards.

I flipped open the case — inside, at the bottom, lay the Elder's golden card. But I didn't touch it. Instead, I carried the case over to the Patriarch, who was still hacking violently.

"Y-you..." he snarled. "What have you done?!"

"Nothing much," I shoved the half-dead treasurer off his chair and sat in his place.

The Patriarch's entire face was scarlet, and blood trickled from one of his ears, which had swollen. I felt weak myself, and my entire body itched — I was sure red blotches had appeared on my face, too. But I was a Weak Evolver. I wasn't that easy to kill.

"All I did," I pushed the case closer to the Patriarch, "was hit you with your own weapon. Radiation."

Jiahao's eyes widened in shock. A crimson welt had risen on his cheekbone.

"You thought I didn't know about your death card?" I scoffed, shoving the case aside. "A radioactive card — designed to kill its recipient within days. That's how you got rid of your brothers, isn't it? And if anyone opposed you, you'd swap out their card to let them waste away slowly. Then, a convenient accident would take care of the rest..."

The Patriarch spat out a glob of bright red. A thin stream of blood trickled from his open mouth.

"You know," I said in a languid voice, "I personally asked Delong and Liang to tell you about me." I couldn't help the urge to gloat. My enemy — my father's murderer — was about to die. And with his death, the Li family would be left leaderless.

"Delong reported directly to you that I knew about my father's death. And Liang informed you that I planned to destroy the family from within — by becoming an Elder and seizing power. That was all it took for you to send me the death card."

Unfortunately, the Patriarch died before I could finish my story. I drew a sigh and pulled a packet of Geyser powder from my pocket. I used the wind to disperse a little less than a gram into the air. Radiation was deadly — but some might survive. And I couldn't allow that.

Once finished, I tucked the bag away, walked to the door, and dropped to my knees. I swung the door open — and collapsed onto the floor.

A second passed. Then chaos erupted. The weakness engulfing me was so overwhelming that I passed out.

* * *

I woke up in a hospital bed. Oleg sat beside me, scowling as he read something on his tablet.

"They haven't patched me up yet?" I rasped, my body weak.

Oleg looked up and shook his head.

"The Chairman himself is involved in the case now. Every intelligence agency is digging through the rubble, trying to piece together what happened."

"How long was I out?"

"Thirteen hours."

"The aftermath?"

"All seven Li family leaders are dead. Another ten people were radiation-exposed. The media is calling it the Gruesome Ceremony — it's all anyone is talking about. No one doubts that the blame falls on Patriarch Jiahao."

"What about Yanling? Is she gone?"

"Yes, she's already in Slavia."

"The intelligence agencies?"

"All evidence points to Jiahao Li's golden card and an Evolver's Poisoned Object ability."

"The Crystal Finger — do we have it?"

"The Evolver in charge of your treatment has

it. When the time comes, they'll completely cleanse you of the radiation. But not yet."

I nodded and closed my eyes.

"And the Li family?"

"They've chosen a new head — Ming Li, Jiahao's third son. The Prince already spoke to him. Ming has agreed to cooperate."

I pictured my grandfather screaming at poor Ming Li and couldn't help but chuckle.

The Li family needed to be dismantled. I had promised my mother that I would avenge my father within two years. But I hadn't needed that long.

At first, I wasn't sure how to eliminate all the dead weight in the Li family. I had considered using Geyser powder, but that was too obvious — I could have been exposed. The powder was impossible to detect in a corpse, but if the entire leadership died and I was the only survivor, it would have been too suspicious. Then I remembered Jiahao's death cards — his radioactive assassinations — which had become public knowledge after his death. The plan came together on its own.

Through Liang and Delong, I had fed Jiahao a story — that I knew the truth about my father's murder, that I was furious at the family, and that I planned to destroy it from within. That was enough to earn a death card. The perfect opportunity to receive it was when I became Elder. Those seven men — the golden cardholders — were the most powerful figures in the Li family. And they had to be present at the ceremony.

Next came Yanling, with her additional ability, Poisoned Territory. Getting her inside the banquet hall was easy. And the moment I entered the room, she activated her skill. My subsequent use of Geyser powder guaranteed a silent, absolute death for the entire leadership.

The final phase involved me being treated with the white Crystal Finger from the ship, which was specifically designed for full radiation cleansing.

So, Patriarch Jiahao and the entire Li leadership were all dead. All blame had been pinned on Jiahao himself. His secrets had all gotten exposed — including the many people he had killed using radiation. But this time, he had miscalculated — choosing to use an Evolver ability instead of a death card. The radiation killed everyone in the room. Except me. I was poisoned, too, but a Weak Evolver's young body was resilient. In everyone's eyes, I had survived by miracle — an unlucky victim who barely made it out alive. Ming Li, the next in line, was an inexperienced nobody. He had already bent the knee to my grandfather and would do whatever he was told.

The only problem as I saw it was the Chairman of the Asian Commonwealth getting involved. I hoped he'd lose interest quickly.

"Investigators will be here soon," Oleg warned.

"I understand."

I began drifting off again.

For two days, I stayed in the hospital, just to avoid suspicion. Then I flew to Yekaterinburg — at my grandfather's insistence. He said he would personally oversee my recovery.

On the plane, an Evolver with the Synthesis Atomeus ability used a Crystallite artifact on me. I was fully healed. And when I arrived in Yekaterinburg, I had to take part in a very difficult conversation.

Oleg drove me straight from the runway to my grandfather's mansion and escorted me to the right room. He gave me a sympathetic look, and then left. They were already waiting for me inside.

"Hey," I smiled at my mother and grandfather. They glared at me with matching scowls. In moments like this, they looked a lot alike.

I found an empty chair and was about to sit down when my mother's cold voice stopped me.

"Stay standing."

I froze.

"Have you completely lost your mind, you damn bum?" Grandfather snapped. "What the hell do you think you're doing?!"

"You've exposed the entire Li family leadership to radiation — including yourself? Do you even understand how dangerous radiation is?" My mother's anger was rising.

"Hold on a second," I raised my hands. "Everything was calculated. There was no way I would die."

"How did you know that? Did you experiment on people? Did you test how Evolvers with the Radiation ability affect Weaklings? How did you know you'd survive, Vladislav?!"

The longer she spoke, the angrier she got.

I didn't have an answer. I couldn't tell her that in my past life, every nation — including Slavia — had already conducted those experiments. And I had access to that data. I had been absolutely certain that I wouldn't die. And with my grandfather's Crystal Finger, any side effects would be erased.

"How did you convince Yanling to go through with this?" Grandfather grumbled. Why would she agree to kill so many people — and injure you?"

"Don't pretend you didn't know!" My mother snapped at him. "Vladislav! Explain yourself — right now!"

"Mom."

Our eyes met.

"I avenged Father. It was the Li leadership that had killed him."

A long silence.

"You're sure of this?" My mother's face paled.

"Yes. Absolutely."

"How?"

"Delong Li is loyal to me. He spoke to Jiahao Li. And Jiahao's reaction confirmed his guilt."

I turned to my grandfather.

"Liang reported that I was planning to become an Elder and destroy the family from within. If you were in Jiahao's place... what would you have done?"

"If I were guilty — I'd kill you," Grandfather nodded. "And if I were innocent, I'd sit you down and prove it. Look, you're Delta — the future of the family. No one should harm you unless it's absolutely vital to avert a greater evil."

My mother frowned, glancing between us.

"You planned this together, didn't you?"

"Mom—"

"How did you subdue Delong? He's loyal to the family to the bone."

"I proved to him that I could wipe out the entire family — alone."

"That made him help you?" My grandfather was skeptical. "How did you prove it?"

"Let's change the subject, all right?" I grimaced, unwillingly recalling what I had done. Back then, I had taken Delong to the outskirts of the city — to a hideout of a gang of assassins controlled by the Triad. In my past life, around 2072, this gang had been responsible for wiping out a small family, which was how they had gained notoriety. Right now, though, they were still nobodies — doing petty robberies and occasional killings.

Delong had watched with his own eyes as over thirty men collapsed, one after another, without ever realizing who was killing them. I had stood beside him, hands in my pockets, spreading Geyser powder with the wind. At that moment, I think Delong had either started worshipping me — or become convinced I was some omnipotent evil force. I wasn't quite sure. But he had agreed that I could wipe out the entire Li family alone. And so he had helped me — to minimize casualties.

"How did you find out about the Patriarch's secret?" my mother asked, shifting the topic. "That he was using radioactive cards?"

"I have my own secrets..."

"May a pack of bums eat you alive."

"In any case, you've botched the execution," she continued. "You've made the Patriarch look like an absolute idiot. He wouldn't have made such a mistake. And because of Yanling's ability, innocent people near that room were affected."

"All the evidence points to him," I shrugged. "Besides Poisoned Territory, which is Yanling's ability, there's also Poisoned Object. I've planned everything meticulously — all the blame will fall on the Patriarch."

"What if someone saw Yanling?" my mother asked. She was calmer now. Apparently, the fact that I had avenged my father was justification enough for the risks I had taken.

"We're not idiots, sending her in without disguise," I flashed her a smug grin. "She dressed as a male servant. No one will recognize her."

"How did you convince her to help?" my grandfather pressed again.

"I promised her that, when the time came, I would help her kill the person responsible for her father's death."

Silence settled over the room. Then my mother stood up, walked over to me, and hugged me tightly.

"I missed you," she whispered into my ear, pressing a light kiss to my cheek.

"I missed you, too." I hugged her back. "And I worried. Why didn't you order someone to return to Earth?"

"Every single person was needed."

"Didn't you have any wounded?"

"None. Only the dead."

My mother's expression darkened. We stepped apart, and I finally sat down.

"Tell me — how did the crossing go? And what's it like on Ape Mountain? What's your next move?"

Since my mother's return, I hadn't managed to speak to her yet. I had been in the hospital, suffering from radiation poisoning, occasionally dealing with investigators. The last few days had been anything but pleasant.

"I found the girl you were talking about," my mother said unexpectedly. "Lily, right?"

"Really?" I couldn't believe my ears. "And how is she?"

"You can't get near her. She's surrounded by apes — and not just any apes. Alphas. I was only able to observe her from afar. And she has an unusual ability. I watched her turn sand into water and drink it."

"Matter Transmutation?" I muttered. "Did she have a white tattoo?"

"She did. At first, I thought it was Matter Transmutation too. But that ability isn't rare. I've seen Evolvers with that skill, and none of them can turn sand into water in seconds. This girl's power is much stronger."

"Try talking to her," I suggested. "Tell her you're Vladislav's mother. I'm sure she remembers me."

My mother nodded.

"And what's your next move?" she asked. "Did you know that the Clowns have already tried twice to kill a Sentient Monster? And both times, they only wounded it."

"Yeah, I read about it online."

Xiuli had worked hard to get as many people as possible to follow the Clowns' attempts to take down a Sentient Monster — the Red Centipede.

Their website had daily updates from the frontline. At first, no one had believed them. But after the first attempt, photos of the Centipede's severed legs had appeared online. One had shown up in the United States of Europica, the other in the Asian Commonwealth. The Clowns had handed them over to the governments, and within a day, the media in both regions reported that the Red Centipede's legs were harder than any Alpha's carapace. That was when people finally believed that the Clowns were indeed hunting a Sentient Monster. At the same time, merchandise featuring the Clowns' logo and individual members had started flooding stores.

"What do you think?" my grandfather asked. "Will the Clowns kill the Centipede?"

"They will. Sooner or later, they'll cut off all its legs. And then killing it will be a piece of cake."

"You're too calm," my mother observed. "Do you have a plan?"

"I sure do. And it's one I've had for a long time — ever since I encountered a Sentient Monster on Xin Shang Peak. That's the one we'll be hunting. And by then," I continued, turning to my grandfather, "I hope your lab will have completed the first potions."

"You mean the leader of the Snakes?"

My grandfather frowned.

"No. There's another Sentient Monster on Xin Shang Peak. And it's not on the descent..."

CHAPTER 13

A BRIEF RESPITE

THE DEATH OF THE LI FAMILY'S LEADERSHIP shook the entire Solar System. One of the Asian Dragons had been beheaded. As expected, the other noble families immediately began pressuring the Li family. Aside from the weapons business, the Li family had been dominant in several industries. Before, no one dared to encroach on their territory. Now, everything had changed.

I had anticipated this. The Li family was in a precarious position — teetering on the edge of collapse. The current family head was incompetent, the Patriarch was dead, and his platinum card was unclaimed. At this moment, the two most influential figures in the Li family were the new family head and me — the last surviving Elder.

Thanks to the financial and political backing of my grandfather and mother, the Li family stayed afloat. We had to abandon many positions, sell off some factories, and focus entirely on the most critical sector — weapons manufacturing. Despite the leadership's deaths, the factories kept running. And I had no intention of losing control over them.

All mentions of Geyser had vanished — as if the powder had never existed. As if the Li family had never been involved. Clearly, intelligence agencies had covered the tracks, burying all evidence. Only a few Li family members had known about Project Olympus and that Geyser was being manufactured on the family's territory. And every one of those people had died in that room.

I had no problem with that. Let the Chairman and the other noble families believe that the Li family was finished.

After my conversation with my mother and grandfather, I called Meili. Due to the investigation, she hadn't been able to visit me while I was in the hospital. We hadn't spoken yet.

"Vladislav," Meili's worried face appeared on the screen. "How are you?"

"I'm fine. Are you having any trouble?"

"No. I was interrogated a few times, that's all. Is it true the Patriarch tried to kill you, but miscalculated the Evolver's ability, and died himself?" She sounded doubtful. "It's hard to believe," she continued. "He was so intelligent — how could he make such a stupid mistake?"

I gave a bitter chuckle inwardly. Looks like Mother was right. The Patriarch's death was too suspicious.

"I think someone's planned this on purpose,"

Meili said. "To kill both you and the entire Li leadership."

"Let the investigators handle it." I shook my head.

"You've already survived two assassination attempts in a short time. First they bombed your car. Then they poisoned you with radiation. Do you ever leave the hospital?"

"Let's talk about you," I cracked a stiff smile. I had orchestrated both attacks myself — but Meili didn't need to know that. "What's your DNA purity?"

"Eight point two percent. Right now, the entire main group is focused on the Centipede. We're hardly hunting Alphas anymore."

"Tell me about the Clowns. Did you find out Black's gender, at least? Are they a man or a woman?"

"I know almost nothing about Black," Meili shook her head. "He's very secretive — only speaks to Red, who is the strongest and most dangerous of the Clowns. She can fire lasers."

I nodded. Red was Xiuli Cheng, Princess of the Cheng family. I was very aware of her combat abilities.

"Besides her, I get along well with White. She's a woman, too, and she's the best healer I've ever seen. Gray is a very gloomy man. I've never seen his face — he's always masked. His ability is disgusting — he can control flesh. He can grow it, create tentacles..."

"Flesh Manipulation?" I was surprised. That ability was as rare as Bone Manipulation — maybe even rarer.

"Yeah, probably. Blue is a Magnetic Fielder. But he's not like the others. His second ability isn't Control — it's Magnetic Storm."

"You sure have joined a team of freaks," I chuckled, feeling a chill down my spine.

"Violet is an Electricity Fielder. The three of us — Blue, Teal, and Violet — work together. I use Air Field. They use Magnetic and Electric Fields. You should see how powerful our attacks are. Especially when Blue activates Magnetic Storm. Even Alphas drop like flies, let alone beasts."

"I can imagine." I nodded. "We don't have a team like that in the Syndicate."

"Who else is there? Yellow? Orange?"

"We have two Whites. One is in charge, and the other is a guy with Cold Manipulation — her subordinate. Two Yellows — one has Dirt Manipulation, the other Sand Manipulation. Two Oranges — one has Pressure, the other, Barrier. And one Clear — a newbie. She can create portals like Anish. That's all for now. And every single one I mentioned is Weak. There's also the Circus, but they're still developing — not much use yet."

"Damn," I muttered. "The Clowns aren't standing still. They've even found a Portal user... I'm impressed."

"Yeah. Want me to tell you what I know about Sentient Monsters?" Meili asked. "Might be useful to you."

"Go ahead." I nodded. I doubted I'd hear anything new, but at least I could compare Black's intel with my own sources. Maybe that would help me figure out Black's origins.

"Sentients differ wildly from each other. Some are very weak. Some are extremely strong. They're classified differently depending on their species. For armored monsters, their natural shell patterns determine strength — the more patterns, the stronger the monster. Others can be identified by size or color — it all depends on the species."

I nodded. Black had an in-depth understanding of Sentients. No surprise.

"The Red Centipede we found is a very weak Sentient. And it's still a juvenile, so it's not very intelligent. It only has twenty pairs of legs. An adult Centipede can have over fifty. Blue said he didn't believe it when Black led them to the Centipede's nest and claimed it was a Sentient. He thought it was just a particularly tough Alpha."

I nodded again. In my past life, Sentients were often mistaken for powerful Alphas. But the only way to confirm whether a creature was one or the other was to kill it. Sentient Monsters didn't have Liquid Cores — the stronger the Sentient, the harder its Core.

"Beasts usually don't have clearly defined abilities. Or, at the very least, they can't control them. Alphas can already control their abilities well. But Sentients — they *are* their abilities. The Centipede can ignite at any moment, breathe fire, or heat its entire body until it glows red-hot. And on top of that, Sentients have incredibly tough bodies, they're fast, and they're strong. Take our Red Centipede. It may be a weak Sentient, but we still have to mobilize the entire team just to keep it at bay.

We only attack its legs, tearing them off one by one to slow it down. And when we run out of Neutrinos and Quarks, we retreat and rest. None of our attacks can pierce its carapace — only Red's lasers leave scorch marks."

I listened to Meili in silence. Sentient monsters were indeed incredibly dangerous because of their sheer durability. Initially, I had planned to kill my first Sentient by combining the abilities of my two virtual DNA spirals. If I had taken a second ability related to fire, I could have gathered a swarm of Air Fielders and a squad of Nuclear Atomei — those with Fire Manipulation and tanks of blood propane. Then it would have just been a matter of execution.

The Atomei would create fire, and I'd take control of it using my ability, amplifying it as much as possible, twisting it into a firestorm. Then, I'd switch my DNA spiral to Bai Hu, seize control of the Fielders' wind, and combine fire and air. I'd be able to turn an entire region into an inferno. And that was just one possible synergy. Others included sand and wind, water and wind, electricity and wind, and a few more devastating combinations.

But since I'd needed mental protection and cognitive enhancement, I didn't go down that path. My abilities weren't very compatible at the moment. Even if I tamed a monster that breathed fire, the effect wouldn't be nearly as powerful. That's why I had to plan every detail before attempting to kill my first Sentient Monster.

"When will you kill the Centipede? Do you have

an estimate?" I asked.

"Three or four days, probably," Meili said after a moment of thought. "Will you have time to kill your Sentient by then?"

"I don't know," I said, shaking my head slowly. "But I'll do my best."

"All right, Vladislav. I need to get back to the Primordial World. I've already missed several days because of the ceremony... I don't even know what's going to happen to our family next."

"Don't worry. The Li family won't fall — I can promise that much."

"Thank you," Meili murmured before disconnecting.

I put the tablet aside and spent a few minutes thinking about my relationship with Meili.

In my past life, she had despised me — resented me, believing that our father loved her less because of me. And I had felt nothing for her. I had been completely indifferent. Now, though, we were more like real siblings. Meili actually listened to me and treated me like an older brother. It was completely different from how things had been in my past life.

A day had passed since I arrived in Yekaterinburg. I had spent the time dealing with my affairs — waiting for my grandfather's lab to finish the first elixir and preparing for my journey to the Primordial World.

For my first Sentient target, I had chosen the Crystal Worm we encountered in the ravine where the Black Monitor had lived. I needed to plan everything meticulously, accounting for every variable. My Silkworm DNA and cold rationality helped with that. Plus, I had already created ten Mental Threads — it was time to put them to use.

That afternoon, I decided to check on Miroslava and her Institute. I couldn't show my face, so I wore a mask. Miroslava was delighted to give me a tour of the campus, explaining everything with enthusiasm.

"After the event, I got six Alpha Cores," Miroslava boasted. "And we already have over a thousand people! Just imagine — if every single one of them becomes an Evolver, they'll all join the Syndicate!"

Her eyes burned with excitement as she described the Institute's future. She was completely invested in her vision, genuinely striving for success. It was refreshing to see her like that.

"Want me to introduce you to my father? He's probably training right now. He told me he wants to become the Prince's personal bodyguard."

Miroslava lifted her chin with pride.

"Honestly, I really want to help him with Liquid Cores. My share would be more than enough to turn him into a Weak Evolver. That way, he'd have a better shot at becoming the Prince's guard. What do you think?"

I scratched my nose awkwardly. I had nothing good to say about a man who had been beaten half to death by his wife and her lover before getting kicked out of the house. I could only hope he actually cared about his daughter and wasn't just stringing her along to squeeze some Liquid Cores out of her.

I decided not to interfere in their relationship. Last time, it had nearly ended in tragedy. Miroslava was happy and proud of her father — better to let things stay that way.

"I'd love to meet your father," I said carefully, "but I don't have much time."

"Yeah, I understand," Miroslava sighed. "I wanted to take you to the Evolver Plaza — it's beautiful, and there's always something interesting going on... But when are we going to hunt the Sentient?"

"I'm not sure yet. I want to wait until my grandfather's lab finishes working on the elixir. It'll give us better odds."

Grandfather's lab was trying to recreate Hu Hongwen's first potion, which increased the Neutrino count of a Weak Atomeus. It had a simple formula — its main ingredient was the blood of lizard-type monsters.

"By the way, have you heard what's happening on the eastern side of Xin Shang Peak?"

"Yeah."

I had been keeping a close eye on the situation. The snakes had taken over a considerable area and showed no intention of returning to the lower slopes. Honestly, it was a bizarre turn of events. After carefully analyzing the situation, I came to the conclusion that something had driven the Sentient Monster from the forest on the second mile — something more powerful had emerged in that region, forcing the previous ruler to flee up the mountain. The death of the White Silkworm alone couldn't have caused such a reaction — it made no sense.

As a result, some people could no longer enter the Primordial World. Those whose binding location was near Mayor Hansh's settlement were in serious trouble. If they logged in, they'd be devoured by the snakes instantly. The mayor himself had exited the world as well — and was immediately targeted by three assassination attempts. Luckily, Hansh Khattar survived and went into hiding, while unrest in India grew daily.

Grandfather, acting on my tip, was supporting Khattar as much as possible. If, by some miracle, the Indian actor-turned-politician managed to seize power, he wouldn't forget our help.

"When do you think the snakes will leave?" Miroslava and I continued walking. "Some of the Syndicate members can't enter the Primordial World at all. Xiao Jin is one of them. I talked to her — she's really upset that our building was destroyed. Remember? You put her in charge and told her to turn that shack into a proper headquarters for the Syndicate? Well, she did it. And now all her work was for nothing."

"Xiao doesn't belong in the Primordial World," I replied. "She's moving to Shanghai to help manage the local branch of Syndicate Epsilon. Her Scholar ability is useful for paperwork — she should stay on Earth, where it's safe. By the way, do you know where Allen lives? I know he's from Britannia, but I don't have his exact address."

"Thinking of bringing him to the institute?"

"Yeah. He's so young, and already an Evolver. And right now, Allen can't enter the Primordial

World either."

"I don't know where the kid lives," I admitted, thinking of Hu Xuan Jian whose head looked like a block of cheese. I wasn't the only one who had considered recruiting him — Grandfather had sent people to him almost immediately, somehow tracking down his actual residence. But unfortunately, Hu Xuan Jian refused to join us. He even claimed he was done with the Primordial World for good, shaken by the beetle massacre. A shame — his ability would have been extremely useful against large groups of monsters.

"Oh, look. That's Yanling. Let's go say hi."

As we neared the institute's training grounds, Miroslava spotted Yanling Wu sitting on a bench, dressed in a black sweater and matching pants. She was staring blankly ahead, paying no attention to anything around her.

Seeing her reminded me of Liang, who still hadn't stopped messaging her. After the Li family had gotten decapitated, Delong had helped Liang move his sick mother to a hospital in the United States of Europica, with my approval. Liang had refused to go to Slavia and had no desire to remain in the Asian Commonwealth. He said his mother wanted to return to her homeland. I hadn't opposed his decision.

"Hey!" Miroslava waved at Yanling. Finally, she acknowledged us.

"Hey," she said absentmindedly, her gaze shifting to me. The moment our eyes met, recognition flickered in hers.

"Could you please ask the Prince to let me go

to Beijing?" she said suddenly. "He says it's too dangerous right now, that I could be killed at any moment. But I really want to go."

"I have no influence over my grandfather," I let out a chuckle. "But I'll talk to him."

Yanling turned away.

"I promised I'd help you kill the ones responsible for your father's death," I reminded her. "And I'll keep that promise. But only if you stay alive. If you die, I won't bother dealing with the big players in the Commonwealth or the Triads."

Yanling grimaced, but nodded.

My phone buzzed — a new message. I pulled it out and read the text from Grandfather.

The first decoction from lizard-monster blood is ready. Trials completed — it increased a normal Evolver's Neutrino by thirty percent and a Weak Evolver's by ten. Duration: one hour. Forty doses will be ready by morning. You'll take them with you.

I smiled and turned to Miroslava.

"Tomorrow morning, we're heading into the Primordial World to hunt the Crystal Worm — our first Sentient Monster."

*   *   *

I stood on a boulder at the edge of the ravine, gazing down at the floor below littered with the corpses of beasts and Alphas. The team was in position, each member knowing their role. We were waiting.

Finally, the ground at the bottom of the ravine

trembled. The bodies of monsters began to slide toward the center.

"It's about to go down," I murmured, raising my hand to signal the beginning of the operation.

183

Chapter 14

The Crystalline Worm

Several hours before the operation

"THE ONLY CHANCE WE HAVE at killing the Crystalline Worm is attacking it from the inside," I explained, watching Wang Bolai gutting the White Monitor Lizard's carcass. "We can't even scratch the worm's armor from outside."

"Will the explosion be strong enough? You've seen how huge it is. It swallowed our bait in seconds — makes hunting it terrifying," Liang approached the gutted lizard, heavy backpack on his shoulders, and began stuffing canisters of blood propane into its body.

The whole Syndicate had gathered on a small clearing near the ravine where we'd spotted the Crystalline Worm, with the exception of Jiao.

"To kill it outright — no. I'll have to handle that

part personally. I'll hold the worm in place with Mental Threads, forcing it to freeze with its mouth open."

"Boss, you don't mean sending me into that worm's mouth, do you?" Wang Bolai looked anxious. He'd been gloomy lately — after the snakes attacked the mountain, Selena had vanished, leaving him heartbroken over her betrayal. I wasn't concerned — Selena would surely appear again when she needed bolts and propane.

"No, I'll be going in myself. If my calculations are correct, I'll have just enough time to reach the Core. But first, we need to remove everything unnecessary from inside the worm."

"What do you mean?" Miroslava asked, confused.

I didn't answer, only shook my head slowly. I wasn't about to tell her that the Sentient Crystalline Worm was alive on the inside, too. Every organ and every muscle was composed of countless worm-like tendrils that regenerated quickly and intertwined tightly. If we didn't clear them first, getting to the Core would be impossible.

"We've got five Alpha corpses and over twenty beasts, all stuffed with blood propane," Natsuko reported.

"Anish, your role will be one of the most crucial," I looked at the Indian, who sat beside Nitya under a tree.

"I understand, Boss," Anish nodded solemnly.

Footsteps approached as Andrei, one of Grandpa's soldiers, entered the clearing. His Explosive skill would aid us greatly.

"Everything's ready."

"Then let's get started."

* * *

The ground at the bottom of the ravine trembled as numerous monster corpses sank into the opening pit.

"It has begun," I muttered, signaling the operation's start.

Almost simultaneously, everyone except Miroslava took out bottles of the new potion and drank. My Neutrino count spiked by ten percent.

I intensified my DNA fusion, my body now covered in stiff white bristles. A massive circular mouth ringed with triangular saw-like teeth emerged from underground. The worm's body was encased in a dark matte crystal shell, its insides hidden behind rows of sharp teeth.

The monster corpses, along with soil and stones, vanished into the worm's massive jaws, taking the blood propane canisters with them. Time to act.

Two Mental Threads shot from my eyes, invisible to the others but clearly visible to me. Following the first pair came another, and then another. Ten Mental Threads pierced the Crystalline Worm. Fully subduing such a monster was impossible, but slowing it down — why not?

All ten threads penetrated the worm's brain, freezing it in place. I felt the threads wrapping around its consciousness, failing to dominate it fully.

"Anish!" I shouted.

A portal opened above the worm's gaping mouth, raining down canisters of blood propane. I'd prepared more than a thousand canisters for this mission. I'd waited not only for the potion to be ready, but also until we'd accumulated sufficient propane.

One Mental Thread snapped. The worm's body trembled slightly.

As the last canisters disappeared into the creature's mouth, the portal closed. Then Andrei began his move, triggering an Explosion as deeply within the worm as possible. The team had intentionally punctured several canisters to leak blood propane inside.

There was a loud bang.

The blast was so powerful my ears rang. A fiery column shot upward, radiating intense heat. Three Mental Threads burst at once — the worm struggled desperately, its body convulsing. The monster corpses it had swallowed were also ablaze deep in its gut.

"Miroslava!" I yelled.

This stage was optional. If the worm had destroyed more than five Threads, I would have skipped it, but it had only broken four.

Another portal opened, pouring a spinning column of metallic sand into the worm's mouth. Miroslava directed it, grinding away everything inside to clear a path to the Core.

The fifth Mental Thread snapped. The sixth and seventh strained, ready to break any moment.

"I'm going in!" I canceled my skill and reactivated it, merging with the virtual spiral of the Lord of the Wind. Unsheathing Bai Hu's Claw, I flew upwards and then dove down, encased in wind. Through experimentation, I'd discovered Mental Threads didn't vanish after canceling the skill, provided they targeted monsters. They embedded in the target's brain like parasites until death. Unfortunately, Mental Threads didn't affect humans — they dissolved instantly, as I'd found out when trying it once on Wang Bolai.

Having switched DNA from Silkworm to Bai Hu, I'd lost my ability to sense the Mental Threads. The worm could break free at any second, meaning my life would be over.

As I approached the worm's maw, Liang activated Grapple, pouring every last Neutrino into it. A gigantic translucent hand appeared in the air, plunging underground to seize the worm's upper body.

I flew into the monster's jaws. Most of the Worm's teeth had been shattered by the explosion and Miroslava's attack. Its flesh was charred from the heat and ground down by the metallic sand. But even after such a devastating assault, the Worm hadn't taken much damage. Its flesh was already regenerating — tiny worm-like tendrils sprouted one after another, writhing grotesquely as they smeared mucus across the wounded flesh, accelerating the growth of even more tendrils.

I knew where the Crystalline Worm's Liquid Core was — inside one of its hearts, located in the upper third of its body. The third or fourth heart, counting from the head. It had more than ten hearts in total, and as long as so much as one remained intact, the Worm wouldn't die. But if I could rip out the Liquid Core, the beast would perish, just like any other monster from the Primordial World. Worm-like monsters had been slain before in my previous life, so I knew their anatomy well.

The wind shielded me from the smoke and the nauseating stench as I sped downward, scanning the Worm's flesh. The areas around the hearts were particularly dense with tendrils, resembling vile tumors. I passed the first heart, then the second... There it was.

Bai Hu's Claw plunged into the Worm's writhing flesh, piercing the heart buried within the tendrils. From the inside, the Crystalline Worm was far weaker than its armored exterior.

The monster's entire body convulsed, its flesh thrashing wildly. I ignored its agony, carving deeper into the heart until a silvery substance was exposed. It resembled a piece of soft rubber. Without hesitation, I tore out the Liquid Core and was about to press it to my tattoo when the Worm's flesh came crashing down on me. The force sent me tumbling sideways, and the slippery Core slipped from my grasp. My breath hitched, darkness swam in my vision.

What was happening?!

Smack!

Something struck my head so hard I passed out...

The One Who Changes the Future

* * *

From the very beginning, Vladislav's plan had seemed far too risky to Natsuko. To climb into the maw of a colossal Worm the size of a train and find a tiny Liquid Core? How was he even planning to locate it? Did worms even have hearts?

But Vladislav had long since proven himself trustworthy, and Natsuko followed him without question. She hoped his plan would succeed and that he would become the first to kill a Sentient Monster. The Syndicate's prestige would soar.

Many had come to watch the hunt. They weren't even trying to hide — Natsuko caught glimpses of movement in the treetops and, more than once, had to turn away in irritation when a lens flare from someone's binoculars hit her eyes.

After the massive explosion — which had singed off her eyelashes, much to her annoyance — she inexplicably felt calmer. She believed, for the first time, that the hunt would succeed.

When Vladislav plummeted like a stone into the monster's maw, her heart clenched with anxiety. The first few seconds, nothing happened. Then, the Worm's mouth began to spasm, and the monster slid into the pit.

Something made a loud hissing sound.

Natsuko's eyes widened as she watched the bottom of the ravine collapse, swallowing the Crystalline Worm into a gaping abyss...

* * *

I woke up suddenly, with a jolt. I had no idea how I was still alive — breathing was nearly impossible. My entire body throbbed in agony, especially my legs. The Worm's rancid slimy flesh smothered me in a suffocating shroud.

I moved slightly and immediately groaned in pain — my legs were broken. Tears welled up in my eyes against my will. Clenching my teeth, I pushed my fusion of virtual and real DNA to the limit and began crawling forward, one hand holding up the Worm's flesh, the other dragging my battered body. I needed to find the Liquid Core. Fast. Otherwise, everything would have been for nothing.

A crunch sounded nearby. The Worm's body jerked, and I was dragged along with it. The pain nearly made me scream. It felt like I could pass out again at any moment.

Where was the Liquid Core?!

I stretched my hand forward and churned the stale air. Pouring all my remaining Neutrinos into the effort, I unleashed a stream of wind from my palm, carving a small tunnel through the Worm's flesh. I moved my hand slowly, guiding the tunnel as it twisted and expanded with each motion.

The crunching intensified. Another jolt rocked the Worm's body. It felt as though it was being torn apart from three different directions.

A flash of white — Bai Hu's Claw. I crawled toward it and sheathed the undamaged blade before continuing my search for the Liquid Core. But I was getting nowhere.

Bracing against the agony, I turned, forcing myself to stay conscious, and resumed searching in the opposite direction — toward the tail, or maybe the head. I wasn't sure. I didn't want to consider that too much time had passed, that the Core might already be gone, or that some other monster had swallowed it. I refused to give up.

There! A silver glint flickered between the folds of disgusting flesh. I crawled toward it, digging my claws into the soft tissue and pressing my chin to my chest.

Crunch!

A chunk of flesh behind me vanished with a wet squelch and a sickening rip, releasing a wave of stale air and filth. I kept crawling, but when I glanced back, I froze. Panic shot through me like lightning, and I clawed forward twice as fast.

Two Crystalline Worms were feasting on the remains of their fallen comrade, drawing ever closer. They weren't as massive as the Sentient Worm — likely juveniles whose Liquid Cores had yet to solidify.

Another crunch echoed ahead. And I knew exactly what it meant. I activated my tattoo, forcing the pyramid to manifest, and reached toward the spot where I had seen the silver glint. My fingers closed around something brittle. There was a snap. I brought my hand up to my face and let out a strangled groan. It wasn't the Liquid Core — it was the inner lining of a broken canister catching the light.

A sudden spasm of agony nearly knocked me out. I screamed at the top of my lungs.

One of the Crystalline Worms had reached me. It lunged forward in a blur, its maw snapping shut over both my feet. It reeled back, preparing for another strike. If it managed another lunge, at least half my body would be gone.

Blinded by rage, I unleashed every last drop of my Neutrino. A tornado of razor-sharp wind blades erupted around me, blasting the Crystalline Worm backward. Deep gashes tore across its body. Shredded flesh splattered my face, and I squeezed my eyes shut as the storm of gore rained down.

A deep guttural howl erupted from the monster.

I quickly wiped my eyes and cracked them open just enough to find the transparent pyramid.

Crunch!

Another section of the monster vanished, revealing more worms. But I barely registered them — my entire focus was on a piece of flesh shaped like a shallow boat. It must have been hidden beneath other chunks of meat until my tornado ripped them apart. At the bottom of that fleshy cavity, a clear liquid shimmered, cradling a tiny silver speck. The Liquid Core had almost completely dissolved.

Two Crystalline Worms behind me. Three more ahead. The "boat" just a couple of feet away, on the other side of the pyramid.

There was no time to think — my body moved on instinct.

I pushed off with my hands, launching myself

toward the boat. The adrenaline rush dulled the pain.

Reality fractured into a kaleidoscope of images. I was falling, my right hand outstretched. My wrist, marked with the triangle, descended straight into the boat. Instantly, I yanked my hand back to escape the worm's snapping jaws — but not fast enough. The monster's razor-sharp teeth sheared off half of my palm.

Using my knees and left hand, I kicked off the ground, propelling myself backward with my back to the pyramid. There was another crunch from above. A hole split open, and another Crystalline Worm slithered through. The same was happening below. My path to the pyramid was cut off.

Operating purely on reflex, I ripped Bai Hu's Claw from its sheath and drove it into the upper worm at an angle. Using the blade as leverage, I twisted midair — my head and legs swapping places in a diagonal flip as I vaulted over the lower worm.

I had just enough time to wrench the sword free before plunging straight into the pyramid, vanishing into the teleport.

The last thing I saw before disappearing was three more Crystalline Worms piling on top of me all at once...

* * *

I woke up abruptly in a spacious room, lying on a soft bed.

I felt... fine. More than fine — I felt great. And,

most importantly, all my limbs were intact. For a brief moment, I thought it had all been a dream. That the hunt for the Crystalline Worm had yet to happen. Then my heartbeat quickened, and my throat went dry. Holding my breath, I checked my status:

Name: Vladislav Li-Vavilonsky
Race: Strong Human
DNA Purity: 10.08%
Evolutionary Branch: Atomeus
Base Skill: Full Transformation (absolute)
Additional Skill: DNA Fusion
First Virtual DNA Spiral: Bai Hu, Lord of the Wind
Second Virtual DNA Spiral: White Silkworm, Lord of Monsters
Third Virtual DNA Spiral: -

I started breathing harder, barely believing my eyes.I had become a Strong Human. In my past life, the first Strong Human, an Indian monk named Ganesh, had only appeared in 2073 — three years after the Eclipse. But now... it had been just a little over two months.

The door opened. My grandfather stepped inside, scanning me with his usual dissatisfied expression.

"This time, I'll let it slide," he said gruffly. "The Liquid Core was more useful to you."

"What do you mean?" I asked, confused.

"When you appeared in the pyramid, no one recognized you. You looked like a bum who had first been hit by a truck, and then crushed by a falling plane. They called the medics immediately. But before they could get you to the hospital, you started regenerating. And your tattoo—" he gestured at my wrist "—grew a second mark."

I glanced down. He was right. At the base of the triangle running parallel to my wrist, in the lower right corner, a solid black dot had appeared. Just like the one at the triangle's apex, pointing toward my elbow. I had undergone my second transformation. I had evolved again.

"The video made it to the net. The entire Solar System knows the Syndicate has killed an Intelligent Monster. You're the first human to surpass ten percent DNA purity. What's your count, anyway? Thirteen? Fourteen?"

"Ten point zero eight."

"Pff," Grandfather sneered, looking at me with mock disdain.

"The Liquid Core was almost gone. I got lucky it worked in the end," I said, ignoring his expression.

"What abilities did you get?"

"A third virtual DNA spiral. And a new skill — DNA Fusion. I don't know what it does yet."

"Fusion... Maybe you can use two abilities at once? Or merge them in some way? Or something else weak and insignificant?" he huffed, narrowing his eyes.

His expression made me want to laugh. For some reason, it reminded me of a bitter old granny who had just found out her neighbor got a pension raise.

"What are you smirking at, you bum?" he snapped. "Feeling proud of yourself, huh?" His temper flared. "I want a Sentient's Core on my desk by tomorrow! Not a day later — your time's running out!"

"What?" I blinked. "Running out?"

"Of course! The moment your mother gets out of the Primordial World and finds out what you did, she's going to gut you like a fish, pull out your intestines, and strangle you with them! So hurry up and bring me a Core before she gets to you!"

"What did I even do?" I still didn't get it.

"You almost died," he said bluntly. "You were hanging by a thread. Your regeneration saved you — if not for your breakthrough, you would have bled out. Your legs were eaten. Your goddamn hand was eaten. Whatever. I'm done. My mood gets worse the longer I look at your bum-ass face. Lying here all smug while everyone's worried half to death about you. Dinner's at sundown."

He turned and left without another word. I drew a sigh as I reached for the tablet on the nightstand and powered it on. I needed to check my messages. My inbox was probably flooded with emails from family, friends, and acquaintances.

The moment I logged into ReChat, a message popped up from Xiuli Cheng.

Hi Vladislav. Congratulations on killing a Sentient Monster — you've managed to beat us to it. Black wants to meet you. What do you think?

CHAPTER 15

CLOSE ENCOUNTERS

Hi Vladislav. Congratulations on killing a Sentient Monster — you've managed to beat us to it. Black wants to meet you. What do you think?

I STARED AT XIULI'S MESSAGE for a few seconds, lost in thought. Black wanted to see me after I killed an Intelligent Monster. Interesting...

I agree.

After sending my reply, I skimmed through the rest of my messages. The Syndicate members had written to me, along with Meili, Delong, and Lilit. Even Peizhi had sent congratulations, despite normally being reluctant to reach out.

After replying to everyone, I turned my attention back to Xiuli.

We'll hold a video conference today. At 20:00 Ural Principality time, I'll contact you.

I chuckled and turned off my phone.

Book Three

*　*　*

The wind played with my hair, ruffling it playfully. Below me stretched the estate grounds — an expansive lake shimmered at the center of the perfectly square park, delivery drones buzzed faintly in the distance, and the occasional white crow flapped its wings. About ten years ago, for reasons unknown, Grandfather had bought an entire flock of these artificially engineered birds and released them onto the estate. That was the beginning of the legendary war between the white crows and the drones, a conflict so infamous in the Ural Principality that only the laziest hadn't heard of it. Someone had even written an entire novel about it.

A few crows soared past, and I chuckled, remembering how I had read that novel when I was thirteen. It was still unfinished — new chapters came out every month. Currently, the birds and drones had a truce, but it could be broken at any moment, sending the world into the thunderous chaos of cawing and mechanical screeching.

All right, maybe I was exaggerating. But the sound of crows cawing and drones wailing, often followed by a flurry of scattered feathers, had become so commonplace that the Ural Principality had even developed a tradition of gifting a white crow's feather to their child upon reaching adulthood. I had no idea what it symbolized. Never cared enough to ask.

Beyond the park lay a vast training ground

spanning miles — Evolvers honed their skills there. Grandfather's laboratories were also there, where potions were brewed and specialized suits were developed. Further still was the military post.

I stood on the mansion's rooftop, listening to the distant thunder of the training ground. Massive chunks of stone shot up into the sky, sending up plumes of dust. Grandfather was training.

After savoring the quiet chaos of daily life, I closed my eyes and activated DNA Fusion. Once again, I saw the image of three DNA chains — one primary, two virtual. The moment the ability activated, I felt my other two abilities kick in simultaneously. All three chains began merging.

I grew taller. Claws sprouted from my fingers. The wind, which had been playfully tugging at my hair moments ago, now swirled tightly around me. Simultaneously, coarse white hairs emerged across my torso, and my mind entered a state of cold rationality.

I was indeed merging two virtual DNA chains at once...

I glanced at my Neutrino reserves, which had increased significantly after my evolution. The count was slowly decreasing. I figured I could maintain DNA Fusion for about thirty minutes — assuming I didn't expend any additional Neutrinos. In combat, though, the duration would shrink drastically, possibly down to just a few minutes.

I canceled the ability and took a deep breath, steadying my nerves. The potential of DNA Fusion was enormous. At the very least, I could attack monsters both physically and mentally at the same time. And in a state of cold rationality, multitasking became effortless.

I pushed off the mansion's rooftop and took flight. There was still time before dinner with Grandfather and the video call with Black. I had things to do — contact Muhiddin and issue my next orders, check on the new Evolvers Grandfather had recruited based on my recommendations, speak with Egghead about our website, and get a haircut before the meeting.

*   *   *

Shanghai
The Cheng Family Estate

Xiuli was nervous. Delta had agreed to meet with Black, and Xiuli would personally oversee what was sure to be a legendary video conference.

The moment news of Vladislav's feat exploded across the network, Xiuli had gone to meet Black.

His reaction still seemed strange to her. Their conversation had gone something like this,

"Delta has killed a Sentient Monster!"

"Mmm-hmm..."

"The strongest organizations have already begun talks of unification! If even thirty percent of giants like Han or the Celestial Empire join forces on one mountain, we'll no longer be the strongest organization! My projections show this will happen within six months!"

"Mmm-hmm..."

"I propose we meet with Delta. At the very

least, it would be invaluable to discuss strategies for hunting Sentient Monsters and establish trade routes for reinforced weaponry and blood propane. There are even rumors that the Ural Prince's people have developed potions that boost one's Neutrino count... Regardless, an alliance with the Syndicate would be beneficial for the Clowns. Once these massive government factions unite, we'll be overwhelmingly outnumbered. We need every advantage to stay afloat!"

"Mmm-hmm... Who is Delta?"

"I've told you about him before! Vladislav Li-Vavilonsky, head of the Syndicate — the organization currently considered the strongest. You're joking, right? There's no way you haven't heard his name..."

"Mmm-hmm... Vladislav? Vladislav. I see. I want to meet him."

"Meet him?! You?!"

"Yes. Is that a problem?"

"No, of course not! I'll contact him immediately and arrange a meeting!"

"I'm not going anywhere. Do it online."

"Understood. A video call, then... Black, will you show your face?!"

"Mmm-hmm... Leave. You're annoying me."

"Yes, my apologies..."

Xiuli had the distinct feeling that, as time passed, Black was becoming more absentminded. He was always lost in thought, barely listened to her, and didn't seem particularly interested in anything. She was afraid he would eventually abandon the Clowns altogether and simply walk away, leaving the organization behind.

That was why she had to push him. She needed to put him face to face with someone equally talented. And, if she was being honest, she had no intention of giving up her position at the top. Right now, the Clowns' influence and popularity allowed Xiuli to multiply her profits — several times over, and that was without selling resources from the Primordial World. Themed merchandise, advertisements, insider information — she had a finger in every pie. And she had no intention of losing that revenue.

Time crawled forward sluggishly like a sedated snail. For the first time in ages, Xiuli was back at the Cheng family estate. She had already set everything up for the video call — all that was left was to wait for 8 PM Ural Principality time.

As she wandered through the family's massive garden, a labyrinth of lush green hedges, she turned a corner and nearly collided with her sister — Xiuying Cheng.

Xiu sat crouched, staring intently at a giant snail inching along the path. As she saw Xiuli, she cast a blank look in her direction before refocusing on the snail.

Xiuli curled her lip in disgust. Everything about her sister irritated her — those short multicolored dreads, those dead, empty eyes, that vile perfume, and, most of all, her revealing outfits. It drove Xiuli crazy. She never wore the same thing twice, and every item in her wardrobe cost a fortune.

"Can you dress like a normal person?" she

hissed. "Stop walking around like a whore!"

Xiu scoffed and tapped the snail's shell with her finger. For some reason, that small act infuriated Xiuli. She raised a finger, aimed at the snail, and a laser beam erased the poor creature from existence.

"The Kim family is assembling a caravan to cross the Great Ridge and reach Xin Shang Peak. You're going with them. You'll join the Syndicate. I'll arrange it."

Xiu said nothing. She just stared at the scorch mark where the snail had been.

"Remember," Xiuli continued, voice sharp, "we have your bastard. If you want him to live, you'll listen to me. Sister."

Spitting the last word out like venom, Xiuli turned and walked away. Xiu lifted her head, watching her go. For the first time in days, her eyes weren't empty. They burned with pure undiluted hatred.

The Chen family held many dark secrets. One of the worst was Xiu's pregnancy at fourteen. But the rumors were wrong — she hadn't aborted the child. She had given birth. And they had taken him from her.

Another dark secret was Xiu being the only legitimate daughter of the family head. The so-called Princess of the Chen family was a fraud. Xiuli was the daughter of a servant. Only a handful of people knew the truth.

"I'll make you pay," Xiu whispered, rising to her feet. She wiped her damp eyes and walked deeper into the maze. "For my son. And for my mother…"

Xiu's mother had seen Xiuli's brilliance for what it was — a threat. With the support of her faction, she had tried to poison Xiuli's food. But Xiuli, ever ruthless, had fed the poison to Xiu's mother instead. The woman had died, and in the aftermath, one by one, Xiu's allies had either been killed or defected to Xiuli's side.

Xiuying became an outcast while Xiuli became the Princess of the Chen family — its crowning jewel and its hidden ruler. She didn't just hold Xiu's son in her grip. She controlled the entire family.

For years, Xiu had believed she could never change her fate. That she would live out her days as Xiuli's slave, crushed under her half-sister's heel. But then she met Vladislav and the long-extinguished spark of hope reignited. His words echoed in her mind.

"In the future, they'll call you the Fire Goddess. With a single thought, you'll be able to burn entire forests. With a wave of your hand, firestorms will rain down on your enemies. You'll transform into flames at will, becoming almost invincible. They'll compare you to the goddesses Dianmu and Houtu. Millions will admire you. Worship you. And most importantly… a princess is nothing next to a goddess, right? Even if she's a Chen princess."

The One Who Changes the Future

* * *

Time passed quickly, and soon, it was time for dinner with Grandfather. We ate alone, and the dinner had started in silence.

"Well?" he finally grumbled. "Tell me. How does the new ability work? Any other differences between a Weak Human and a Strong Human? Where's Atlantis?"

"DNA Fusion allows me to use two virtual DNA spirals at once," I said, pushing my empty soup bowl aside and pulling a plate of salmon and cheese waffles closer. I really loved waffles, soft and warm...

"Answer the damn question!" Grandfather snapped when I fell silent, distracted by the food.

"Right, sorry." I swallowed. "The difference between Weak and Strong Humans is in their Neutrino count. A normal Evolver has, say, around a hundred Neutrinos. A Weak Human? Five hundred. A Strong Human? Five thousand. That's the ratio. With more Neutrinos, I can push my abilities further, and the results are completely different."

I stretched out my palm. A small tornado spun above it. I poured more Neutrinos into it, and the vortex collapsed inward, condensing into a sphere, surrounded by shifting rings of glowing blue energy.

Beautiful. And deadly. The sphere kept growing until it was the size of a bowling ball, glowing a brilliant neon blue.

"This attack alone could reduce the mansion to rubble," I boasted.

"I'll reduce your head to rubble if you don't put that thing away!" Grandfather barked.

I started breaking down the sphere, peeling away its layers. A gust of wind tore through the room. Grandfather nearly fell out of his chair.

"You goddamn bum!" he roared, hurling a mug at me.

I caught it reflexively, still focused on the sphere. I had overcharged it with Neutrinos, and now it didn't want to dissipate.

Dishes shattered against the floor. Chairs crashed over. Servants rushed in, only to recoil, shielding their faces.

"I'm working on it!" I shouted, wiping sweat from my forehead.

"You clumsy bastard!" Grandfather hurled a plate of dumplings next.

I managed to catch it, but the dumplings weren't as lucky — they tumbled out, splattering all over me.

Clearly on a roll now, Grandfather snatched up a tray of roasted quail.

"Enough already!" I yelled. "Help me instead!"

"Handle it yourself!" he shouted back, but at least he put the tray down. Instead, he waved his hand, and the floor split. Stone slabs rose around me, sealing me inside an impromptu prison.

I broke into a cold sweat. If the sphere exploded now, I would become a smear on the floor.

Drenched and trembling, I carefully unraveled the sphere, dissipating the compressed Neutrino wind. Finally, I exhaled in relief.

"Done! You can put these damn walls down now!"

"Hell no! Stay in there!"

I jumped, soaring over the stone barricade.

Grandfather scowled from his chair as the servants hurried to clean up the wreckage. I landed beside him and sat down across from him.

"You saw how much stronger an Evolver becomes after a breakthrough," I said, smoothing my sleeve with exaggerated calm.

"When are you bringing me a Core?" Grandfather scoffed. "I'm organizing a caravan and searching for Atlantis right now — I don't have time to hunt Sentients. Otherwise, I'd have done it myself, obviously..."

"I have an idea... If it works, I'll get a Sentient Core in the next few days."

Grandfather's mood noticeably improved.

"Have you picked your third monster yet?"

"Not yet," I answered evasively. I had some thoughts, but it was too soon to say them out loud.

The servants brought us tea.

"Ever think about moving to a different mountain?" Grandfather asked casually. "I'm planning to gather sixty percent of the Golden Lions in one place. It'll take a little over a year, but by then, the Golden Lions will be one of the strongest organizations."

"It'll take longer than that," I shook my head. "Don't compare it to what my mother did. She built a small, powerful group of Weak Evolvers, which is why she made it in a month. And even then, there were casualties. If you gather a whole caravan, you'll move slower, and the combat strength won't compare to my mother's squad."

Grandfather chewed his lip in irritation.

"Andrei is leaving soon, too. He won't be around to help you."

"That's fine," I smiled.

"What's your plan, then? Staying on Xin Shang Peak and killing monsters? When are you going to start looking for Atlantis? Or are you just going to keep ignoring something that important?"

"As soon as I choose my third DNA chain and raise the purity of all four of my spirals past ten percent — then I'll start searching for Atlantis," I promised. "As for what I'll do next... I don't know."

That was a lie. I had an idea — to claim a mountain no one had settled yet and build a city there. It could become an invaluable asset in the future.

"Do you even have a rough idea where Atlantis is?" Grandfather pressed.

"No."

Grandfather sighed, leaning back in his chair. "The government finished studying the Crystallites' technology," he said, clearly disappointed with my answers. "With my connections, I can buy or trade for some of it."

"Oh, that's good," I nodded, taking a sip of tea. "It'd be great if you could get a few more green artifacts."

"I have some scans of those fingers. Take a

look and tell me what they do."

We spent some time discussing Crystallite technology. Before long, it was time for my call with Black.

As I climbed the stairs to my room, my thoughts drifted to Adele. I wanted to call her and ask how she was doing, if she was managing the branch well. Find out about Axel — a Weak Atomeus of Synthesis had visited him already. He probably hadn't said anything new, but I just wanted to hear Adele's thoughts.

Who was I kidding? I just wanted to hear her voice.

I'd accepted that she wasn't my Adele, the one I had loved. But that didn't make me miss her any less.

In my room, I changed into a formal three-piece suit and combed my hair. I was the son of Rosa Vavilonsky and Xing Li, after all. The grandson of Boris Uralsky. I had a reputation to uphold — I wasn't just some nobody.

Once I was ready, I sat in my chair and powered on the massive screen that took up half the wall. Right at 8 PM, Xiuli called on ReChat.

"Hello, Vladislav," she greeted me, looking as stunning as ever. Dressed in white slacks and a matching blazer, she radiated both grace and authority. Her hair was tied in a simple style, and her sharp amber-brown eyes gleamed, drawing my attention.

"Hello, Xiuli," I nodded. "Where's Black?"

A message at the bottom of the screen showed that another call was in progress, but the recipient wasn't answering.

"Don't worry, he'll be here soon," Xiuli reassured me with a smile.

I looked away, feeling an odd restless energy stir inside me.

"Let's talk business. Are you satisfied with your sister's progress? She fits in surprisingly well. Respects her elders, follows orders, and never argues."

"I'm glad to hear it."

"I'm sending Xiu to your mountain with the caravan. It'll take two months."

"That's too long. I'll pick her up myself."

Xiuli's smile widened. Finally, the call connected, and the screen split into three sections — me, Xiuli, and... Black.

In a dark room, seated in a black chair, was... someone.

They wore a loose, hooded robe. A clown mask covered their face, complete with a round black nose. Gloves concealed their hands. Boots covered their feet. Every inch of them was hidden. Even their eyes were obscured by dark lenses.

For a while, I simply studied Black. Black, in turn, stared at me. Their reaction struck me as odd. Their body trembled slightly. Their hands clenched and unclenched.

"I am Vladislav Li-Vavilonsky, known as Delta," I introduced myself, placing a hand over my chest. Whoever Black was, they had seen the future. It was best to establish friendly relations.

Black slowly raised a shaking right hand and pointed at the screen. Then their feed cut off. It was just me and Xiuli again.

Silence fell.

"Ahem," Xiuli cleared her throat awkwardly. "I apologize. The boss is… a unique individual. I'll ask why he left. He might not answer, but I'll try… Until next time, Vladislav."

She hung up hastily — and, just like that, I was alone. I turned my head, catching my reflection in the mirror. Neatly combed hair. Perfectly tailored suit.

"Ugh," I muttered, standing up. "I should have called Adele instead…"

Still in a sour mood, I decided to check in on Grandfather. I needed to talk to him about my plan to hunt Sentients — and it was time to tell him about the Music Box.

But when I walked into his office, I stumbled upon something… unexpectedly personal. Grandfather sat at his desk, counting money. His eyes shone with emotion. His expression was almost tender, as if he were gazing at a long-lost grandchild for the first time. He sorted the bills, binding them with colored rubber bands, then stacked them neatly. Each stack had its own designated color.

I quietly stepped back and left. It was best not to interrupt. We all had our sacred little joys.

I stepped out of the mansion and took to the skies.

I pushed everything out of my mind — Crystallites, their artifacts and ships, the Amphibians, the Primordial World, my future city, the Crystalline Worm lair, and the beasts I would soon tame.

Book Three

I just flew over the vast expanse of the princi-pality, thinking about nothing at all. Moments like this were rare. And they'd become even rarer in the future. So I let myself savor it.

213

Chapter 16

The Millionaire

United States of Europica
Germany, Berlin Suburbs

MUHIDDIN SAT BY THE FIRE, staring into the flames with a gloomy expression. He was waiting for orders from the leader — his last mission was already complete.

"Hey! Will you look at that! Doesn't the moon look just like a croissant?"

A girl, no older than eighteen, sat on a tree stump a meter away, excitedly comparing the croissant she was holding in her hand to the crescent moon. "Come on, tell me it does!"

"Shut up, you freaking moron," growled their other companion — a dark-skinned young man sprawled out on an improvised bed of stones.

"But it does look like one," the girl murmured, holding the croissant up to her eyes.

She was short, with black hair cut into a sleek bob. Dressed entirely in red, with a well-proportioned figure, she might have been beautiful — if not for her hypertelorism. The space between her eyes was unnaturally wide.

Muhiddin sighed internally. He hated working with these two. The former — Abdullah al-Kaabi — was a psychotic criminal who had murdered his entire family and several police officers. Getting him out hadn't been easy. But thanks to their leader's tip, Muhiddin had known when Abdullah would be transferred to another prison — and ambushed the convoy.

The latter — Rumiko Naruse — was just as unhinged. Muhiddin stole a wary glance at her. Her ability still gave him chills. Both of them had rare and terrifying powers.

Abdullah, an Atomeus of Transformation, had a strange skill called Corpse Body. It was useless on its own — it just made him incapable of feeling pain. But when he became a Weak Evolver and gained Berserk, he turned into an unstoppable killing machine. At the Schmidt estate, he lost all control and slaughtered everyone. Muhiddin had been forced to use his own ability just to stop him.

Rumiko, on the other hand, was an Atomeus of Synthesis — and her skill was the most horrifying Muhiddin had ever seen. Uncontrolled Mitosis. With a single touch, she could trigger rampant cell division, turning human flesh into a writhing cancerous mess. Muhiddin shuddered, forcing the gruesome images from his mind. And then there were her eyes. Bulging, fish-like. An indeterminate color, slightly crazed. Every time she stared at him, his skin crawled.

"It's an exact copy of a croissant!" Rumiko declared. "Commander, don't you agree?"

Muhiddin said nothing.

"Commander, if you don't answer, I'll eat the croissant."

Silence.

"This is your final warning."

Muhiddin closed his eyes.

Rumiko ate the croissant.

A phone chimed.

Muhiddin snapped to attention and checked his inbox. The first thing he opened was a video. His eyes burned.

On the screen, his wife sat anxiously, listening as a doctor explained their son's illness. Every time their leader sent a new video, his wife looked healthier. Now, she was barely recognizable — a radiant beauty. Muhiddin wiped his eyes discreetly and focused on the doctor's words. Their son's treatment would be long and expensive. He had been born with the disease, and curing congenital conditions was far harder than acquired ones. Finding the right specialist was nearly impossible.

The video ended. Muhiddin took several deep breaths, calming himself. Despite the blatant blackmail, he was grateful to the leader. After all his travels, he had seen enough to know that the leader hadn't lied. There was no cure for his wife's illness. She would have died.

After the video came his next orders:

Head to Brussels. There, you will receive a package and power up. Further instructions to follow. Kill Ronald Von Belga. Lars Thorvald, son of Chris Thorvald…

Muhiddin quickly skimmed the list of eight names and read on:

After Brussels, go to Warsaw. You will recruit another Evolver there — I'll send details later. If I don't contact you, proceed to Shanghai. You will eliminate the local Triad branch. That is all.

He reread the message twice before carefully stashing his phone. Was the leader really planning to wage war against the Triads?

Muhiddin licked his lips. He remembered how Triad members were treated in prison. Like kings. Meanwhile, he had been a pariah. And now, the mere thought of cutting them down sent shivers of excitement through his body.

"Captain, are you happy?" Rumiko asked, stepping closer. Her fish-like eyes locked onto him. "We're going to kill, right? Who's our next victim?"

Muhiddin immediately looked away. Her gaze killed his enthusiasm instantly.

"We're leaving for Brussels in the morning," he ordered, standing up.

"Captain, I've run out of croissants…"

The One Who Changes the Future

*　*　*

"Hello, Adele," I couldn't help but smile at the screen.

"Good evening!" Adele was visibly nervous. "Congratulations! Both on becoming a Strong Human and on your stocks skyrocketing!"

"Thank you," I nodded.

I had spent the night flying over the city and its outskirts. Then I went home and fell asleep. And when I woke up...

I was a millionaire.

Several sensational headlines had spread across the web overnight like wildfire. First came the revelation that I, Delta, had advanced to the next stage of evolution. I had surpassed Black and everybody else. Then came the explosive news about Grandfather's new potions. I had no idea how that information got out. Honestly, I wouldn't be surprised if Grandfather leaked it himself. And to top it all off, Xiuli had used the Clowns to stir the pot — flooding the info sphere with news of my secret meeting with Black. She made sure the whole world heard about it.

Article headlines were along the lines of:

"The Mysterious Connection Between Two of the Strongest Evolvers!"

"A Legendary Meeting of Two Leaders — What Was Left Off Camera?"

"Will the Syndicate and Clowns Become Partners? Read Our Article to Find Out!"

"The Secret Bond Between Delta and Black!"

One news story after another crashed into the ocean of the infosphere, sending wave after wave of hype rippling outward. Cumulative effect in action. The Syndicate and Syndicate Epsilon stocks skyrocketed as a result. At this moment, the Syndicate's market capitalization stood at six hundred million yuan. Still far from the true market giants, but for an independent organization that hadn't even existed for three months yet? A fantastic result. The Clowns' stocks had surged as well, albeit not as dramatically. Demand for our virtual currency had tripled. Our chief economist had sent me a report that morning.

Syndicate Epsilon's stocks had also climbed, and Adele — who owned a stake in the organization — couldn't hide her excitement.

"We finally have a flood of applicants! We've already received over fifty Evolver profiles! Can you believe it — there's even a Weakling among them!"

"I'm glad," my smile widened. "How have you been?"

"Great," Adele nodded confidently. "My DNA purity is already over seven. And I'm making an effort to hunt monsters myself instead of using the warehouse."

"How's Axel?"

"He's working," Adele's enthusiasm dimmed slightly. "He's preparing a presentation — he wants to show you something. He has a few proposals."

"I'd be happy to see them."

"Um... Do you know who keeps sending me black roses every day?"

I scratched my nose.

"Maybe a secret admirer?"

Adele gave me a flustered look.

"I was told that it was you who ordered them."

"Oh? What were you saying just now? Yeah, how's Carlos? Doing a good job?"

"I was told it was you..."

"I have a very important mission for you," I cut in, suddenly serious.

I needed to find the blabbermouth who ratted me out and rip their tongue out.

"What is it?" Adele straightened, her focus sharpening.

"My people will arrive shortly. Hand them twelve Liquid Alpha Cores. Contact the Beijing headquarters to clarify the details — they'll explain everything."

"Understood. Anything else?"

"You're not throwing away the roses, are you?" I asked, furrowing my brow in mock severity.

"Uh... no."

"All right. See you later, then."

I ended the call and let out an excited grunt. My mood was excellent. Adele was safe — Felix had fled the country, and the Von Belgas wouldn't dare make a move for years. Ideally, I'd hunt Felix down and kill him, but I had no idea where he'd gone. Even Grandfather's men had lost his trail. No matter. The important thing was that Adele was out of harm's way. In essence, I had prevented the tragedy that would have led to her coma. I had killed Sam with my own hands (a moment of weakness — I shouldn't have let my emotions take over), and I had crushed Felix's empire before it could take root, even though Felix had moved faster and more effectively in this life than in the last. Solomon Von Belga, though — that old dog knew whom he could bite and whom he couldn't. He wouldn't be a problem.

But there was still one disgusting bastard left — Ronald Von Belga. A depraved beast who wanted to take his sister by force. He wasn't even an Evolver. A coward who wouldn't set foot in the Primordial World anytime soon. But the moment Muhiddin reached Brussels, he'd be dead. As for Nikita Von Belga and Adele's other brothers — I had decided to spare them. Many of them had played a hand in Adele's downfall, but Felix and his six-man team had orchestrated everything. And I had ordered Muhiddin to kill every single one of them. It wasn't the most rational move. But my heart demanded it. And I wasn't about to go against my heart.

The seeds I had so carefully planted were finally bearing fruit. Muhiddin would soon raze several Triad bases and empty their vaults — he'd grow stronger, and I'd begin fulfilling my promise to Yanling. I had a feeling she'd be leaving soon. Syndicate Epsilon was already generating revenue in the form of Liquid Cores. For now, only beast Cores — but it was a start. And Grandfather had gathered more unique individuals in his principality than any other faction. Once they all became

Strong Humans, no one would be able to match Boris Uralsky in power.

Maybe, when this was all over, I'd write a book about him. I'd call it Grandpa's Chronicles. That would be hilarious.

My phone beeped. Liang was asking when we were returning to the Primordial World. I checked the date — June 28th. The height of summer. Instead of asking for a break — flying to the beach, relaxing, and so on — they all just wanted to get back to the Primordial World. Even though we had money. None of them wanted to rest. Each one had messaged me, asking when we'd go back. Wang Bolai had spent all of yesterday whining about how he hadn't received his reward. He had even threatened to commit seppuku to cleanse his shame.

After my conversation with Adele, I went to find Grandfather. I needed to wrap things up here — and, if possible, return to the Primordial World tomorrow. The monsters weren't going to kill themselves.

Having learned that Grandfather was at the training grounds, I stepped outside — only to run into Miroslava.

"Oh, hey!" she greeted me with a bright smile. "I was just heading to see Miss Majewski. She's with the Prince."

"He's at the training grounds. Let's go together."

"Sure! Oh, did you hear? The Brittas have announced a raid."

"No. Is there a big turnout?"

"Not yet — they only just made the announcement... Oh! Look over there! That crow's fighting a drone! What is it doing? It's shaking so much..."

"Let's keep moving..."

We reached the training grounds before I realized it. Grandfather was already coming out — scowling and dressed in workout gear. Behind him, a bald man scurried along, wiping his forehead with a handkerchief.

"Sir, I couldn't do anything... The company's profits plummeted, the margins shrank to critical levels. I had to act fast — I couldn't predict—"

"You should have predicted it," Grandfather interrupted coldly. "Albert, you've made a mistake. Do you understand?"

Albert trembled. His eyes darted wildly, as if he were on the verge of passing out from sheer terror.

"I-It won't happen again..."

"Of course it won't. Resign from your position, Albert."

"D-D-Do... Yes," Albert's face filled with bleak resignation.

Grandfather turned, his sharp eyes locking onto me. His frown deepened. With long strides, he marched toward us and yelled,

"You damn bum! I hope my crows peck you to death! Why the hell didn't you tell me about your meeting with Black?! You—"

His furious tirade continued as he stomped closer.

"Oh, right!" Miroslava perked up. "How did your conversation go?"

I scratched my nose in embarrassment.

"We... didn't really get to talk. The connection cut off. Technically, we didn't say a single word to each other."

Grandfather exhaled sharply.

"You're not a person," he declared. "You're an animal — stuffed inside a bum's corpse."

"We need to talk," I said with a smile.

"Don't act like some mangy stray dog!"

"All right, all right... or I won't bring you a Sentient Monster's Liquid Core."

"You dare threaten your grandfather?!" he bellowed in my face. But he calmed down just as quickly, grumbling, "You cowhide sack... Fine, let's go to the lounge — you can tell me everything there."

Then, turning to Miroslava,

"And what are you doing here? Begging for more houses for your little bum brats again? Why the hell do you keep dragging riffraff into my city?!"

Miroslava shrank behind me.

"I wanted to talk to Miss Majewski," she muttered.

I wiped Grandfather's spit off my face.

"She's over there," he gestured toward the training grounds.

Miroslava hurried off while we made our way to the lounge.

"We'll be trading potions and blood propane with the Li family," Grandfather started without preamble. "After your breakthrough, they'll be left alone for a while. And I've also started negotiating for Crystallite technology."

"How do you manage all of this..." I shook my

head. I already knew Grandfather's motives. He wanted to secretly acquire the weapons manufactured by the Li family — specifically, the kind reserved for the military. The same type Felix had used to wound me. But it was a dangerous game. If the Chairman or the Czar found out, Grandfather would be in serious trouble.

"I don't do anything," he said smugly, slapping his belly. "I give orders."

My phone rang.

Xiuli's icon popped up on the screen.

"Yes?" I answered coolly.

"Hello, Vladislav," Xiuli's enchanting voice softened my annoyance a little. "I spoke with Black. He didn't talk to you because he wasn't feeling well. You saw how he was shaking, didn't you? He's sick, and he—"

"I don't care," I cut her off and hung up.

I didn't buy it. I didn't believe Black was sick. But he had acted strangely. It felt like he recognized me. But why now? My photos were all over the internet. My identity as Delta was public knowledge.

Grandfather let out a mocking imitation of Xiuli's voice.

"Hewwo, Wladislaw..."

"Cut it out," I muttered.

Grandfather burst out laughing. Or, perhaps, cackling would be a better word.

We stepped into the lounge.

"You've simply been had," he declared gleefully, still chuckling. "Black didn't even bother talking to you."

I grimaced. We sat across from each other.

"Has Mother returned yet?"

"No. Anyway, what did you want to talk about?" Grandfather wiped tears of laughter from his eyes, still clearly entertained by my humiliation. I drew a sigh inwardly.

"I'm heading to the Primordial World tomorrow morning. My biggest concern right now is India. I'm worried that the Asian Commonwealth will start a war over the territories that have slipped out of India's control. And the Moon and Mars — do you know what the world governments are planning for them? Is a big war coming?"

Grandfather studied me for a long moment, chewing his lip in thought.

"You wouldn't be able to change anything even if you knew. Leave it to me — I know what to do. There won't be a war."

"All right," I nodded.

But the situation still troubled me. Not much time had passed since my rebirth. I had technically prevented the Indo-Asian Conflict that had led to the Slavic War and, ultimately, the Last World War. But things were still far from ideal. War could break out at any moment.

Before, I had been sure that the Amphibians would attack in twenty-two years. After all, no matter how much I changed history within the Solar System, it was unlikely to affect the entire Universe. But after seeing Black, that certainty wavered. What if the Fish attacked sooner?

The only solution I saw was becoming stronger. Strong enough to single-handedly stop the war. And I needed to reach Atlantis as soon as possible. I had to retrieve the Chaos Stone and the Crystalline Slate.

"You should be focusing on bringing me a Sentient Core," Grandfather said pointedly. "I'll handle everything else. Your job is to work your ass off. Politics, economics, intellectual nonsense — leave that to me. As the saying goes: 'To each their own — man to mankind, bum to bumkind…'"

"I have a weapon blueprint," I interrupted before he could keep stroking his own ego. He could go on forever, alternating between praising himself and insulting me, twisting proverbs into ridiculous nonsense along the way.

"A weapon?" Grandfather stiffened. "Something like blood propane?"

"Yes, but much stronger."

"Tell me more."

We talked for a long time. About the Syndicate. About the Primordial World. About trade and politics. The most important takeaway? Grandfather had agreed to share the first potion recipe with allied factions in exchange for a cut of the profits. It was another push for humanity's progress. Who knew what new recipes the laboratories of different nations and noble families would uncover? Or how far alchemy — as the internet had started calling it — would advance in this timeline?

Grandfather had been reluctant to part with the formula at first. But I convinced him. For some reason, I felt an urgency about it. I didn't know why. But the feeling had crept in ever since I saw Black.

The One Who Changes the Future

The next morning I reentered the Primordial World as planned. I never got to see Mother before I left, although I was very curious if she had managed to establish contact with Lily.

At the designated time, the entire Syndicate — except Jiao — gathered at the clearing that was our chosen rendezvous point.

"Well," I swept my gaze across the eager faces of my people. "Are you all ready? These next few days will be really challenging. Our goal is to collect as many Sentient Liquid Cores as possible. And we'll start with the Crystalline Worm nest..."

CHAPTER 17

THE FIRST MONSTER

United States of Europica
France, Paris

LIANG SAT IN A ROCKING CHAIR, staring blankly ahead, lost in thought. The past two weeks had turned his life upside down completely.

The door creaked open. An old man, dressed in black-and-silver robes, stepped inside.

"My lord," he said with a ceremonious bow. "You must not return to the Primordial World. Now is the perfect moment to restore the Fo family."

Liang didn't answer. After the Li family had started blackmailing him, he was contacted by a group of strangers claiming that he was the last surviving member of the Fo lineage. Two decades ago, the Fos had been one of the three heads of the Triad.

At first, Liang hadn't believed them. But the

evidence they provided was irrefutable.

"Your father—"

"Leave," Liang cut the old man off. "I am going to the Primordial World. That is not up for discussion."

"As you wish." The old man bowed and left.

Liang had no memories of his childhood. Only one face surfaced from the depths of his mind — the woman who had cared for him all his life. He had called her Mother, though he had always known she wasn't his birth parent.

The Triad men claimed she was his nanny. And that when the entire Fo family had been massacred, she had somehow managed to escape with him. But that night was so horrifying that his young mind had erased it.

"Father..." Liang murmured.

He had never known him. These men swore they had remained loyal to the Fo family. But the last order from the head of the clan had been clear. If Liang grows up weak, do not intervene in his fate. And so they hadn't. They had deemed the heir too weak. But the Eclipse had changed everything.

Since childhood, Liang had longed for a friend. But living in a foreign country, he had always been different — too different. Then he had met Vladislav. And for the first time, he had thought — finally, I have found one. A true friend. He had never felt more at peace. But as time passed, Liang began to see the glaring differences between them. The Syndicate leader was chasing some unknown goal. Every ounce of his energy was devoted to strengthening himself and his group. Vladislav didn't need friends. Liang had realized that after the bar incident.

And when he agreed to spy for the Patriarch, feeding him information about the Syndicate, he had finally let go of his naïve delusions. He was alone. Again.

And now, he didn't know what to do. The Fo family had once commanded immense power. Their base had been in Hong Kong. And for the first time, the thought crept into Liang's mind that perhaps he might want to take back what was his by rights, after all. But first, he needed to become a Strong Human. Once he pushed his DNA purity past ten percent, he would make some decision. For now, though, he needed to prepare for the next deployment.

* * *

Primordial World
Xin Shang Peak

"Where do we begin, Boss?" Natsuko asked cheerfully. Her mood was exceptionally good today.

And she wasn't the only one. Most of the squad looked pleased. Dumisa sat on a tree stump, cracking his knuckles. His face was grim — but his eyes betrayed his anticipation. Miroslava smiled at me. Anish and Nitya radiated excitement, admiring their new combat suits.

But two people stood apart from the rest — Wang Bolai and Liang. The former kept glancing at me miserably, dabbing at his eyes. And the latter seemed completely distant, lost deep in thought.

"You'll set up our hunting ground," I told them. "Right around that pit where I fell in with the Crystalline Worm. Meanwhile, I'm going to subjugate a monster. One that will be useful to us."

"Which one?" Miroslava asked, sounding intrigued.

"A Giant Gorilla," I flashed her a lopsided grin. Now that I was a Strong Human, my Neutrino reserves had increased significantly. And I had already formed ten Mental Threads.

"You mean the one that almost killed Selena?" Natsuko gleefully reminded Wang Bolai of the girl who had bolted at the first opportunity.

"Yes. Natsuko, handle the preparations. We need blood propane and fortifications around that pit. Have the Evolvers specializing in construction work on it."

"Boss," Wang Bolai whimpered, "I don't think I can hold back my desire to die anymore—"

"Selena will come back," I cut him off. "She needs bolts and propane. Don't worry. And your personal weapon is already in the works. You wanted twin warhammers, right? They'll be ready in a few days."

Wang Bolai was the only one among us without reinforced weapons. I had the Claw of Bai Hu. Dumisa had his knuckle dusters. Miroslava had throwing knives. Natsuko, Anish, and even Nitya had daggers from our collection of fortified weapons. But Wang Bolai couldn't use a knife. He needed hammers — or something similar.

"You think she'll come back?"

"I know she will."

"All right..." Wang Bolai hesitated — and then sighed, rubbing his temple.

"Fine. I believe you. I won't kill myself. Even though it's really hard to resist the temptation..."

Then his expression shifted.

"Boss, who's getting the first Sentient Core?"

The entire squad suddenly went silent. Everyone was listening.

"The first three Cores are mine," I said. "I'll upgrade all of my DNA chains — and I'll give one to Grandfather. After that, we'll see. It depends on which monster we hunt next. Where Miroslava's Magnetic Field is useful, Liang's ability might be useless. And vice versa."

"I already know I'll be the last one to get a Core," Natsuko muttered. She looked dejected.

"I'm the most useless of us a;;. Dumisa and Wang Bolai have higher damage and defense than me, even though all three of us are melee fighters. So what's the point of me being in the Syndicate?"

"Your greatest strength is your speed and the sharpness of your blade-arms, I countered. "And who knows how you'll evolve once you absorb a Core? It's too early for disappointment."

Natsuko smiled, but the sadness in her eyes didn't disappear.

"Let's begin," I ordered and took off. I was determined. After reaching ten percent DNA purity, the next threshold was thirty. And after that — fifty. In my past life, it had taken eight to nine years before the first people reached thirty. By the end of my life, my DNA purity had been forty-nine point nine percent. I had never managed to break the fifty-percent threshold. But this time it would be different.

It took me less than an hour to reach the rocky outcrop where Selena had once been trapped. Now, I could fly freely over the mountain without worrying about an ambush.

I landed near the cave where the Giant Gorilla lived and strode inside with confidence. Had I not unlocked DNA Fusion, I would have been much more cautious. But now there was nothing to fear — I could remain fused with Bai Hu, keeping my semi-beast form's physical strength.

My confidence wavered the moment I stepped into the cave-tunnel. The skeletal remains of Giant Gorillas were still sitting there, facing each other with their backs against the wall. A sudden, instinctive aversion gripped me. I really didn't want to go any further.

"...Hey!" I called out. Let the gorilla come to me, I thought.

"Ey... ey... ey..."

My voice echoed down the tunnel. One of the skeletons — by the looks of it, the oldest — cracked and crumbled.

A deep growl rumbled through the dark. Then red sparks flared to life. Not long after, a ten-foot-tall Alpha emerged from the shadows. The Giant Gorilla had finally decided to show itself.

I acted immediately — activating DNA Fusion and merging my two virtual spirals. My torso bristled with coarse white fur. My vision shifted. The feline sight of Bai Hu vanished, replaced by the thread-sensing vision of the White Silkworm. Everything turned blue.

The Gorilla growled menacingly, but it didn't attack. Could it be it didn't want to fight among the bones of its ancestors? Or was it simply warning me to leave its den? Didn't matter.

A Mental Thread shot from my right eye — piercing the Alpha's mind. The Gorilla recoiled. It resisted. But compared to the Sentient Crystalline Worm's consciousness, its struggle was child's play. I crushed its will by force. The Gorilla's growl faded. Then — slowly, reluctantly — it sat down, lowering its head.

"Well then. Lead the way," I exhaled, wiping sweat from my forehead. Subjugating a living creature wasn't easy. And I still didn't fully understand how Mental Threads worked. Did they turn monsters into obedient puppets? Or simply alter their perception of me?

I deactivated DNA Fusion — there was no point in wasting Neutrinos. The Gorilla's behavior didn't change. The Mental Thread had already embedded itself in its brain — it wouldn't disappear until I commanded it to.

The Alpha led me deeper into the tunnel. After about three hundred feet, the corridor widened into a spacious cavern. I had heard shuffling earlier, but only now could I see the source.

Two tiny black gorillas were playing on the cave floor. Their Liquid Cores hadn't even formed yet — they were too small. At the far end of the cavern, resting atop a pile of pelts and leaves, sat another Giant Gorilla. This one was crippled. Both feet had been gnawed down to stumps. Several fingers were missing from its upper limbs. Its fur was partially gray. The creature looked ancient.

The moment it saw us, the old beast growled. The little ones froze — then scampered to its side.

"Let's go," I muttered, shaking my head. I really didn't like the smell in here. Rot. Decay. Dead leaves...

"Grraaaah!"

The old gorilla lunged, lumbering forward on its forelimbs — its body expanding as it moved.

I started gathering wind in my palm, but I didn't get to attack. The Giant Gorilla I controlled suddenly stepped forward and slammed into the old one. A dull boom echoed through the cavern, and a gust of wind rushed past. Both gorillas were immense. If not for its missing feet, the old one would have been twenty feet tall. My Gorilla had grown from ten to fifteen feet. It was weaker than the elder.

Both of them growled, but hesitated. They weren't attacking. Family? Brother and sister? Husband and wife? Father and daughter?

I could hear the mental struggle in my Gorilla's growl. It was fighting back against the Mental Thread. But it couldn't overcome it.

I extended my hand, poured a substantial amount of Neutrinos into my palm, and attacked.

There was a loud bang.

I created a wind battering ram loosely based on Liang's Gravity Fist. The old gorilla was blasted into the cave wall. With a heavy thud, it crashed against the rock — then slid to the ground.

My Gorilla flinched.

"Let's go," I repeated. And walked out of the cave.

The Gorilla hesitated — but followed.

"Don't worry," I muttered. "They won't go hungry."

I hadn't subjugated the old ape. It was useless in battle. Better for it to stay behind and watch over the little ones. Outside, I spent some time hunting. Two Ironhide Boars. Three birds. I even found an Alpha — a Dark Fox. I didn't take the Cores. The Giant Gorilla hauled the corpses back to its den. That should be enough to keep the little ones fed for a while.

"Well?" I asked. "Happy now?"

The Gorilla didn't answer.

"Follow me."

I took off — soaring toward the pit I had fallen into not long ago. The Gorilla ran after me. It wasn't obeying orders... If I wanted proper communication, I'd need to switch to Silkworm Form and connect through the Mental Thread. For now, though... It simply knew that it had to follow me.

When the ape realized it was lagging behind, it was forced to activate its ability and grow larger. I adjusted my speed, ensuring it could keep pace. Occasionally, people crossed its path, scattering frantically in all directions upon seeing the gigantic monster. Some screamed hysterically — how had any of these idiots survived this long?

Yet the ape never harmed anyone — it was fully focused on keeping up with me. And from my altitude, choosing easier routes posed no challenge.

It took four hours to reach our destination. Natsuko had done excellent work — sturdy stone walls had been built around the hole, along with several simple buildings housing tanks of blood propane. There was a sizable group of Evolvers diligently busy with construction. In fact, the number of Weak Earth Gravitei seemed to grow by the day. It wouldn't be long before governments and powerful families kicked off massive fortress-building projects. I was certain blueprints and preliminary budgets already existed — they only lacked enough skilled workers to start.

The Giant Gorilla's appearance on the horizon immediately stirred panic among the workers.

"It won't harm you, don't worry," I called from above, my voice clearly reaching everyone below. They tilted their heads upward, quickly spotting me as I hovered near the pit, waiting for the Gorilla.

"I'll check out the worm den first. We'll start afterward." With that, I descended into the hole, focusing intently on every sound and mentally counting each foot. About a mile down, the tunnel suddenly expanded into an enormous cavern, riddled with numerous openings.

There was silence.

Where had the Crystalline Worms gone? I chose one of the wider tunnels, intent on exploring it. It ran parallel to the surface and quickly became narrow, forcing me to maneuver cautiously to avoid colliding with the low ceiling.

The scouting took longer than expected. Several times I considered turning back, yet convinced myself repeatedly that the end had to be near. Eventually, after nearly ninety minutes, the tunnel opened out into fresh air — right onto a slope. I wasn't sure exactly how far down it was, probably no deeper than two or three miles at most.

I decided to return. I had barely traveled a hundred yards into the tunnel when a vague unease gripped me. The walls were vibrating subtly.

"Crap—" I spun around instantly, hurtling toward the exit, burning Neutrinos without a second thought. Razor-sharp wind whirled around me as I accelerated, but I was too late — the tunnel collapsed.

The wind surrounding me drilled through earth like an industrial auger. My heart thundered, and my Neutrino count plummeted rapidly.

An explosion!

I burst free onto the slope, gulping down air.

A sharp hiss sounded above as a massive shadow fell across me. Instinctively, I drew Bai Hu's Claw, deflecting a barrage of bluish feathers — sharp as finely-honed blades. But the real shock was seeing deep scratches now marking my sword.

"A freaking Cerulean Condor," I muttered, staring up at the gigantic bird, easily the size of a small plane, hovering overhead and piercing me with its intense gaze.

Clearly, I'd walked straight into a trap. Whether I should feel annoyed or impressed, I wasn't yet sure.

Evocom had once posted a semi-humorous classification of Sentient monsters: dumb, average, and smart. Translating it into Evolver terms, a Sentient with ten to fifteen percent DNA purity qualified as dumb — the Crystalline Worm I'd killed had fit perfectly into this category. Fifteen to twenty-five percent meant an average monster — neither intelligent nor particularly stupid. But from twenty-five to thirty percent? You absolutely didn't want to mess with those.

I now had little doubt that the Crystalline Worm leader belonged to that third category — a smart Sentient. Witnessing the death of its kin, it had evacuated its pack and carefully set a trap for anyone foolish enough to return. Clever bastard.

The Cerulean Condor finally ended our staring contest, its massive body glowing faintly blue as razor-sharp wind currents formed, spinning dangerously around it.

I reacted instantly, surging toward it, activating DNA Fusion, and launching Mental Threads straight at its mind. A quick glance at my Neutrino count — forty-seven percent. The Cerulean Condor was an incredibly dangerous Sentient. Fighting it midair would be suicidal, but there was nowhere to hide on the unfamiliar terrain below. That left only one viable option.

The Condor effortlessly shredded my Mental Threads, its mental defenses vastly superior to the Crystalline Worm's. Yet it hesitated briefly, giving me exactly the opening I needed to pierce its wind barrier. I executed a sharp maneuver, landing securely on its back. I instantly canceled DNA Fusion and transitioned fully into my were-form, pushing my Bai Hu DNA integration to the absolute limit. Covered from head to toe in black and white fur, I likely looked like a humanoid tiger — though thankfully, a tail hadn't emerged.

I dug my claws deeply into the Condor's flesh as I pressed myself flat against its back.

The bird shrieked violently, twisting its head as it desperately tried — and failed — to snatch me with its massive beak. I had chosen my position perfectly.

Realizing it couldn't dislodge me, the Condor suddenly surged upward. I activated my tattoo immediately, frantically calculating how I could reach the pyramid, now hovering about six feet to my right.

The Condor twisted viciously, nearly throwing me off as dizziness overwhelmed me. Too late, I realized the bird had turned sharply downward, hurtling straight toward the glassy-blue surface of a perfectly circular lake below.

Chapter 18

Friends

THE WIND WHISTLED IN MY EARS, and my eyes were watering. The Cerulean Condor was plummeting downward at breakneck speed, its wings tucked in. A razor-sharp wind wrapped around the bird, forming a protective shell of sorts. If I jumped now, I'd break my neck for sure.

Splash!

The Cerulean Condor dove straight into the lake. I barely managed to hold on, my arms and legs trembling from sheer exertion.

The bird twisted in the water, trying to shake me off. But it didn't work — I clung to it like a leech. With a sudden burst of speed, the monster shot upward and broke through the surface.

I coughed violently. The Condor rocketed into the sky like a bullet. Judging by the splashes below, it had angered some creature living in the lake. From up here, I couldn't see what had emerged from the water.

The Condor suddenly veered, flying belly-up for a few seconds. Out of the corner of my eye, I caught a glimpse of tentacles reaching skyward.

The bird spun a few more times, but I held on. Neutrino was already down to twenty percent — if this thing didn't settle down, I'd have to risk a jump.

However, the Condor quickly realized its attempts were pointless. Letting out a loud hissing screech, it began to descend. A few minutes later, I was jolted as it landed. The moment its wind armor dissipated, the Condor folded its wing and prepared to roll onto its back to crush me.

I hastily unsheathed my claws and leapt toward the pyramid. If that massive body landed on me, I'd be dead.

Bluish wind blades materialized out of nowhere. A barrage of razor-sharp feathers shot from the Condor's wing straight at me.

I hadn't expected such a swift attack. The second I was teleported away, I crashed to my knees, gritting my teeth against the searing pain. Three feathers had pierced my body — my stomach, my chest, my thighs. Deep wounds gaped, some all the way to the bone.

Swearing to myself that I would subdue this damned bird no matter what, I collapsed forward and passed out. The hunt for the Sentients had failed.

The One Who Changes the Future

* * *

The tense wait dragged on. Hours had passed, and Vladislav still hadn't emerged from the pit.

"Guys, what if he was attacked and has already gotten out?" Wang Bolai asked.

"We wait. If that happened, we'll get word from the settlement," Dumisa rumbled.

Wang Bolai nodded. The Syndicate had an unspoken hierarchy, one even Vladislav wasn't aware of. In his absence, command fell to two people — Dumisa and Natsuko. The former took charge in battle, while the latter handled everything else. They were obeyed without question. Dumisa and Natsuko knew their strengths and weaknesses and never clashed. Natsuko didn't interfere with Dumisa's decisions, and he never got in her way.

Beyond those two, the highest authority belonged to Miroslava. She had no ambition and never sought leadership. But the simple fact that she was closer to Vladislav and his grandfather than anyone else made the others heed her words. She rarely spoke, but when she did, her opinion carried weight.

Anish and Nitya stood apart, yet both were key Syndicate members — the Portalist and the Healer. The two Indians never argued and always did their jobs flawlessly. If they had concerns, they waited for Vladislav to return and asked him directly.

At first, Wang Bolai had seemed like little more than an errand boy. But after that incident —

when he mercilessly shattered an Indian girl's legs — people started watching him warily. And with good reason. Everyone had seen how much Vladislav valued him. Sometimes, it even seemed like he favored Wang Bolai over the others.

Within the Syndicate's hierarchy, the fat man had become Dumisa's right hand. In combat operations, he only deferred to the African. But Dumisa knew it wasn't due to his own authority — Wang Bolai had simply joined the Syndicate much later. If Dumisa ever showed weakness, the fat man would seize leadership without hesitation. Despite his clownish behavior around Vladislav, he was serious — and sometimes even cruel — when the leader was absent.

Jiao had followed Vladislav's orders from day one, paying no mind to anyone else. And ever since she'd stopped entering the Primordial World, little had changed. In fact, things had gotten easier — there was no longer an extra non-combatant to protect. Still, Jiao's authority in the Syndicate rivaled even Miroslava's. She was indispensable.

And then there was Liang... The one who had once been closest to Vladislav, the first member of the Syndicate. Now, he kept his head down, silent and withdrawn. He felt guilty, distancing himself from the others more and more. Strangely, the only person he spoke to was Anish. Liang followed Dumisa's and Natsuko's orders without a word. And he watched.

Lately, he'd come to a realization — the Syndicate existed solely because of Vladislav's charisma and unquestioned authority. Natsuko was an Elder of an Asian Dragon Family belonging to the Ishida bloodline, and held power beyond his imagination. Dumisa — the First Evolver, the pride of the entire African Confederation — was as well-known as Delta or Black. Miroslava — the Princess of Magnetism, adored throughout Slavia — needed no introduction. Wang Bolai — slightly unhinged but brimming with potential — was bound to make a name for himself, at least in the Asian Commonwealth.

Many in the Syndicate were larger-than-life individuals, united only by Vladislav. If something happened to him, or if he chose to leave, the Syndicate would collapse.

And Liang understood exactly why things had turned out this way. Without Vladislav, none of them would be who they were today. They would have died in a monster's maw long ago...

"I hear something!" one of the Evolvers suddenly shouted. He was a Listener, hired for the raid in exchange for a reward. "Something's crawling out of the hole! Hey! There's a lot of them!"

A buzzing sound filled the air as bugs began pouring out of the pit. Ants, centipedes, worms.

"Fall back!" Dumisa barked. "Miroslava, Liang! Anish, the portal!"

Miroslava immediately unleashed a rain of blades upon the creatures, while Liang used his Gravity Fists.

The translucent fists crushed insects into pulp with ease, while the silvery blades sliced through them like paper. Most of the creatures emerging from the pit were beasts, but there were a few Al-

phas among them as well. There were too many —
Miroslava and Liang couldn't hold them off alone.

Anish opened the portal, and the squad began
retreating. Dumisa, Wang Bolai, and Natsuko
joined the fight, covering the evacuation. Besides
the Syndicate's core members, there were also
some Epsilon Syndicate fighters and hired Evolvers.

Liang wasn't holding back, burning through
his Neutrino reserves, crushing insects like... well,
insects. His blood was boiling, as it always did in
the heat of battle.

There was a loud clicking sound as a massive
brown centipede shot toward Liang, its countless
legs moving in a blur. A Gravity Fist slammed into
its head... and dissipated. Liang tried using a
Grapple, but it was just as ineffective.

The centipede didn't even slow down — it was
only a couple of feet away now. He barely had time
to draw his dagger. Staring at the charging Alpha,
he realized he had almost no chance of survival.

A yellow comet streaked past. The centipede
just two feet away when Dumisa lunged forward
and slammed his knuckles into it, effortlessly cav-
ing in its chitin. The massive body was sent flying.

Two yellow beetles suddenly dive-bombed from
above, spraying something onto Liang. He
flinched, momentarily distracted — and missed
the airborne attack. Something yanked him by the
collar and threw him aside.

"Don't just stand there, dammit! Agh, it's
acid!" Wang Bolai shouted.

Liang tumbled to the ground right in front of a

brown worm. The monster barely had time to react before it was split in two by Natsuko's blade-arm.

"Get up!" she yelled, covering him.

He leapt to his feet, just as a shadow loomed over him. But the dog-sized black fly never had a chance to strike — Miroslava's knives skewered it from multiple angles, and the Alpha's corpse crashed to the ground at Liang's feet.

"Get to the portal! Now!" Dumisa's roar was deafening. "I'll cover you!"

Liang surged toward the portal vortex, sending creatures flying with his Gravitational Fists. Despite the chaos raging around him, a foolish grin spread across his face. He realized he had never been alone. He had always been surrounded by comrades — people he could trust with his back, his life. In moments of crisis, they would come to his aid. And if that wasn't true friendship, then what was?

*　*　*

I woke up on a hospital bed, wrapped in bandages. On instinct, I immediately activated my ability and merged my primary DNA with my virtual strain. The doctors noticed I was awake and rushed around, but I ignored them. My mind was elsewhere — thinking about how to kill my next Sentient monster. I needed to take down another one to increase the purity of any virtual spiral. After that, things would get much easier. My wind power would finally be able to harm Sentients, and my Mental Threads would be able to control them.

The door opened. My grandfather entered, looking displeased. Miroslava followed behind him.

"You almost died again."

"The feathers I brought back. I need them," I said abruptly.

It was the only solution I could see — using the Condor's feathers. It would improve my chances, even if it meant risking lives. The other option was waiting for my grandfather's lab to produce a Music Box. But there was no telling how long that would take.

Grandfather stopped in his tracks. His expression darkened.

"Do you realize your guts were spilling out?" he said flatly. "You survived because of your reinforced body. A weaker Evolver would have been sliced to ribbons."

I said nothing. There was nothing to say. I had underestimated the Crystalline Worms and overestimated myself. I should have been far more cautious.

"Insects flooded out of that pit. It was like the serpent attack earlier on — thousands of monsters swarming part of the mountain. People had to evacuate en masse from the Primordial World. An entire settlement was destroyed. And they blame the Syndicate. They're demanding compensation, calling for you to exterminate the insects."

"How long was I out?" My mood plummeted.

"A day. But a lot has happened in that time." He sighed.

"Well, rest up, Vladislav. Don't worry — we'll

handle it."

Then he turned to leave.

"Thanks," I muttered, pressing my lips together.

A wave of warmth surged through me. My grandfather hadn't yelled at me. Hadn't berated me. Hadn't said he was disappointed. In the moment I needed support the most, he was giving it to me.

I had miscalculated. Badly. Sentient Monsters with intelligence on par with humans usually stayed below the hundred-mile mark. They could strategize and set traps. I wasn't ready to face such an opponent yet. But all of that was just an excuse. A leader was responsible for every failure.

Only after my grandfather left did Miroslava step closer. She stood there, biting her lower lip, fingers laced together at her stomach.

"There's news about the Clowns," she said. "They killed a Sentient. Yesterday. And Black became the second Strong Evolver."

I closed my eyes. Black's power was Decomposition. And I knew exactly what a Strong Evolver could do with that ability. The Clowns would start hunting Sentients one after another. If they hadn't already begun.

"I made a wrong move..."

"What do you mean?"

"I should have planned the attack on the Crystalline Worm differently. Made sure the Liquid Core went to one of you. Like I did before. If you had become Strong, Miroslava, we could've tried going after a Sentient with a metallic body. The

Stag Beetles, the Chromed Bears, the Armadons. There are Sentients like that on the descent — I even know where they live. But I got greedy. And one Core isn't enough for me. I need at least one more if I want to fight Sentients. Virtual DNA spirals won't help me until their purity is over ten percent."

I fell silent. I didn't even know why I was saying all this to Miroslava. After my confession, she was quiet for a few seconds. Then she sat down beside me and took my hand.

"You did the right thing," she said, her voice unwavering. "It's your name that should go down in history. You're the first human in the Solar System to become a Strong Human. Right now, you are the vanguard of humanity. Black and the Clowns have always been behind us. And that's all thanks to you. So you did the right thing. I believe that. And I can't imagine how else it could have been planned. You nearly died inside that worm. Anyone else would have failed."

Looking at Miroslava's stubborn face, I felt confused. My thoughts were a mess. I needed time to process everything and come up with a plan.

"The patient needs rest," came the doctor's irritated voice.

"Oh! Right," Miroslava quickly pulled her hand away, blushing. "I'll check in later. Get some rest, Vladislav."

She hurried out of the room, leaving me alone with the doctor — a plump woman with a perpetually disgruntled expression. I ignored her and slipped into a cold and logical mindset. Or, rather, my brain was busy analyzing all the data, trying to find a solution, while my body remained on high alert, ready for anything.

But no matter how hard I thought about it, there was no easy way to kill a Sentient. I had marked a few on the descent whose weaknesses I knew and could exploit. But to take them down, I'd need at least thirty people, and there would definitely be casualties. The raid would take around five days, and there was no guarantee the Sentient wouldn't escape.

There was another option — subjugating several beasts and attacking the Sentient alone, using them to my advantage. With proper coordination, it was possible. Before my recent failure, I would've done just that. But my confidence had been shaken. What if I ran into two Sentients? What if the one I targeted was stronger than I expected? What if a pack of Alphas attacked me mid-hunt? Any mistake could cost me my life. If I got another Sentient Core, all these problems would disappear. But where the hell was I supposed to get one?!

The doctor left, and I decided to distract myself. I grabbed my phone and checked my messages. The folks were worried — there were a lot of unread texts. I started replying to everyone. And then I stopped at Xiuli's message.

Hey, Vladislav! Black wants to talk to you. Audio call. Let me know if you're up for it.

I hesitated for a moment before replying that I was. Then I continued answering the rest of my messages. Just as I was about to put my phone down, it rang. Caller ID hidden. The call was coming through ReChat's messenger.

"Hello?" I pressed the phone to my ear cautiously.

"I have a proposal," a quiet raspy voice said.

"Black?"

"I'll give you two Liquid Cores. You return six in a week."

"Liquid Cores? From Sentient Monsters?" I clarified, my heart pounding.

"Yes."

"I'm in."

"My people will deliver the Cores to Dumisa tomorrow morning. He'll hand them over to you."

"Who are you?"

"In a week, all my Clowns will be Strong."

With that, Black — if it was really him — hung up.

I lowered my phone slowly and checked my wounds. There was no way they'd heal by tomorrow morning, especially the gash on my stomach. But it didn't matter. I'd manage. I needed to contact Dumisa immediately through Grandfather's people.

I refused to believe that Xiuli or Black were messing with me. I didn't want to believe it. Two Liquid Cores from Sentients… This changed everything.

I sat up, wincing from the pain. Then I stood and started dressing. The doctor rushed back in, yelling about something, but I wasn't listening. One thought was stuck in my head — who the hell is Black?

The phone rang again. For a second, I thought it was Black, but then I saw the caller ID. Mom. So she was out of Primordial World?

"Hello?"

"You alive?" she asked, sounding exhausted.

"Yeah."

"I already know everything. The insects, your injuries... Don't worry. I think I've found a Sentient Monster. My analysts are working on a plan. Want to take a look?"

"Uh... yeah, of course," I said, caught off guard.

"If it works, I'll become Strong and start killing Sentients. You'll get your second Core. I wanted to give you the first one, but—"

"I don't need it," I cut her off. "I'll manage. Have you gotten in touch with Lily?"

"I have. But she doesn't trust me yet. She wants to see you. She's the one who pointed out the Sentient. Even said the monkeys would help kill it if I go for it."

"What kind of monster?"

"A Silver Hedgehog. It comes up from the descent once a week to hunt monkeys. Even the Alphas can't handle it."

A Silver Hedgehog... Didn't ring a bell. I needed more info.

"I'm flying to Yekaterinburg tonight. We'll talk then. Right now, I just want a shower..."

"I'll be waiting. See you."

"Don't stress. Everything will be fine."

She hung up. I smiled involuntarily. Whatever was going on in the media must have been really bad if neither Mom nor Grandfather was being sarcastic or trying to push me around. But I'd sort this out later. For now, I needed to contact Dumisa.

Chapter 19

The Second Raid

MOM COULDN'T MAKE IT to Yekaterinburg — too many responsibilities had piled up in her principality. She had to postpone the trip. She sent me information on the Silver Hedgehog overnight, but I hadn't had time to look at it. I decided to deal with it later.

Early in the morning, despite the doctors' protests, I headed to the pyramid. I didn't tell Grandfather about my conversation with Black — what if the Clown leader really was just messing with me? He had named his organization for a reason, after all.

Miroslava came with me.

"Have you read the news?" she asked, staring anxiously at her phone screen. "It's like they're all in on it. They're saying we failed the raid, that the snakes came to the mountain because of us, that people died because of our mistakes. And now these insects…"

I didn't answer. I had already assessed the media assault. People had realized just how far ahead I had gotten. Even governments were still only drafting plans to kill Sentients, while I had already become a Strong Human. And in the eyes of many, the Syndicate's growth needed to be slowed down. Black's name hadn't made waves across the Solar System like mine had, and he hadn't made as many mistakes as I had. That was probably why they'd been leaving him alone so far.

"They're writing about the Clowns, too," Miroslava added, as if reading my thoughts. "Listen to this: '…*The Clowns will stop at nothing to achieve their goals. There is indirect evidence linking them to the deaths of several groups at the peak of Senepid. Reports confirm threats and assaults on Evolvers. Our editorial team urges the authorities to conduct a full investigation into the Clowns…*'"

She stopped reading and looked at me.

"They're trying to pressure them through the police? But the Clowns keep their identities hidden."

"They're also calling on people who know them to expose their real names. Any idea why this is happening?"

"It's a race for influence," I said, shaking my head.

I wished the car would move faster. Right now, I wasn't thinking about Black's motives — I needed to change the situation in the Primordial World as soon as possible. People had started filing lawsuits against the Syndicate, blaming us for their misfortunes. For the deaths of Evolvers. For psychological trauma. For their inability to enter the Primordial World... Obviously, it was all nonsense. People died by the hundreds every day — that was the reality of the Primordial World. But here, on Earth, things were different. Neither Grandfather nor Mom had control over Slavia's judicial system, let alone the Asian Commonwealth's. If I let this go unchecked, the Syndicate would get into real trouble. And the more public opinion swayed against us, the worse it would get.

Finally, the car reached the pyramid. We got out, and I immediately winced, touching my stomach instinctively. A wave of noise hit me — the clamor was overwhelming.

"You okay?" Miroslava asked with a concerned look on her face. "Why are you entering the Primordial World now?"

"Let's go." I strode toward the pyramid with firm resolve, ignoring everything around me. I didn't care about the heat, the hovering drones, or the journalists being held back by security. I didn't hear any of the questions and accusations hurled at me. I had a goal, and I was moving toward it.

A minute later, I stepped into the pyramid and entered the Primordial World. The summer heat of Yekaterinburg vanished in an instant, replaced by the coolness of the forest. My nose was immediately flooded with a hundred different scents, and my vision swam in a sea of green. But I had been long used to these sudden shifts in environment — long before this life.

I lifted off shot toward the clearing where I had arranged to meet Dumisa. My heart pounded in my chest. I was nervous. Even the pain from my stomach wound faded into the background. The other injuries? I ignored them entirely. If I had to fight in this condition, though... that would be unpleasant.

Dumisa had already arrived. He was sitting on a fallen tree, polishing his bone knuckles with something.

"Boss," he greeted me, rising to his feet as I landed beside him.

He pulled his backpack off his shoulder, set it down, and opened it.

"Here."

Dumisa handed me two cubes. Suppressing the slight tremor in my hands, I took them. I forced myself to stay calm as I sat on the same fallen tree and pulled out a glove. A sharp pang of pain shot through my stomach.

"Is this what I think it is?" Dumisa asked. "Sentient Cores?"

"I don't know yet," I muttered, shaking my head as I opened the lid. I gave the cube a thorough scrutiny, and then gingerly removed the Core. It wasn't as liquid as an Alpha's. My fingers could feel its pliable texture.

Holding my breath, I pressed the Core to my wrist. A message appeared before my eyes:

Select DNA.
Strong Human. Purity: 10.08%
Bai Hu, Lord of the Wind. Purity: 9.95%

White Silkworm, Lord of Beasts. Purity: 9.98%

I closed my eyes and took a deep breath, then exhaled. If the main spiral was listed, that meant it could be upgraded. Which meant...

I selected the second spiral — and felt my blood boil. My heartbeat surged. The wind on the clearing picked up. Hot blood trickled from my nose.

"Boss, you good?" Dumisa asked, concerned.

"...Yeah."

I couldn't hold back a grin as I felt all my wounds heal. Even half-healed old injuries had vanished. Already knowing what I would see, I checked my status:

First Virtual DNA Spiral: Bai Hu, Lord of the Wind.

Bai Hu, Lord of the Wind DNA Purity: 10.3%

It worked. I couldn't believe it actually worked.

"You guys here?" Miroslava finally found us.

"Come here," I gestured for her to approach. "There's something important I need you to do. Go to the settlement. Find Grandfather's people. Have them send this message to Earth..."

Book Three

* * *

KanOn Channel: Herald of the Primordial World

Attention! Message for all those tethered to Xin Shang Peak! The Syndicate has announced a new raid! Today, July 1st, at 6:00 PM Moscow time, Delta will attack the insects! The Syndicate calls on everyone to follow the raid and, when the time comes, join in collecting the spoils!

Our editorial team has adopted a wait-and-see approach. Everyone is curious how the Syndicate's second raid will turn out — another embarrassing fiasco or a resounding victory? Subscribe to our channel and stay updated with us!

Magazines, media outlets, and chatrooms worldwide buzzed with news about the Syndicate's latest raid. This time, however, something unprecedented was happening — the Syndicate had invited everyone to participate in gathering loot.

Many clearly understood that, regardless of how this Syndicate raid concluded, it would make history. But exactly how future generations would remember this day depended entirely on its outcome.

The One Who Changes the Future

* * *

I asked Miroslava to spread the news about the event. Afterward, I located Natsuko to discuss the upcoming battle.

Incidentally, after I left the Primordial World, the Giant Gorilla had fled back to its den. But no matter — I'd retrieve it later, as I'd definitely need it again.

"We have a total of thirty-one Air Fielders," Natsuko reported with less than an hour remaining until the event began. "Five of them are Weaklings. Is that enough?"

"Yes," I nodded. "I could handle it alone, but any help is appreciated."

We were seated in a tent six hundred feet from the insect-infested territory. The insects' territory continued expanding, although the expansion has slowed down. Underground creatures still emerged from the hole in waves every few hours, rather than continuously.

"I've also briefed the collectors. We're ready," Natsuko said, casting me a nervous glance. "Are you absolutely sure? If we fail, we risk becoming laughingstocks."

"I'm sure."

Checking my status once more, I smiled faintly. The name Bai Hu, Lord of the Wind, remained unchanged. That was because humanity hadn't yet named the Sentient White Tiger. Even though the monster bore the same name, the difference in the abilities I gained was immense — I'd already tested them.

"Then we'll definitely succeed," Natsuko smiled.

"You did great," My praised was sincere. "You've managed to organize so much in just a few hours…"

"I need to be useful somehow, right?" Her smile grew strained. "I don't want you to abandon me because I'm useless. You remember my goal, don't you? I want to evolve."

I chuckled softly, awkwardly patting her shoulder.

"I'd never abandon you — don't even think that."

Blushing slightly, Natsuko excused herself, citing work, and left the tent.

The raid's scheduled time arrived soon. The Air Fielders had gathered atop a small hill, awaiting my arrival. No monsters interfered — in this area, they'd already been exterminated. As time passed, fewer monsters remained atop the peak. Within a few years, newcomers would need to descend into deeper regions to obtain their first Core.

"Vladislav," Ulysses greeted me with a nod. All the Air Fielders assembled by Natsuko worked under his command. I'd known Ulysses since the first raid and trusted his competence.

"Your task is to use your Quarks to the max for generating wind currents above us. Many of you have done this before, so I'm confident you'll manage. Begin."

At Ulysses' command, the Evolvers activated their abilities. Blue-tinged wind currents began to swirl in the air. I could now sense precisely how these currents formed. Roughly speaking, each Fielder emitted Quark streams to alter and command the surrounding air. Ordinary Evolvers released Quarks aimlessly, while Weak Fielders produced significantly more energy and controlled the streams skillfully. The difference was unmistakable.

One by one, the Evolvers stopped applying their skills, and I gradually took control of their wind. Minutes later, only Ulysses remained active.

"Done," he announced, wiping sweat from his forehead.

"Thank you, everyone." I soared upward, absorbing all the Quark-infused wind. A vortex began forming around me. Taking a deep breath, I steadied my nerves. This was my first time performing something on this scale.

The insect-infested territory loomed ahead, visibly devastated — grass and leaves devoured, earth churned up, rivers and lakes stained pale brown. And this was only the second day of the invasion!

Continuing to spin the vortex, I advanced forward. In my past life, a powerful Indian Evolver named Paramahansa Vivekananda had used a similar technique. He would create a massive tornado, lifting hundreds of monsters into the air. Known as the Lord of Wind, Paramahansa, albeit a Weakling, had fought evenly with Strong Evolvers. His incredible talent made him someone worth studying closely.

I was now employing his technique, which he'd

described in detail in a written interview posted on Evocom. The crucial point was avoiding getting accidentally caught in your own storm — that could prove fatal.

The distinction between Strong and Weak Evolvers extended beyond superior physical prowess and a larger Neutrino count. Strong Evolvers deepened their Evolutionary branch, mastering their skills with greater efficiency and precision. Talent was crucial. Some, like Paramahansa, were true virtuosos of their element, while others merely relied on increased Neutrino count without achieving deeper mastery.

I was aware of this and strove not merely to control the wind, but to merge with it — to feel its essence. Bai Hu's form was helping tremendously — without it, such mastery would've been impossible. An ordinary Air Fielder could do nothing of the sort.

Yet even this wasn't enough. Training, new strategies, and advanced techniques were essential. But that could wait — right now, it was time to kill.

As I reached the insects' territory, my vortex brushed the ground. Trees groaned as the earth lifted in large chunks. No longer holding back, I poured Neutrinos into the storm, rapidly expanding it until it turned a vibrant shade of blue.

I was deafened by the roaring wind and thunderous noise. I could no longer see anything beyond the swirling walls of the tornado. Adrenaline surged violently through my veins, my pulse hammering in my head. One wrong move, and the storm would tear me apart — I knew that clearly. I'd spun the tornado up until the vortex no longer needed me to sustain it. The tornado would now grow on its own until reaching a critical point. All I could do was struggle to maintain its trajectory — and desperately try not to die.

A fierce grin formed involuntarily on my lips. Moments like these were exactly when you truly felt alive.

* * *

Standing side by side, mouths agape, Natsuko and Miroslava stared as the massive bluish-brown tornado ravaged the insect-infested lands. The scene was awe-inspiring — almost surreal. It seemed impossible that a human could unleash something on this scale.

Dumisa clenched his fists tightly, his breathing heavy. Once again, he was convinced that the Spirits favored Vladislav. Liang stared at the tornado unblinking, eyes ablaze. Anish and Nitya watched Vladislav's creation with superstitious terror, believing only a god — or perhaps a demon — could command such power.

Wang Bolai felt a faint stab of envy. He longed to achieve something equally spectacular, but deep down, he knew his strength lay elsewhere. Recently, he'd tried his hand at cooking and found it too easy. He hadn't yet discovered a new purpose, but watching Vladislav's tornado, he sensed a mysterious wave rising within, one he didn't fully understand.

Besides Syndicate members, hundreds of

other Evolvers who had gathered for the event watched the spectacle unfold.

Their expressions formed an encyclopedia of astonishment — each face capturing awe in its unique way. No one had expected Delta to execute something so monumental. Trees were uprooted, and flying insects had no chance to escape, sucked helplessly into the deadly vortex. Worms, centipedes, larvae — all creatures that had previously seemed terrifying — were now tossed lifelessly within the storm.

The tornado soon reached the hole from which the insects had emerged, and the vortex darkened.

Suddenly, several Crystalline Worms were pulled from the pit, appearing tiny and insignificant against the vast scale of the tornado.

Natsuko gasped when she saw them. These worms were smaller than the one Vladislav had killed earlier — but even so, they were massive...

The tornado moved on, but attention shifted to the rain of corpses falling from its peak. Dead insects had been plummeting in a gruesome downpour of slime and shattered carapaces for a while now.

"Get ready!" Natsuko snapped back to her senses. "On my command, we move out and collect the Cores!"

"Yea-a-ah!" The Evolvers shouted awkwardly, slowly returning to reality.

The One Who Changes the Future

* * *

My Neutrino count had dropped to ten percent by the time the tornado had finally dispersed. My entire body ached, as though I'd endured a brutal training session, and my clothes were drenched with sweat.

Yet I felt deeply satisfied — I'd achieved exactly what I'd intended. Now it was unlikely anyone would dare provoke the Syndicate again. Imagine unleashing a tornado like this on a city or some rival family's territory... The damage would be catastrophic.

People had already started collecting the Liquid Cores, resembling insects themselves as they sifted through monster remains, occasionally shouting in excitement. Others hunted surviving creatures, finishing them off. I didn't interfere and descended to the ground.

"That was amazing, Boss," Liang approached, grinning. "Hey, can we talk? There's something I want to tell you."

"Let me speak with Natsuko first, then we'll talk." I studied Liang carefully — he looked refreshed, as if he'd found some kind of inner harmony.

"Cool," Liang replied, giving me a thumbs-up.

I found Natsuko in the tent, issuing orders to a subordinate.

"Vladislav!" She brightened immediately when she saw me. "That was incredible! How did you even manage to control something so massive?!"

"I surprised myself, honestly," I grumbled. "How's the collection going? Will we have enough funds to build a new settlement here?"

I caught an intriguing idea, chuckled, and continued,

"Actually, scratch that — settlements are so last-century. Or even last-month, literally speaking. We're setting a new trend — we'll build a fortress!"

"It's rare to see you in such a good mood," Natsuko's smile widened even more.

"True enough," I agreed. "Our next target will be the snakes. I want to take down the Sentient controlling them — or perhaps bring it under my control. We'll see."

"You'll use another tornado?" Natsuko asked curiously.

"No, this time I'll try a different strategy. Also, I need to figure out where exactly I encountered that Cerulean Condor. A Sentient bird would be useful — I could ride it to the other mountain to find Xiu. And another thing..."

Just then, a young woman dressed in dark green rushed into the tent.

"Commander! Something huge is crawling out of the hole!"

"A worm?" I turned quickly to her.

"No! It's a giant brown beetle with blade-like legs!" she replied, clearly panicked. "That thing's already killed three Evolvers!"

"How big exactly?" I demanded, immediately calculating my next move.

"Enormous! Like one of those old three-story

buildings on the outskirts of my hometown!"

"Natsuko, get the squad ready," I said grimly, glancing at my Neutrino count, still at ten percent. "Another Sentient has made an appearance, and we'll need everyone's help.

Chapter 20

The Praying Mantis

THE BEETLE THAT EMERGED FROM THE PIT was indeed a Sentient. And I even remembered what they had called it in my past life — the Devastator Praying Mantis. A monster related to the Atomei of Decomposition. It had appeared on Xin Shang Peak once — and brought nothing but death. Back then, I had been traveling along the Great Ridge with Selena's caravan, so the whole event had passed me by.

The Devastator Praying Mantis looked like a colossal mantis, but every one of its legs was a razor-sharp blade, and its torso was covered in a heavy brown carapace. Because of that armor, its speed wasn't as high as it could have been. But even so, it moved far faster than any Evolver.

I hovered in the sky, carefully studying the Mantis. It occasionally paused to devour the corpses of its fallen kin, giving me a clear look at its armor and the patterns on it.

"Dumb, but close to regular," I muttered.

If monsters had DNA purity like humans, then this Mantis was sitting at around thirteen percent. A far cry from thirty, of course. But enough for what we needed.

The Mantis suddenly twitched and lunged forward. A scream rang out — someone crawled out from under the pile of corpses and tried to flee. They didn't make it. A bladed limb speared straight through them.

The Mantis tossed the body into its mouth and crunched down, glancing around. Many of the looters had fled the moment they heard about the giant monster, but some hadn't made it — or hadn't wanted to.

It was time to end this. I descended to my squad, who were already prepared for a long and grueling battle. I shrugged off my backpack, pulled out a cube, and locked eyes with a frowning Liang.

"Take this and use it."

Liang took the cube, looking utterly confused.

"It's a Sentient's Core," I explained. "Use it and become Strong. I can't handle the Mantis alone."

Originally, I had planned to keep the second Core for myself. But plans had changed. My Neutrino reserves were dangerously low. And even if evolving the Silkworm granted me the power to subdue — or at least immobilize — the Mantis, I might not have enough energy left to use the skill.

Liang didn't believe me. He just stood there, mouth slightly open, catching the envious stares of Wang Bolai, Anish, and Natsuko. Miroslava was smiling, and Dumisa showed no emotion.

"Well? Hurry up," I urged.

Liang finally moved.

"He'll use Grapple, and we'll all strike the same spot — the temple," I instructed. "Dumisa, Wang Bolai, Miroslava — you'll have to put in some work. That thing's armor is tough, breaking through won't be easy. Anish, you handle the portal."

As I spoke, Liang pulled a glove from his pocket, opened the cube, and absorbed the Liquid Core. Then he froze.

We all watched him, waiting.

"...My skills have disappeared," Liang muttered, turning his head toward me. "I got something called Gravity Palm, but everything else is gone. What is this?"

"Your skills always transform or vanish," Natsuko grumbled. "Why doesn't this happen to anyone else?"

"I don't know," Liang admitted, looking shaken. "And my tattoo has activated — even though I've been here for less than a day. Vladislav, how?"

"Don't worry," I mused aloud, realizing I could activate mine as well. I had forgotten about that detail. When an Evolver became Strong, they no longer had to wait twenty-four hours to leave the Primordial World. They could enter and exit at will.

"As for your skill..." I continued. "Try activating it. Feel it. Understand what it can do. But do it fast — the Mantis is about to start mowing people down."

"Got it."

Liang raised his palm. A translucent copy of his hand materialized in front of it. The phantom hand clenched into a fist. Then opened. Then it grew in size.

Liang lifted his other hand, and a second Gravity Palm appeared.

"I see," Liang exhaled in relief. "I can still use Grapple and Fist, just through the Palm. Cool. And it consumes fewer Neutrinos than before."

"Your job is to restrain the Mantis. Keep it immobilized. Understood?"

"Yes, Vladislav."

Liang canceled the skill and gave a firm nod.

"I'll do my best."

We had chosen high ground for the battle. I had deliberately picked a spot that would lure the monster in.

"Everyone ready?"

The team nodded. I fired an air bullet at the Mantis. It did no real damage, but that wasn't the point. The Mantis, which had been busily gnawing on corpses, snapped its head up and immediately turned toward me. An instant later, it charged — its bladed limbs scything through the air at terrifying speed.

"I'm scared," Wang Bolai admitted.

"Liang, get ready."

At my signal, Liang activated the Gravity Palms. But this time, he pumped far more Neutrinos into them. Both hands expanded until they dwarfed the monster itself.

When the Mantis was less than a hundred feet

away from the hill, I gave Liang the sign.

The two translucent hands surged forward...

SLAM!

The Mantis crashed into them like a wall. Its entire body groaned under the force. Its head snapped back. Liang flinched, sweat beading on his forehead.

"Guys — my Neutrinos are draining fast," he said.

"Go!" I shouted, launching myself toward the Mantis. Anish opened a portal — Dumisa, Miroslava, and Wang Bolai stepped through.

I descended, pulled out a pre-prepared spray can, and marked the exact spot where they needed to strike — the left temple.

The Mantis groaned, struggling against Liang's grip. And, little by little, it was succeeding.

Miroslava attacked first. Her reinforced knives struck the insect's armor with a metallic clang and bounced off. But she didn't stop, hammering the same spot over and over. Then she paused — to avoid interfering with Dumisa.

The African warrior leapt onto the Mantis's body and used his strongest attack.

There was a loud bang. Cracks rippled across the carapace. The monster shuddered.

"Faster, guys!" Liang yelled. "I'm down to less than half my Neutrino count!"

Wang Bolai reached the Mantis slightly later than Dumisa. His attack wasn't as powerful, but it widened the cracks, giving Miroslava an opening to drive her knives into them. Now it was my turn.

"Twenty percent!"

"Get out," I ordered Miroslava. She immediately withdrew her knives — all but the ones embedded in the cracks — then stepped through the portal.

The Mantis seemed to sense danger. Its bladed limbs ignited with black fire, and a thick mist began pouring from its carapace. Until now, it hadn't seen us as serious threats. That's why it hadn't used its decay abilities. Not that they would have protected it from Liang's Gravity Palms anyway.

"Too late," I shot an air burst, pouring seven percent of my Neutrinos into it.

There was a loud sickening crunch.

The cracks shattered, sending the knives and shards deeper. The Mantis let out a piercing high-pitched screech as its body erupted in black smoke.

In a swift motion, I pulled out Bai Hu's Claw and threw it. Liang's palms flickered and vanished. My blade sank straight into the Sentient's head, piercing its brain.

This didn't kill the creature — the upper half of its body tilted, paralyzed. But the smoke kept billowing, and its flaming blade-limbs twitched, as if still trying to strike.

I returned to the squad. The entire Syndicate watched, transfixed, as the Mantis writhed in agony. A sight like this could only be witnessed in the Primordial World.

"This area is off-limits. Fence it off," I said to Natsuko. "The monster isn't dead. The wound is severe, but if we give it time, it'll regenerate. I'm leaving. I need sleep. Once I recover enough Neutrinos, I'll deal with it."

"What about us?" Wang Bolai asked. "Maybe Liang and I should go hunt the Snakes? He could just squash them with his palms like bugs."

"Listen, I'm low on Neutrinos, too," Liang spread his hands. "So count me out for now."

"It's too risky," I shook my head. "We don't know who's controlling the Snakes. What if they're natural enemies of Gravity Gravitei?"

"Like that centipede..." Liang shuddered. "Vladislav, let's talk before you leave. There's something I need to tell you."

"Right, you did mention that... Let's go."

"Let's fly," Liang grinned, activating his skill. A Gravity Palm materialized in front of him, reshaping itself into a boat-like cradle. He hesitated for a moment before carefully climbing inside. And it worked! Everyone — including me — stared at him, wide-eyed, as he settled in comfortably.

"Look at me! I'm a monk's alms!" he yelled, grinning like an idiot.

Wang Bolai burst into laughter, tilting his head back before collapsing onto the ground. He started rolling around, pounding the dirt with his fists, letting out incomprehensible noises between fits of laughter.

"Let's fly, then," I nodded, forcing a smile. Liang's ability was indeed strange. I needed to study it — back in my past life, I had only heard faint rumors of skills like this.

Surprisingly, Liang handled his power well. The Palm carried him smoothly as he gleefully observed the ground below.

"I've always dreamed of flying like this! Using my own abilities!" he shouted.

"We're descending."

After a couple of loops, we started our descent near the camp. Liang deactivated the skill a second too early and fell from a ten-foot height. But he quickly adjusted mid-air, landed on his feet, and pressed both hands to the ground to keep from toppling forward.

"Phew!" Liang dusted his hands off with satisfaction. "So it turns out that I'm the last scion of the Fo family! Do you know them?"

"Fo...?" I didn't recall the name.

"Yeah. One of the former heads of the Triad. I'm the last surviving heir. And apparently, I've been under surveillance by my family's old subordinates this whole time. They're the ones who secretly helped me move my mother to the Asian Commonwealth. Helped out with a bunch of other things, too. I used to think I was just lucky. Once, they were about to expel me from university — but then the rector suddenly changed his mind. They even started paying me a stipend, can you believe that? Anyway, that's what I wanted to tell you. Oh, and those subordinates? They want me to return to Hong Kong and take my rightful place as one of the Triad bosses. What do you think?"

I studied Liang carefully. I hadn't expected this. Fancy Liang being the last surviving heir of one of the Triad's most prominent families?

"Did your family's people push you into volunteering?" I asked. Liang had always stood out among the other volunteers because of his youth.

That was how he had bonded with Dumisa, Natsuko, and Miroslava — they had been the only ones under twenty in that settlement.

"Yeah. I think they were just trying to get rid of me that way," Liang admitted, rubbing his cheek in embarrassment. "Because of them, I was one hundred percent sure the Primordial World wasn't that dangerous. And that I'd find a cure for my mom there."

"How is she, by the way?"

"Better." Liang exhaled. "Back when I was still in Beijing, I asked a Weak Atomeus of Synthesis to take a look at her. But none of them could heal her. Do you think Strong ones could?"

"I don't know," I admitted, ashamed that I hadn't asked about his mother's illness before. "But I think it's possible."

We fell silent for a while, each lost in thought.

"What do you want, Liang?" I finally asked. "Do you want to go back to Hong Kong and restore the Fo family? If that's your choice — I'll support you."

"You know, sometimes I wish it rained in the Primordial World," Liang said, tilting his head up toward the cloudless sky. "Right now would be the perfect moment — so cinemic — cinemagraphic — cinemaphotographic?

"Cinematic," I corrected with a chuckle. "There are mountains in the Primordial World where it rains," I added. "Some places where it never stops raining, twenty-four seven. Haven't you heard?"

"Nope. Wait, don't distract me. Let me think."

Liang went quiet, deep in thought.

"Triads are robbery, death, and corruption," he

said at last. "That means my parents were criminals. I get that in the Asian Commonwealth, parents and children's fates are intertwined. Tradition and all that. A good son is expected to reclaim his family's name. To avenge them. But... I don't want to."

Liang paused before continuing:

"I'll take my father's last name. And I'll start a charity. I'll help kids. The sick. Atone for my ancestors' sins. I have money now — I can afford it. What do you think?"

"I... didn't expect that," I admitted.

"Look, a lot of people need help right now. After the Eclipse, after everything that happened. Maybe this is my fate? I mean, I met you for a reason, right? Sometimes I get this feeling... like I was meant to die in the Primordial World. But you saved me. So... that's how I see it."

I met his gaze.

"And what about the Fo family's subordinates?"

"They serve me until death," Liang shrugged. "Since they've revealed themselves, they might as well be useful. And I need to find a reliable assistant, anyway — someone to handle things while I'm in the Primordial World."

He furrowed his brow.

"I have a candidate for you," I said slowly. "You're in Paris right now, yeah?"

"Yeah."

"I'll send you her details. She's European. Help her with her problems and offer her a job — she'll agree."

"Oh, cool," Liang perked up. "I'll be waiting then!"

"I'll do it as soon as I log out." I activated my tattoo.

"I'm heading out too. Need some rest... and something delicious to munch on. Wish they had cakes here. I love cakes. Do you?"

"I don't care either way."

"I love them. Poppy seed cakes, lavender cakes, banana and caramel, warm waffles with chocolate spread and berries..." Liang practically started drooling. "They say people who crave sweets are lacking love. Do you think I—"

I stepped forward and returned to Earth. Liang could go on forever about random nonsense, but I had no time to waste. The Mantis would regenerate if I didn't act fast.

First I messaged Xiuli, hoping she was still on Earth.

Do you need a Sentient Mantis-Devastator? Ask Black what he's willing to offer for its Core and body.

I deliberately didn't mention my debt — if Xiuli wasn't aware of it, I wanted Black to decide how to respond.

Grandfather's people met me and drove me to the nearest hotel. I told them I was only back for a short rest — just long enough to sleep. I had seven hours before the Mantis recovered. Ideally, I'd get a reply from Black and regain my strength. Neutrino restored faster during sleep. Unfortunately, Grandfather's potion was useless for a Strong Human. By the way, the internet had named his concoction the Ural Neutrino Elixir. Not a bad name, in my opinion.

I didn't bother checking my inbox — there'd be time for that later. I just sent Liang the contact information for the European woman I'd considered hiring as my secretary. But there were other candidates, and soon, one of them would need help.

After four hours of sleep, my Neutrino was back to sixty percent. I surmised it should be enough to finish off the Mantis. I read Xiuli's message in the car on the way back to the pyramid.

Add Black's contact — he's messaging you on ReChat.

I did as she said and received a message.

The full body of the Sentient Mantis-Devastator, intact with all limbs and Core, in exchange for four Cores from your debt. If you agree, I'll send my people to Yekaterinburg.

I paused to think. To Black, the Mantis Core was worth as much as three or four regular Sentient Cores that weren't tied to Decay. And on top of that, he'd get the entire body, every part of which was a treasure. And he'd only forgive four out of the six Cores I owed. But... As Grandfather would say — a stitch in time saves a bum nine. Black had helped me when I needed it, giving me two Cores upfront. I had no problem returning that generosity.

The Mantis body will be ready in an hour.

I sent the message just as the car pulled up to the pyramid. Now it was time to call Grandfather. I hadn't told him about my deal with Black. Wouldn't want him getting pissed that I gave away the Mantis Core instead of keeping it for him...

Grandfather listened, muttered something, and hung up. Seemed like he understood. Now it was time to deal with the Devastator Mantis and carry on with the implementation of my other plans. As long as nothing unpleasant happened unexpectedly.

* * *

United States of Europica
Britannia Province

The stifling heat, constantly broken by heavy rains, had done no favors to the Wyle Square district. A sour stench hung in the air. Allen hated the smell. He didn't like this place one bit. Especially the orphanage where he and his sister, Iris, had spent their entire lives under the rule of cruel caretakers.

Wyle Square was a black stain on London's body. A pit where society's finest gathered — thieves, rapists, drug addicts, and murderers. Every night, someone was beaten or killed. Every morning, new corpses were found.

Allen sat in the orphanage's common room, staring out the window at the miserable reality of Wyle Square.

"Tell me about the Primordial World again," Iris asked.

"I've told you a hundred times," Allen grumbled. "Wait... is that Beakface Patrick? Didn't he freeze to death last winter?"

Allen pressed his hands against the glass, squinting. The backs of his hands were covered in bruises and cuts. He'd been beaten badly for sneaking out of the orphanage and making his way into the pyramid.

"Tell me about Miroslava," Iris sighed dreamily. "Can she really control any metal?"

"Yeah... Where's Patrick running?"

Every winter, thousands died in Wyle Square. Even the state-funded orphanage froze. Iris had weak health. Winters were hard for her — she had barely escaped death several times. Now that Allen had become an Evolver, he felt he had gained great power. No one could hurt him anymore. He could snap the legs of grown men with ease. No one — except the caretaker. Allen had to endure the beatings for Iris's sake. Because if they didn't punish him, they would punish her.

"Can Dumisa really break a boulder with one punch?" Iris asked.

"Yeah. He's insanely strong."

Allen never told his sister about his ability — Pit. It was a worthless skill — something Allen was ashamed of.

"Look, Patrick's bringing someone over... It's the Hatter!"

Allen immediately pulled Iris away from the window. The Hatter was one of Lady's most trusted men. What was he doing here?!

Iris fell silent at the name. Everyone in Wyle Square knew — you never crossed Lady. Even the coppers, who turned a blind eye to every crime in Wyle Square, feared her. It was that way before the

Eclipse. And after the Eclipse, their fear had only grown.

A scuffle broke out outside. Allen crept to the door and listened. The caretaker was speaking to someone...

"...Yes, here. This way."

The door swung open. Allen barely managed to step back in time.

Two people entered. The caretaker, stretching her lips into an exaggerated smile, and... the Hatter. Nearly seven feet tall, gaunt, dressed in black, with a blood-red hat atop his head. He hadn't gotten his name for nothing — years ago, he had angered Lady, and she had cursed him to wear that ridiculous hat for the rest of his life.

"You're Allen?" The Hatter's eyes fixed on him, his hand resting on the pistol at his waist. His grim, humorless demeanor clashed with the absurd hat. But no one so much as smirked. No one wanted a bullet in the head.

"Y-yeah," Allen stammered, stepping back. "I didn't do anything!"

"You're coming with me. Lady wants to see you."

"O-okay."

Allen shot Iris a quick warning glance and followed the Hatter out.

The ride to Lady's sanctum took a long time. At some point, Allen was ordered to tie a blindfold and lower his head. Then they led him through corridors for five minutes before stopping.

"You may remove the blindfold," a beautiful husky voice said.

Allen obeyed and saw her. Lady. Dressed in black, veiled, and mysterious. Allen bowed, trembling. There were all sorts of myths and legends about Lady. Seeing her was a great honor for an orphan like him.

"You were in the Primordial World," she said.

"Yes," Allen whispered, fear rising. What if they killed him for it?

"And you met the Syndicate. Even received a Liquid Core and became an Evolver."

"Y-y-yeah," he admitted, cursing himself. Why had he bragged about it?!

Lady snapped her fingers. A masked man stepped from the shadows, setting a chest filled with cubes before Allen. Another brought a chair and forced him into it. Cold, unyielding fingers grabbed his wrist and rolled up his sleeve, exposing his tattoo.

"You will become a Weak Evolver," Lady said as her men opened cubes of liquid helium-3. "Then you will return to Xin Shang Peak and join the Syndicate. Understood?"

"Huh?" Allen gaped. He didn't even notice the first Liquid Core being pressed to his tattoo.

"Haven't you heard me?" Lady asked with a mocking grin.

"I... I understand. My sister, Iris. She lives in the orphanage and—"

"We'll move her. From now on, you'll work for me," Lady cooed. "You won't suffer anymore, my dear boy."

She raised a hand, and a servant placed a wine glass in it. As she tilted her head back, her veil lifted slightly, revealing the tattoo of a spider on her neck. Allen barely registered it — his eyes were locked on the notification flashing before him.

DNA purity increased...

CHAPTER 21

IN SEARCH OF CORES. PART 1

WHILE I HAD BEEN SLEEPING and taking care of business, the Devastator Praying Mantis had nearly regenerated. The breach in its temporal lobe had sealed, leaving a swollen lump with the hilt of Bai Hu's Fang protruding from it. The monster's brain hadn't fully recovered yet, and the Mantis couldn't move properly — it thrashed its sharp limbs, jerked its head, and spewed black smoke and fire. The entire area around it had turned into a lifeless scene of desolation. Not only the plants, but the very soil itself had wasted away.

I hovered about a hundred feet away, considering my strategy. The weak point of any Mantis was its temporal lobes — the least reinforced part of its exoskeleton. That was where I'd strike first.

I conjured a ball of wind in my palm. My Neutrinos drained rapidly — I wasn't holding back. At my command, the sphere elongated into a spiraling drill, lifting dust from the dead and blackened ground. The projectile strained to break free from my grip, and the more energy I poured into it, the harder it became to contain.

When my Neutrino reserves had dropped to half, I descended lower, extended my palm, and released control of the drill, aiming straight for the swollen lump on the Mantis's temple.

BANG!

The shockwave sent me flying as a deafening blast echoed through the wasteland. A shard of something sharp embedded itself in my left leg — I hissed in pain. Only after regaining balance did I see the Mantis' headless corpse. It had no chance of survival — its brain had turned to mush, and shards of its skull had scattered in all directions, one of them injuring me.

Muttering curses under my breath, I plucked the bone shrapnel from my leg and landed next to the Mantis' body. I activated my tattoo. While the pyramid was forming, I found Bai Hu's Claw and picked it up. The blade had taken a beating — rust-colored stains, nicks, chips, and cracks marred its surface. It looked nothing like it had when I first acquired it. I'd have to show it to Jiao — maybe it could be repaired.

The pyramid took shape. Carefully, to avoid cutting myself, I grabbed the Mantis by a leg and stepped into the pyramid, bringing its entire carcass with me. A feat I wouldn't have been able to pull off before — Weaklings couldn't transport such massive cargo from the Primordial World.

Back on Earth, I spent the next two hours assisting Black's people with the Mantis' body. There was no way to drag it far, so the only option was to carve it up. And as quickly as possible — we needed to get to the Liquid Core before it vanished.

Black had sent professionals who knew their work. Using military-grade tools, they meticulously dismembered the Mantis and took everything, down to the entrails. The process partially halted operations in the pyramid, which Grandfather certainly wouldn't be happy about. But he wasn't the first to call me — Mother was.

"Hello, son. I'm in Yekaterinburg. Fly over to the Prince's estate — we need to talk."

By then, night had fallen, and unfamiliar stars lit up the sky one by one. I decided to postpone my trip to the Primordial World — it wasn't going anywhere. And I had time to settle my debt with Black, now down to just two Cores.

Mother was waiting for me in Grandfather's office. He was there too, seated at the head of an oval table on a raised platform. Mother sat apart, arms crossed, leaning against the wall. All the chairs had been removed, leaving only a single small, battered wooden stool in the center of the room.

"Well, sit down, agent of chaos," Grandfather grumbled. "Why'd you hand over a Sentient's body to outsiders? We could've used it."

"I already explained," I began, deciding I could stand my ground. "I'm paying off my debt to Black."

"And why would they do you such a generous favor in the first place?" Grandfather's frown deepened.

"It's strange. How did they get two more Cores?" Mother added.

"Black is a powerful Atomeus of Decay. After becoming a Strong Human, killing a Sentient isn't hard for them."

What I didn't tell them was that Black had possessed knowledge of the future. Like me, they'd been able to choose a powerful first monster and awaken an exceptionally rare ability.

"Sit down. A bum finds no truth standing," Grandfather gestured at the stool.

"I don't mind standing," I replied with a slight smile, glancing at Mother. "Did you bring information on the Silver Hedgehog?"

"Yes, it's on the table."

I spent some time studying the details on the Sentient Monster. The Silver Hedgehog had been called something else in my past life — the Metal Porcupine.

What was the main difference between Hedgehogs and Porcupines? On Earth, among ordinary animals, the distinctions were clear. But among monsters, the external differences were often subtle. However, their abilities made them easy to differentiate. A key detail was that Porcupines were always related to Atomei of Transformation, while Hedgehogs were typically Gravitei.

Both could fire quills, but differently. Hedgehogs released a few quills in a straight line at midrange, while a Porcupine's attack covered a broad area — more like a bombardment. And even if you survived that, getting close meant facing the monster in melee combat. All in all, it was better to kill multiple Hedgehogs than a single Porcupine.

"Don't go after this monster," I set the files aside and looked at Mother seriously. "It's too dangerous. The whole team could die."

"Why?" she frowned.

"It's not a Hedgehog — it's a Porcupine. Have your analysts compare all available data on the two species. Then you'll understand why I'm saying this."

Mother and Grandfather exchanged glances.

"Besides, this Porcupine isn't just any Sentient. If we compare it to a human, it's like a Strong Human with fifteen to seventeen percent DNA purity."

"How do you know that?" Mother pursed her lips.

"Intuition," I lied. "If it freely climbs the descent, then it owns the territory."

Mother gave me a suspicious look, and Grandfather gave a disdainful snort. In truth, I had figured it out based on the number of quills. If the report was accurate, there were about seven to eight million of them. Earthly animals had, on average, thirty thousand, but monsters of the Primordial World were far larger.

"You'll be able to handle this creature when you have Strong Magnetic Fielders in your group," I continued. "That porcupine is metallic — an ideal prey for a Fielder."

"We'll have to look for a new Sentient," Mother grimaced.

"Give it a few days. I'll get both you and Grandfather a Core," I promised.

I had an idea. While dealing with the Mantis' body, I had time to think with a clear mind and sketch out a new plan. If it worked, I'd be able to gather a sufficient number of Cores in a short period.

"Son," Mother stepped closer and unexpectedly hugged me. I was caught off guard.

"Grandson," Grandfather stepped forward, arms outstretched, sniffling dramatically.

What the hell was going on?! Panic nearly set in. Grandfather stepped back and gave me a bras d'honneur.

"Not a chance," he declared smugly. "No hugs for bums like you."

Thank the nonexistent gods...

"I need to talk to you seriously," Mother pulled back and grew solemn, smoothing my hair. She rarely showed affection, but it felt warm. Pleasant.

"What's the conversation about?" I asked cautiously.

"Your grandfather and I want you to get married."

"Uh..."

"I need a grandson!" Grandfather suddenly bellowed. "Who am I supposed to pass the princedom to?! Certainly not a good-for-nothing brat like you."

Mother smiled sadly. As the wife of the last Vavilonsky, she had no right to pass the princedom to her descendants. After all, I wasn't a Vavilonsky from my paternal side — I was Xing Li's son. And the Czar would never approve of Novgorod's princedom passing to me. It was an impossible matter, even if theoretically feasible. That was Slavia's internal politics. Because of my surname, many assumed I was of Vavilonsky lineage. But in truth, if not for Mother's whim, my name would have been Li-Uralsky. Or maybe it wasn't whim but calculation — I didn't know. Complicated business...

"Well?" Grandfather stared at me expectantly. "Where's my grandson, you ungrateful bum?"

"Where am I supposed to get one for you?" I retorted indignantly.

"From Miroslava," Grandfather announced triumphantly. "She's a fine girl. Fertile."

A silence stretched for several seconds. I stared at him in disbelief. Fertile?! Seriously?! Even Grandfather seemed to feel some embarrassment — he cleared his throat and then yelled:

"Enough of that! Anyway, you have no objections, so go propose. Then start making grandchildren. We'll keep one here, send another to Rosa, a third to the Li family, a fourth—"

I didn't understand. Did Grandfather look at Miroslava and see... a breeding sow?

"Dad," Mother interrupted irritably. "Enough nonsense. Vladislav, what do you think?"

"What does it matter what he thinks?" Grandfather snapped. "He's not the one giving birth!"

Mother shot him a scorching glare before turning back to me. As for me... I wasn't shocked or taken aback — Grandfather had brought up grandkids in my past life, too. But now wasn't the time.

"Let's put this aside for now," I suggested carefully. "Please don't try to find me a wife. When the time comes, I'll handle it myself."

Mother lifted a hand, silencing Grandfather's growl. Then she smiled at me.

"But think about it, alright?"

"Of course. I'm heading back to the Primordial World, if that's alright. We'll talk business later — I need to pay off my debt to Black and find you both some Cores."

"Go, go," Grandfather waved dismissively, wrinkling his nose. "And don't come back without ten Cores, got it?"

"Yeah, sure... Have your people stand by the pyramid — I'll be bringing Sentient corpses."

Mother and I embraced, and I stepped outside. Deciding to take the faster route, I opened a window and jumped. The wind caught me, carrying me upward.

"Caw! Caw!"

A bizarre procession flew past. Two white ravens had mounted a damaged drone and were viciously pecking at it while cawing hoarsely.

"Caw!"

"Caw!"

"What the hell..." I muttered, shaking my head.

I was starting to think Black had visited the Ural Princedom and drawn inspiration from it when naming his organization.

Reaching the pyramid and entering the Primordial World was easy. A short half-hour flight later, and I was at the clearing near the insect-ravaged settlement. People were already moving through it, sketching things in their notebooks. Construction would begin soon, with accommodations for Weak Earth Gravitei taken into account in the design.

The entire Syndicate had gathered today. Even Jiao had come.

"Look, Boss!" Wang Bolai hefted two bone hammers as I descended. "Look! I'm Thor!"

"Hey," Miroslava smiled at me. I hesitated, remembering the recent conversation, and for some reason, the word "fertile" echoed in my head. I cringed inwardly.

"Leader," Jiao bowed. "My apologies for only arriving now."

"It's fine. Can you take a look at this — can it be repaired?" I handed her Bai Hu's Claw.

There was a loud bang as Wang Bolai clashed the hammers together.

"Oh my gods!" he rolled his eyes. "What a sound!"

"Bone on bone," Liang nodded approvingly. "A beautiful sound. Soulful. Brings tears to your eyes — like hearing your daughter's first word..."

"Vladislav," Natsuko cut Liang off. "What's our plan?"

"Lead us, Chief! Oh, can I call you Chief, please?" Wang Bolai clashed the hammers again, rolling his eyes dramatically.

"Clown," Anish muttered disdainfully.

"Our plans..." I tore my gaze away from Liang.

Was it just me, or did he look different? As if he had grown slightly. And the others... they were looking at him with a newfound respect. Was it because he had become Strong?

"Unfortunately, you're all useless to me for now, except Liang," I told them bluntly. "Wait until we get Cores for you. Then we'll continue hunting."

The air swirled around me as I took off. Liang caught my gaze and conjured two Gravity Hands. He leaped onto one, while the other covered him. Under the envious stares of the others, he soared into the sky as well.

"Get on with your own business for now," I called back and sped toward the Great Ridge. The Cerulean Condor and Snakes could wait — I needed to raise the Silkworm's DNA purity to ten percent first.

"Boss, not so fast!" Liang shouted, struggling to keep up.

I slowed down. Liang's speed left much to be desired — at this rate, we'd take half a day just to reach the Great Ridge. In the end, I decided to give him a push with the wind. It would cost me more Neutrinos, but we'd get there faster.

We spent about four hours reaching the Great Ridge. Liang talked nonstop, and occasionally, I responded, so we didn't get bored.

"Oh, I can see that green lake from here!" Liang exclaimed. "Where we killed the tiger!"

"Keep flying."

"So what are we hunting?"

"I'll tell you when we get there."

I wasn't entirely sure I'd find the right monsters. In my past life, they had been killed five years after the Eclipse — by none other than Heng

Huang, the same one I had taken out. Heng had not only become a Strong Human, but had also raised his team's Core level to match. In various interviews, he had bragged about his achievements, detailing how he had done it. After him, there had been cases where people killed Sentient Butterflies using gravity.

I stopped dragging Liang along, and we glided slowly over the Great Ridge. The landscape below wasn't much different from the terrain around Xin Shang Peak — forests, streams, lakes, hills, and ravines.

"Caw!"

Suddenly, a flock of snow-white ravens, each the size of a dog, took to the air. Waves of cold radiated from them — Frost Ravens, Alphas. They immediately reminded me of the birds in Grandfather's princedom.

"Can I squash them?" Liang rubbed his hands together, contorting his face like a cartoon villain.

"No, conserve your Neutrinos," I shook my head. Then I inhaled deeply, gathering as many Neutrinos as I could. The hurricane wind from my breath blasted the ravens away like dust. They didn't even have time to caw.

"Impressive," Liang nodded in respect.

For the next ten minutes, no monsters bothered us. Then another flock of birds — Heavy Geese — decided to test us. I didn't bother blowing them away — there was a reason they were called Heavy. Instead, I hurled a few wind blades at them. That was enough.

An hour later, we arrived at our destination —

a tricolored lake. Because of the algae and fish living in it, the water shimmered in shades of yellow, red, and green, creating a stunning scene.

"Are we there yet?" Liang asked when he noticed me slowing down.

"No, we're heading further down the ridge."

Even the Great Ridges had descents. And monsters from below could climb to the peaks at any moment to hunt. That was why caravans traveled through these regions at great risk — one unlucky encounter with a powerful Sentient, and it was over.

I flew around the lake and began cautiously descending. Liang followed in silence. He understood we were in a precarious position. Especially him. I could escape — I was fast. But his method of transportation...

We went lower and lower. Twice, I heard roars that sent chills down my spine. There were Sentients here — by my calculations, all of them land-based. Aerial monsters wouldn't dare venture into this part of the descent.

"There they are," I finally found what I was looking for.

"Whoa," Liang exhaled in awe. And rightly so.

The descent leveled out into a horizontal plateau upon which lay a flower bud the size of a stadium. It looked like a daisy, except its petals were bright green, and it had three centers. Two of the golden pollen sacs were occupied by massive Butterflies. A third hovered nearby, scattering a brilliant golden dust from its wings.

The sight before us was dazzling, almost hypnotic in its beauty. And yet, in my past life, these same stunning creatures had wiped out hundreds of Evolvers.

"What's the plan?" Liang swallowed. "These butterflies — they're Sentients, right?"

"Yes."

"And what can they do?"

"See that yellow one? The seven-foot-wide one with red circles on its wings? The one that's airborne?"

"Yeah."

"It can create a superheated zone around itself. It would dissolve both of us in an instant. And that green one with the white circles? It can turn its body into plasma. The purple one — the biggest and nastiest — can release radiation waves from its wings. There's no defense against that. If you get hit, you die."

Liang swallowed again, louder this time.

"And... how exactly are we killing them?" he asked cautiously.

"You wanted to squash the ravens, right?" I pointed at the flower. "Squash the butterflies instead."

"Uh... seriously?" Liang gawked at me.

"Yes. Don't worry — Butterflies are the dumbest of all Sentient Monsters. They have no brains at all," I assured him. "Don't let the 'Sentient' classification fool you — it's just a term. Even among humans, you'll find plenty of individuals just as mindless."

"Like lipstick testers?" Liang mused. "I had a friend who was a lipstick tester. Dumb as the offspring of a fish and a plank of wood. She got hit by cars five times, walked into lampposts seven times because she got distracted, and once—"

"Yes, Liang," I cut him off. "Like a lipstick tester. You got it right. Butterflies are stupid. But if we attack them the usual way, they'll kill us in less than a second. We have to strike from a distance. And in a way they can't counter with fire. My wind would get swept aside easily, but your Gravity Hand is impervious to fire. So just squash them. Their bodies aren't as tough as other monsters'."

That was exactly how Heng Huang had done it. He used gravity and the Butterflies' stupidity to take them down. And even then, a seventh of his group died. Before him, no one had even managed to injure a Butterfly — there was a reason other Sentient Monsters feared them. Their lethality was among the highest of any species.

"Summon two Gravity Hands and crush the Butterflies. Just don't miss. If they spot us, we're dead."

"Got it." Liang wiped sweat from his forehead with his sleeve. "I won't ask how you know all this. But... you're sure this will work? One hundred percent?"

"Yes," I lied.

It had been a long time since I'd felt the comfort of absolute certainty. But I had calculated everything. I remembered every word from Heng's interviews and everything I knew about Sentient Butterfly monsters. There shouldn't be any problems.

Except… I hadn't mentioned one thing to Liang — most Butterflies had the ability known as "dichotomy." If the fight dragged on, they would split into two smaller copies. And then those would split again. And again. Indefinitely.

"If you're sure, then I trust you," Liang raised his hands and activated his ability…

Chapter 22

In Search of Cores. Part 2

THE GRAVITY HANDS APPEARED near the bud. At Liang's command, they began to grow and descend toward the flower. He breathed excitedly.

"I can't believe I'm attacking three deadly monsters alone," he muttered and pressed his hands downward.

The Gravity Hands crashed onto the bud. The Butterflies panicked, flapping their wings wildly. One of them fired plasma bursts, but the lethal projectiles passed right through the Hands.

BANG!

The ground trembled as the Hands slammed into it. Through their translucent surface, we watched the Butterflies' bodies break and the flower crumple. My calculations were correct — the monsters didn't have time to react. They didn't even understand what was happening. Stupid

Butterflies.

"Holy crap," Liang exhaled. "That's it? They're dead? Just like that?"

"Yes." I slowly descended, my eyes locked onto the Butterflies' bodies.

In the Primordial World, every monster had its own weakness. Some were slow, some highly flammable or susceptible to poison, and some — like the Butterflies — were simply fragile. But their weakness was balanced by their overwhelming attack power.

Landing carefully in the center of the flower, I transformed my hand into a clawed limb and sliced open a Butterfly's body. I extracted the Core and pressed it against my tattoo.

Select DNA.

Strong Human. Purity: 10.08%

Bai Hu, Lord of the Wind. Purity: 10.3%

White Silkworm, Lord of Monsters. Purity: 9.98%

I canceled the skill and chose the third option without hesitation. The ability activated instantly — my DNA began merging with the Silkworm's. My blood boiled as usual, dizziness hit me, and pain shot from temple to temple. I closed my eyes and endured the transformation.

In my mind, the nine Mental Threads (one still lodged in the Giant Gorilla) began to change — coiling into a sphere, becoming fluid and ephemeral. Something new. I had never heard of this before.

I checked my status and saw that one of the

lines had changed:

Additional skill: Mental Whirlwinds (10).

"Vladislav!" Liang shouted.

A rustling sound. A shadow rushed over me — the flower was closing. And it was doing so fast. Pollen shot from all three centers.

With Bai Hu's DNA inactive, I couldn't fly. But the Silkworm fusion had its own advantages — my reaction to the flower's attack was instantaneous. All ten Mental Whirlwinds erupted from my head. Three struck the centers, while the rest swept through the plant's body.

I felt resistance — the flower had three brains, each with its own consciousness.

Except... this wasn't a flower. This was a full-fledged Sentient Monster, one unknown to me.

My head spun. I dropped to my knees, my vision swimming. With sheer willpower, I ordered the flower to stop attacking and open back up.

It obeyed. Six free Mental Whirlwinds shot back into my head.

I had completely subjugated the monster. Made it my servant, in a way.

"Vladislav!" Liang landed and ran toward me. "My Gravity Hands couldn't stop the flower!"

"Get out of here," I rasped. But it was too late — Liang collapsed too, unable to maintain his ability.

Damn pollen — it completely drained strength!

The flower no longer attacked us. The pollen was just the first stage. I had no idea what would have happened after the flower fully closed, and I didn't want to find out. In my past life, plant-type monsters had been extremely rare. And Heng, that bastard, had never mentioned these buds to anyone.

"Gdwa..." Liang mumbled, barely moving his lips.

I finally activated DNA Fusion. Wind whistled around me immediately. But I couldn't control it yet — I could only burn through Neutrinos and hope it would blow the pollen away.

We took a long time to recover from the flower's effects — especially Liang. I managed to regain partial strength after forty minutes. The first thing I did was trudge back to the Butterflies' bodies — I had to hurry and extract their Cores.

The higher a monster's evolutionary stage, the longer its Core remained intact after death. With Sentients, it could take up to three hours to dissolve — if the corpse was left untouched.

I stored the Cores in cubes and piled the Butterflies' bodies in one place. A resource this valuable couldn't be left behind.

Liang was still lying down, though at least he could move now. For a moment, I considered flying to the second flower alone. But I dismissed the idea just as quickly. Too risky, even with my Mental Whirlwinds.

Thinking about them brought a grin to my face. Mental Whirlwinds — a mutation. This ability wasn't supposed to exist. Apparently, the Mental Threads had transformed under Bai Hu's DNA influence. I couldn't fully gauge their power yet, but one thing was clear — Mental Whirlwinds hit the brain hard. Against a strong opponent without psychic defenses, they could be a game-changer.

I checked my Neutrino count. Less than fifteen percent.

"Aaahh-lalala," Liang drawled, smacking his lips before breaking into a snore.

I decided to take a nap, too, ordering the flower to guard us. No Sentient would dare enter Butterfly territory anytime soon, and I needed to replenish my Neutrinos.

I lay down, got comfortable, and closed my eyes.

When I opened them again, three hours had passed.

"Wake up." I lightly shook Liang, who was drooling in his sleep.

"Huh?" He jolted, eyes darting open. "Am I in Heaven? Or Hell? Vladislav? You're an angel, aren't you? I knew you were either God's or the Devil's messenger..."

"We're inside a giant monster's stomach," I said calmly. "And we need to get out. The monster burrowed deep underground and fell asleep. We're probably going to grow old down here."

I stood up and stretched.

"Huh?" Liang whined. "Vladislav, why aren't you a girl? How are we supposed to—"

"That's enough." I kicked him. "Get up. Time to move. What's your Neutrino count?"

Beams of the nonexistent sun bathed us — the flower was opening at my command.

"So we weren't inside a monster's stomach?" Liang leapt to his feet. "You mean that was a joke?"

"Just fly already." I activated my skill and selected Bai Hu's DNA, taking off.

"I'm at fifty percent," Liang summoned two Gravity Hands.

"That should be enough." I rose above the flower and inhaled the fresh air.

"So... we were out for a few hours? What even happened?" Liang caught up to me.

"You blacked out, and I tamed the monster. Then I slept."

"Slept? Here? With Sentient monsters roaming everywhere?" Liang gawked at me. "What if we'd been eaten? And we're just leaving the Sentients' bodies behind? Maybe I should take them out and sell them. Make some money..."

"The Butterfly corpses aren't going anywhere — we'll be back. Now fly, Liang. Enough talking."

"Where are we going?"

"There should be another flower. And three more Butterflies."

I wasn't worried about losing. We may have had a slip-up with the first bud. And without the Mental Whirlwinds, I'd have been dead, no doubt. Heng, that bastard, had outright lied about these flowers. But it didn't matter — this time, we'd get it right.

We found the second bud quickly. It was larger than the first.

"All right." I focused on the Butterflies' colors.

"Look at that one — it's huge," Liang pointed at a monster. "At least fifteen feet tall. Same as the one on that other flower."

"Yes. It can turn into plasma. The most dangerous of the three," I agreed.

"And that little red one?"

"Laser Butterfly."

"How many types of Butterflies are there with the power of a Nuclear Atomeus?"

"Plasma, Fire, Laser, Radioactive, Explosive, and Light. The orange one — it's an Explosive. It can create blasts just by flapping its wings."

I shuddered, imagining what would happen if such a Butterfly split into hundreds of smaller copies, each retaining even a fraction of the original's abilities.

"What's the plan?"

"Get the Hands ready. I'll try to subjugate them all."

"Subjugate?! What kind of unfair ability is that?!" Liang protested but still summoned his Gravitational Hands. "Hey, maybe you should collect an entire set of Nuclear Butterflies. You'd be invincible. Kill anyone with ease."

"Ready? I'm starting." I activated DNA Fusion and released six Mental Whirlwinds.

To Liang, it looked like a faint ripple in the air. But I saw the gray-neon wind currents plunge downward, striking all at once — the flower with its three brains, and the Butterflies.

The Laser Butterfly was the first to fall. At my command, it flapped its wings and took off.

There was a flash.

The Plasma Butterfly glowed, its body undergoing a full transformation. To my surprise, the Mental Whirlwind simply burned away. The flower obeyed me, albeit reluctantly. But the Explosive Butterfly was still resisting.

"Attack!" I shouted, realizing I had overestimated my abilities. "And activate the pyramid!"

Flap!

The Plasma Butterfly quivered and split into two smaller versions. Damn dichotomy!

Two massive Hands crashed down on the Explosive Butterfly — just as I had finally subjugated it — snapping it apart. The monster died instantly.

But the Plasma Butterflies weren't affected at all. They had fully transformed — no more bones or flesh. Only plasma.

Two laser beams shot straight through one of the Plasma Butterflies, doing nothing. I ordered the Laser Butterfly to fly toward the mountain and wait for me. Meanwhile, the flower began closing. Its command was clear — stall the Butterflies for as long as possible.

Flap!

Each of the two Plasma Butterflies split again. Now there were four.

Flap!

Eight.

"Get to the pyramid, now!" I shouted, bolting toward the first flower. I wasn't sparing my Neutrinos — speed was all that mattered.

There was a flash, and Liang screamed. The lower half of his body vanished. A second later, he disappeared into the portal.

A chill of horror swept through me. I had activated the pyramid long ago — I was sure I'd be able to teleport away if needed. But the Plasma Butterflies were too fast!

Surrounded by a hurricane of wind, I raced toward the flower, hand outstretched, fingers inches from the pyramid. The Plasma Butterflies had incinerated the bud and scattered in all directions — now numbering in the dozens. If even one of them locked onto me, I'd immediately touch the pyramid and return.

I reached the flower and landed beside the Butterflies' corpses. Placing my hands on them, I withdrew all the Mental Whirlwinds from the bud before returning to Earth. It had no chance of surviving — the Plasma Butterflies were about to unleash absolute devastation.

The moment I materialized inside the pyramid, with the Butterflies' corpses at my feet, I finally exhaled in relief. Then I stepped out immediately and tried to contact Liang. No answer.

My phone screen lit up with Grandfather's name. I picked up.

"You alive?" came his anxious voice.

"Yes. What about Liang?"

"They're stabilizing him. The kid lost his legs — what the hell happened?!"

"A Plasma Butterfly," I coughed. "He's alive — that's what matters. We'll make Nitya a Strong Evolver, and she'll gradually restore his legs..."

"Get to me now!" Grandfather barked before hanging up.

I closed my eyes. The Plasma Butterfly had reacted too quickly. But... would it have done the same if Liang had attacked instead of me?

I pushed the thought aside. There were four such flowers on the Great Ridge of Xin Shang Peak. Two closer to our mountain, and the other two near Blue Mist Peak. And in my past life, all four had been destroyed by Evolver squads. Heng had taken care of the first one. As for the others, no one knew who had eliminated them. No records had survived.

The Plasma Butterfly had been too smart for an insect. There were rare exceptions — just like human geniuses.

Mother had already left for home, so only Grandfather was there to meet me.

"You realize that kid had almost lost his most valuable asset?" Grandfather started the moment I stepped in. "A couple centimeters higher, and that's it! Good thing he's Asian and not—"

"Can you send everyone his location?" I cut him off. "We need to visit him. Liang got the worst of it — he won't be able to walk for a while."

"He should thank the Christian God he's even alive," Grandfather grumbled, pressing his lips together. "He'll manage. He may be a bum, but he's not weak. What have you got for me?"

"I brought three Sentient corpses. Not sure what to do with them."

"I'll use them for experiments, what else?" Grandfather muttered. "Our lab recently found that Earth animals exposed to monster meat start changing. They grow bigger, their claws and bones toughen. But if you feed them Alphas' meat, they die. So you have to do it slowly, drop by drop."

"Could we make clothes instead?" I asked. "Butterfly wings would make excellent fireproof coats. Bright ones, just the way you like."

Grandfather paused in thought.

"So I, the Lion, would wear a butterfly? Why the hell not? Worth a try." His eyes lit up. "But we'd need specialists — don't have those yet. This is the first time we've gotten our hands on Sentient bodies. So for now, we'll have to stick to experiments. But once we figure it out, you're grabbing a net and going butterfly hunting. Got it, you ungrateful bum?"

Grandfather scowled again.

"Where are my Cores?! Hand them over!" he bellowed, spitting on me in the process.

"Hold on," I wiped my face in annoyance. "You'll get your Cores. You saw what happened to Liang. Every Sentient is dangerous — they need a tailored approach."

"What about the Cores from those corpses?" Grandfather asked slyly.

"I'll use them to strengthen the Syndicate. We're going hunting for other Sentients today. I want everyone to become Strong before we visit Liang. Should take a day or two."

"So someone else is losing their legs this time?" Grandfather's face darkened.

"There'll always be risks in the beginning. We all know that. And Liang was a huge help with those Butterflies. He's the one who'd really killed the Sentients. Support his fund — give him some money. I'll send some too, once I check my accounts."

"'Give me money,'" Grandfather wagged a finger at me. "Those are bad words. Never say that to me again, got it? Or I'll take all the money and leave you a bum."

"Yeah, sure. I'm going now."

"Wait! Who's getting the two Cores?" Grandfather's face lit up with curiosity — he suddenly looked like a mustached inquisitive child.

WHACK!

A white raven slammed into the window and slowly slid down.

"See that? The future monster army is growing!" Grandfather boasted. "So? Who gets them?"

"Miroslava and Dumisa," I chuckled and walked out.

I was curious — what extra abilities would they unlock? When an Evolver became a Strong Human, their powers expanded significantly, opening various evolutionary paths.

Take Miroslava, for instance — some Magnetic Fielders could unlock Magnetic Storms, capable of wiping out hundreds of people and beasts at once. Others awakened Metal Sense, allowing them to detect ore deposits deep underground, strengthening their bond with metal.

I reached the pyramid quickly and entered the Primordial World. From there, I flew toward the Snakes. Few of them could fight in the air, so there shouldn't be any problems.

Speaking of the Snakes — they were still advancing, but much slower now. They had scattered in all directions, losing their greatest advantage — density. Before, you could find three to six snakes per hundred square feet. Now, you'd be lucky to see one or two.

Because of that, the mountain monsters had managed to push them back. The humans, however, still hadn't made a move.

The land occupied by the Snakes hadn't changed — same trees, sparse cliffs, and lakes. Snakes weren't like insects; they thrived in nature.

Flying over the ruins of Hansh Khattar's settlement — how was he doing, anyway? — I activated DNA Fusion.

I had only three free Mental Whirlwinds left. One was lodged in the Gorilla, and the other, in the Butterfly. Five had burned away because of the Plasma Butterfly. Technically, I had only seen one burn up, but I was certain that area had turned into pure chaos — there was no way the others had survived.

But things didn't go as planned. The moment the Silkworm's DNA fused deeply enough and my vision shifted, I gasped involuntarily.

Threads.

Hundreds of pink Mental Threads stretched from the Snake Alphas, converging at a single point — the start of the descent. I realized immediately what was happening. Another Silkworm, Lord of Monsters! But where had it come from?!

I wanted to turn back but hesitated. The Silkworm was an Alpha. Not a Sentient — an Alpha. I could tell just by the Threads — they were exactly like mine. There was no Sentient strength in them. Which meant I could try to subjugate it. And if I succeeded, this entire Snake army would become mine.

A plan formed instantly in my mind — a way to use these monsters for my own gain. But first, I had to subdue the Silkworm. Even though it was only an Alpha, it was close to a Sentient mentally. This wouldn't be easy.

Decision made, I shot straight toward the point where all the pink Threads converged...

CHAPTER 23

A Personal Army

"THERE YOU ARE..."

I hovered high above, scanning the Silkworm's lair. The monster had hidden inside a mound, guarded by eleven Alphas — each an elite of their species, all capable of becoming Sentient Monsters.

"Let's begin."

I shot a quick glance at my Neutrino gauge and spun a mini-tornado in my palm. Forty percent — plenty. DNA Fusion burned through energy fast, but not critically so.

The Snakes noticed me too late. I acted fast — plummeted down and hurled the bluish mini-tornado straight into the mound. I made sure the wind was soft enough not to kill the Silkworm by accident.

Whooooosh!

The tornado expanded rapidly, cracking the earth apart. Chunks of soil and hissing Snakes shot skyward, whirling together in the storm. The monsters used their abilities to escape, but how could they possibly match the power of a Strong Evolver?

I kept my eyes locked on the battlefield, waiting for the Silkworm to emerge — watching where the Mental Threads converged. I had too few Whirlwinds left — I couldn't afford to waste them.

Wind roared around me as the tornado grew, churning earth, trees, and Snakes into a violent vortex. The crisp mountain air took on a sweet, dusty taste — oddly pleasant.

There!

The moment I saw a fluffy pink Silkworm rising from the mound, I struck with three Whirlwinds at once.

It didn't resemble its white counterpart. That one had been plump, almost fat. But this one was slender, delicate, with elegant wings. Female, maybe?

One by one, my Mental Whirlwinds slammed into the Silkworm's mind. It collapsed, but the force of the storm flung it into the air along with a layer of soil. I extended my hand and tore the tornado apart with sheer will. It hadn't grown too large yet — I was still in control.

To my surprise, the Silkworm resisted. Three Whirlwinds had struck its mind — stunning, disorienting — but they hadn't subdued it.

What the hell?

Even Sentient Monsters hadn't fought back

this hard.

The battle of minds lasted five minutes. If I'd had only two Whirlwinds instead of three, I wasn't sure I could've overpowered the Pink Silkworm. But in the end, it surrendered. And to my satisfaction, its Mental Threads remained intact. Even during our battle, it hadn't retracted them — the Snakes were still under its control.

I was about to cancel DNA Fusion when I felt something strange happening. The Silkworm was trying to communicate. Not with words, but with intent, emotions, and feelings.

It was angry. If I understood correctly, it felt cheated — because it couldn't use its own Threads. If it retracted them, the Snakes would turn on their puppet-master and devour it. The fact that I could even understand the monster surprised me. Was this because Silkworms developed their brains?

I descended. The Snakes didn't attack — the frustrated sulking Silkworm wasn't siccing them on me. Strangest of all — even with three Mental Whirlwinds inside its head, it could still express emotions. And sulk.

I reached out and touched its silky fur. Then I tried to ask — why did you even come up here? What was your goal? The response was a wave of resentment and self-pity. Only then did I realize that the Silkworm was indeed female. And she was on the verge of tears, broadcasting chaotic emotions.

At first, I couldn't make sense of them. I ordered the Silkworm to calm down. Then I focused on the Whirlwinds inside her head — and finally, I understood what she was trying to transmit.

To put it simply — White and Pink were siblings. Someone had thrown them up here from below. And from these same powerful beings, the two Silkworms had felt a call. Pink still heard it. But she didn't know who was calling. Most likely — an extremely strong Silkworm. An elite Sentient. Or maybe even an Ancient Monster.

After I killed White, Pink lost her purpose. For some reason, she believed she could only evolve after devouring her brother. And when she failed, she took her army of Snakes and headed up. Why? No idea. She probably didn't know, either. Maybe out of spite.

"So what the hell am I supposed to do with you?" I muttered.

If I wanted the Silkworm to obey, I'd have to leave at least two Whirlwinds inside her head. Even then, she would resist and obey with much reluctance. Three would be better. But was one Alpha worth three potential Sentients?

After a brief hesitation, I decided it was. If Pink became Sentient, she could subjugate other Sentients. I wasn't about to lose a trump card like that. And her army of Snakes would come in handy.

I gave Pink an order — to keep doing what she had been doing. But with one condition. After she processed the command, I reclaimed one Whirlwind, took off, and canceled DNA Fusion. My Neutrino count had dropped to twenty-six percent during our little conversation. That was interesting. If the Silkworm became Sentient, would she learn to speak, I wondered?

First things first — I flew toward my new soldier — the Laser Butterfly. It was small — just over three feet from the bottom to the top of her wings. It had clearly only recently become Sentient. But with that kind of attack potential, our hunt would be much easier.

The Butterfly was flying over a clearing, far from the Great Ridge. It had followed my order and was waiting for further commands.

"My, aren't you colorful," I said, reaching out to touch the insect's head.

The butterfly glowed — deep crimson and scarlet blending seamlessly across its wings, forming a breathtaking pattern. Its body was rust-colored. Its large, round eyes — as black as obsidian — held no sign of intelligence. Even ordinary beasts had more intellect in their gaze.

"Lipstick tester," I muttered, shaking my head.

It was time to head back to the others. I'd look for the Cerulean Condor later — right now, I needed to collect a solid number of Cores. The Butterfly could fly around on its own for now — I didn't want to stir up a commotion.

I found Natsuko where I'd left her — at the site of the insect massacre. Dumisa and Anish were with her. I didn't see the others nearby.

"Vladislav!" Natsuko exclaimed the moment she saw me. She stood in front of a tent, scribbling on a tablet with a pencil. "What about Liang?! Is it true that he lost... you know?"

"No, he's fine in that regard."

I tossed Dumisa a cube containing a Sentient Core.

"Where's everyone else?"

"I'm here!" Wang Bolai shouted, panting as he ran toward us.

And why the hell hadn't he lost any weight after evolving? His only change was that his skin had somehow gotten even smoother.

"Can you find Miroslava and Nitya? Is Jiao here, too?"

"Sure thing, Chief." Wang Bolai veered off course and took off running.

"This is… for me?" Dumisa held the cube in his hand.

"Yes. Become Strong and help me gather Sentient Cores."

Dumisa was clearly moved. He placed a hand over his chest and bowed.

"May the Spirits bless you, Boss."

While Dumisa carefully opened the cube and put on a glove, Wang Bolai returned with Nitya, Miroslava, and Jiao. And walking beside them was… Allen? What the hell was this kid doing here?

"Vladislav!" Miroslava quickened her pace when she saw me, worry written all over her face. "Liang, he…"

"He's alive, almost fine. Nitya, you'll handle his recovery once he can move on his own."

"Y-yes," Nitya stammered.

"Chief, do you have a Core for me?" Wang Bolai licked his lips. "Just reminding you — Selena still hasn't shown up."

The fat man's excitement dimmed instantly.

"Not for you yet," I shook my head. "Allen, how the hell are you here? The Snakes should have eaten you."

"Pfft," the boy scoffed, arms crossed, feet planted wide. "Me? Pfft. I killed all of them!"

"Allen is already a Weakling," Miroslava praised. "Can you believe it? He reached this level all on his own, without a group. I suggest we keep him with us for now — he's got serious potential."

"What's your secondary ability?" Wang Bolai cut in.

"Great Pit!" Allen declared proudly. "Wanna see? It's huge!"

"Show me," I nodded. I was curious. How had he survived? And gathered so many Cores? Even an idiot could tell something wasn't right.

"All right, I just need some space..."

Allen scanned the area. People bustled around, and a few tents stood nearby. He jogged off to an open patch of ground and dropped to one knee, pressing his hands against the soil.

"Pit!" Allen shouted.

The earth sank. It was a sheer drop — thirty feet across and fifteen feet deep.

"Whoa," Wang Bolai was impressed. "Not bad at all."

"Right?!" Allen stood, dusting off his hands. He looked insufferably smug.

"What's your DNA purity?" I asked.

"Nine point ninety-nine!" Allen placed his hands on his hips, chin raised high. "I'm this close to becoming Strong!"

"You can stay with us for now," I decided, then turned to Dumisa. "Well?"

The African sat motionless, eyes closed. At my question, he slowly opened them.

"Mass Transfer," he frowned. "If I understand correctly, I can increase the mass of anything I touch."

Not bad at all. After Liang's Gravity Hand, I'd hoped Dumisa would unlock something truly unique. But this wasn't the case. This ability had existed in my past life — hundreds of people had it.

"Jiao," I turned to the Asian woman. "Can you reinforce some throwing axes and spears? Dumisa will get more use out of them than brass knuckles right now."

"Of course," she nodded.

I understood why Curtis had sent her here. Obviously, he wanted me to help Jiao become Strong. And if that happened... how would it shift the balance of power? If the Lunarians gained weapons strengthened by Strong Evolvers, every bolt they fired would be lethal to any Weak Evolver. Did I really want to unleash that kind of firepower onto the world this early? I wasn't sure.

"Natsuko, you'll get Jiao some throwing weapons. Ask Dumisa what he's good with, and make sure they're delivered fast."

Then I turned to Miroslava and handed her the second Core.

"Miroslava, take this."

She nodded and accepted it.

"We need to visit Liang," I continued as Miroslava opened the cube. "He's badly injured — lost his legs."

"I was going to suggest the same," Natsuko sighed.

"Nitya, Anish — will you still try to leave? Even after becoming Strong?"

"Nope," Anish shook his head.

"I will," Nitya said softly. "I'm from Jammu — it's no longer under India's control. They don't execute branded people there."

"I'll ask Grandfather to send someone for you. Give me the city and square, alright?"

"Y-yes," Nitya bowed even lower.

"What the hell is happening in India, anyway?" Wang Bolai frowned. "Some kind of uprising?"

"Not yet." Nitya shot him a quick glance. "People are waiting for Hansh Khattar to emerge and lead them. The other leaders are divided — they care only about themselves and their own power. India's government survives only because Hansh Khattar is in hiding."

"So things are that bad?" Wang Bolai scowled. "I wouldn't be so hasty... Especially in India — it's not exactly the strongest country."

"Since the Eclipse, India's population on Earth has dropped by fifteen percent. That's over three hundred million people..."

"Miroslava?" I cut in.

I didn't want to discuss India. I had enough worries already. That country was a ticking time bomb in the fragile balance of our unstable planet. If India grew too weak, its neighbors would start getting ideas. But leaving things as they were wasn't an option either. The situation was already critical. In my past life, Hansh Khattar had been assassinated quickly. The Indian people never saw their messiah. So they suffered in silence. But this time, things were different. And I hoped Grandfather knew how to play his cards right.

"Yes?" Miroslava's head snapped up. "I got a new ability. It's called Magnet Point. I don't know what it does yet."

Magnet Point. I immediately knew our next target. That ability was invaluable against small metallic monsters. Miroslava could create a field of extreme magnetic attraction. The more Quarks she used, the stronger it became. Later, as her DNA Purity increased, she'd learn to move at incredible speeds and set up multiple Points, activating them at different times. In my past life, there had been one master of this ability in the United States of Europica — Thomas Firth. An incredibly skilled Magnetic Fielder, feared by many.

"Magnet Point, Mass Transfer..." Wang Bolai muttered thoughtfully but didn't continue.

"Natsuko, arrange a new raid," I switched gears. "Gather as many people as possible. We're attacking the Snakes."

"You sure?" Natsuko frowned. "There are a lot of Alphas among them."

"Yes, I'm sure. Get it organized. Dumisa, you'll help."

"Understood." Dumisa's expression darkened, but he nodded.

"Natsuko, set it up like the first raid. Spread the word. Let everyone know what we're doing." I flashed a grin. Pink already knew her Snakes had to hold back against humans. That was the hidden condition in my command.

"Hmm. All right." Natsuko studied me. "You've set something up, haven't you?"

"You'll see for yourself."

"Miroslava, you and I are going hunting. If everything goes well, we'll bring back Liquid Cores — for all of you."

I scanned the group.

"For me as well?" Allen pointed at himself, rocking impatiently on his feet.

"Don't push your luck," I snorted and took off. Orders given. Time to work.

* * *

United States of Europica
Brussels

Adele stood behind Axel, gripping the handles of his wheelchair. Her gaze was locked on the lifeless body lying before them. A woman in black sobbed over it. Ronald Von Belga, the fifth son of Solomon Von Belga, had been brutally murdered. His heart had been ripped out. Looking at her half-brother's corpse, Adele felt... sorrow. She hadn't liked Ronald. He had disgusted her. But still... they shared the same father. She felt a faint grief.

"Let's go," Axel patted her hand. "We're not exactly welcome here."

He was right. They were being deliberately ignored. No one spoke to them. No one answered their questions. It was as if they didn't exist. Even Bella Von Belga — the sibling Adele had once been closest to — refused to look at her. To the Von Belgas, Adele and Axel were traitors. Renegades. They had joined the enemy. And Adele hated it. She wanted to cry. She had never wished harm on her family. She knew they didn't love her... But this?

She met Nikita Von Belga's eyes — dark and grim. Then she looked at her father, Solomon. And in his gaze was pure hatred.

"Let's go," Axel repeated.

Adele obeyed. She lowered her head, pushing Axel's wheelchair forward. The crowd parted for them. Recoiled. Like they were lepers.

A car was waiting. Their bodyguards helped Axel inside. The doors closed. They were alone.

"Nikita has changed," Adele broke the silence, wiping her tears discreetly. Inside, resentment burned. She had done nothing wrong. Never betrayed them. Never wished them harm.

"Yes," Axel agreed. "He used to be a hedonist. Lived for pleasure. Laughed easily. But after Felix fell, everything changed. The family began fighting for the right to be heir."

"We have a meeting with Vladislav's contact today, right?"

"Yes, in an hour," Adele answered absently. "At first, he wanted to send twelve Cores. But the plans changed. Now I have to deliver twenty-two Alpha Cores. Why so many? And to whom?"

"Not our concern," Axel shook his head. "All these Cores came through the Primordial World. You're not losing anything. Better to focus on max-ing out your DNA Purity. Vladislav and Liang are already Strong. And this is just the beginning. Vladislav likes you. Try asking him for a Core.”

“I don’t want to ask,” Adele muttered. “I’ll wait until Nitya becomes Strong. Then I’ll ask her to heal you. I read her biography — she’s from Sangar in Jammu. She’s already been identified online. Jammu is safe now. Nitya can leave. But I need to contact her...”

“That’s a waste of a favor.” Axel frowned.

They argued for a while. Neither changed their mind.

The car stopped. Adele and Axel got out. Their loyal secretary was waiting. Carlos Norton. One of the strongest Evolvers in Brussels. His ability was Pressure. Extremely rare.

“The chief’s guest is inside,” Carlos said, his expression severe. He didn’t like the man waiting in their headquarters.

“Bring the case. I’ll speak with him,” Adele tensed. But she forced herself to stay calm.

She and Axel entered the foyer. A man sat on the leather couch.

The moment Adele saw him, she felt a deep instinctive fear. She barely stopped herself from activating her ability. The man radiated dread. A bald dark-skinned Asian in a stiff, ill-fitting suit. But most of all... His tattoos. From them, Adele sensed a power like her own. Decay.

“Hey,” the Evolver nodded at her. “You bring it? I’m in a hurry.”

Carlos entered, handing Adele a heavy backpack. Her legs felt weak as she approached the guest and set it down.

"It's all there."

"Perfect."

The Evolver stood up and grabbed the bag.

"Later."

Their eyes met. His looked familiar — cold and emotionless. She had seen a pair of eyes just like these earlier today.

The eyes her own father.

CHAPTER 24

THE WESTERN DESCENT

MIROSLAVA WAS EVEN SLOWER than Liang in flight, so before long, I gave up and told her to climb onto my back.

"What are we hunting?" she asked, wrapping her arms around my neck.

"Remember the Red and Metallic Sparrows?" I felt a little uncomfortable with her pressed so tightly against me, her breath warm against my ear.

"Of course."

"We're looking for a flock of Sentient Sparrows — monsters that have evolved from their Metallic kin. They're not in the Bestiary yet, but I know where to find them."

"You want to use my ability? Oh, what's that butterfly? It's beautiful."

"Our new companion." I flew closer to the Laser Butterfly, activated DNA Fusion, connected with it, and ordered it to follow me.

"Coo! Coo!" came a familiar cry. A white cloud was speeding toward us — Foul Pigeons.

"Butterfly, oh butterfly, please kill those pigeons," I requested, issuing a mental command.

The butterfly flapped its wings and shot forward at incredible speed. Dozens of laser filaments lanced out from its wings. The Foul Pigeons' death cries rang through the air. Two Airless Pigeons tried to flee, but they didn't stand a chance — the red beams burned perfect circular holes right through them.

"Wow," Miroslava breathed. "That's incredible! Can I ask it for something too? Does it understand me?"

"Of course, butterflies are very intelligent creatures. They can't talk, but they understand everything," I said, keeping a straight face. The guys often teased Miroslava for her naivety — she was too trusting, which made moments like this amusing.

In less than ten seconds, the Laser Butterfly wiped out the entire flock of Foul Pigeons and returned to us.

I set my course for the western descent. Around the five-mile mark, we should find a flock of Solid-Metal Sparrows — Sentient Monsters whose bones, feathers, and even beaks were made entirely of metal. Red Sparrows had steel talons and beaks, Metallic Sparrows had steel feathers as well, but the Solid-Metal ones were pure steel through and through. Highly dangerous creatures. They were smart, capable of mid- and close-range attacks. Their only weakness was magnets. Miroslava was their natural enemy.

"Butterfly, oh butterfly!" Miroslava called. "Dance for us, please!"

I cursed inwardly and slowed down. What command was I supposed to give? I improvised, having the Butterfly weave through the air in zigzags and perform flips.

"That's a traditional butterfly dance," I boasted with fake expertise.

"It's so beautiful!" Miroslava watched, enchanted. "I never thought you could befriend monsters in this world. It's fascinating!"

"Let's keep going. It's still a long way," I said, speeding up. I'd have to tell Miroslava the truth later — otherwise, she might actually try befriending a monster butterfly.

We reached the descent quickly and slowed down. Alphas feared the Laser Butterfly and kept their distance. Only once did a few Lightning Hawks take to the air, but at the sight of the Butterfly, they turned and fled immediately. No one interfered as I searched for the path. I only had a rough memory of the way, but I managed to find the right landmarks. Miroslava dismounted and stuck close — one couldn't afford to rush on the descent.

The first Sentient we encountered was a Coal Mouse at the three-mile mark. If not for the Butterfly tensing up, I might not have noticed the small monster at all.

"A Coal Mouse wields the power of Decay," I murmured, watching warily. The tiny creature peeked at us from the roots of an old blackened tree, its unblinking eyes fixed on us.

"Is it dangerous?" Miroslava whispered, equally tense.

"Yes. Let's keep moving and hope it lets us pass."

Coal Mice were almost impossible to kill. Any attack that touched them simply disintegrated. Their abilities were poorly studied — too few survived an encounter to tell the tale. But they rarely struck first.

We passed without incident, and I let out a quiet breath. Lucky.

Near the four-mile mark, I came across something unexpected — an Ant Nest. A mound the size of a village swarmed with Ant Monsters.

"We need to get out of here before they notice us," I decided.

Only a suicidal fool would challenge an Ant Nest. But why hadn't there been any records of it in my past life? Were other monsters going to destroy it?

We had to take a long detour, but the Butterfly kept the monsters at bay. Even Sentients refrained from attacking — they sensed its power. If we had come alone, we'd be constantly fighting Alphas, not to mention Sentients. Monsters always underestimated humans.

The Butterfly was the first to sense danger. It flapped its wings abruptly, soaring higher. We were a step too slow, so we were yanked toward the ground.

DNA Fusion. Mental Vortex.

Impact!

I slammed into rocky soil, the wind knocked out of me. Nearby, Miroslava groaned.

A flash!

A laser beam from the Butterfly sliced through the air. A deafening roar followed. Another beam fired, and the pressure vanished instantly. I forced myself to sit up. Ten yards away, the smoldering corpse of a Gravity Bear lay still — the next evolutionary stage of the Gray-Eyed Bear. Unlike its lesser kin, this one didn't need to make eye contact to exert its gravitational force.

The Butterfly landed beside us.

"Well done," I patted its wing and stood up, retrieving my Mental Vortex. Miroslava sat on the ground, cradling her right arm, tears in her eyes.

"It's broken," she groaned.

"We have one Core. It should be enough..." I muttered.

"No, I can bear it. I'll secure it with steel threads. What kind of monster was that?"

I told her about the Gravity Bear.

"So the Butterfly has saved us?" Miroslava looked at it gratefully. "Without it, we wouldn't have even had time to touch the pyramid."

"That's right..." I approached the Sentient's body. The lower half was still inside the cave, hidden under grass and branches. That's why I hadn't noticed it — it had been well-concealed and struck at just the right moment. Miroslava was right — Gravity Bears were incredibly dangerous for any human. An Evolver wouldn't even be able to move if caught in its gravity field.

The One Who Changes the Future

I used my claws to cut into the monster's flesh and reached its heart. I sealed the Liquid Core in a cube, and proceeded to pull out its fangs. The Butterfly's attack had left several holes in the Bear, the largest one in its head. The lasers had done their job.

While I worked on the body, Miroslava walked up to me. She had managed to stabilize her arm, but she was careful not to move it.

"You're pale," I noted as I stood up. "Are you sure you don't want to turn back?"

"No. It would be a waste if we left empty-handed."

"All right... We're close to the five-mile mark now. Can you sense anything with your Magnetic Field?"

Miroslava focused, her eyes glowing blue.

"I can feel ore deposits underground. Nothing else."

"Then let's keep moving," I decided. "Monsters will be swarming this body soon."

This time, we flew even slower. I scanned the landscape below, ready to counter any ambush. The western side of the descent was rocky, with barely any plant life. Everywhere I looked there were hills, pits, ravines, empty trenches, and miniature deserts. My field of vision was limited — the lower the descent, the thicker the mist.

"I feel something," Miroslava said suddenly. "Let's go that way."

We veered off course and soon arrived at a massive smooth rock, its surface riddled with hundreds of holes. The stench here was unbearable —

Miroslava nearly vomited. I had to use wind filtration so we could breathe properly.

"I can sense a lot of creatures inside this rock. There are hundreds of them. Some feel weak, but a few are really strong."

"Metallic and Solid-Metal Sparrows," I muttered. "If we wipe them out, we'll get a massive haul. But not yet. This rock is a Bird House. Tens of thousands of bird monsters live in there."

"Like a Nest?" Miroslava asked in surprise.

"A Nest has a leader. A Bird House is just a shelter. There aren't any trees here, so birds can't roost properly — they had to improvise. Let's go. We need to set a trap."

"What kind of trap?"

"We'll use your Magnetic Point. I'll tell you what to do."

There were plenty of rocks of all shapes and sizes in the area. But one, in particular, caught my interest — a black one with blue speckles. It was almost perfectly circular, like a giant watch face. We didn't approach it, though — something was living beneath it.

"Butterfly, oh butterfly," I turned to my loyal soldier. "Scout the area, please."

"Be careful!" Miroslava called anxiously.

The Butterfly turned to her and nodded.

"Uh..." Miroslava's mouth fell open in shock.

I checked my Neutrino count — less than twenty percent. I needed to leave the Primordial World soon.

I sent my last Mental Vortex from my head into the Butterfly's. It could stay there for now. The

Butterfly flew toward the rock and fired a laser into a small hole at its base.

There was a loud hiss.

A clawed limb wreathed in black flames emerged from the hole. I recognized it instantly. A Coal Mole! The next stage of evolution after the Destroyer Mole!

The Mental Vortex shot from the Butterfly and dove into the hole. But the Mole was already attacking — black flames erupted from its claws, scorching everything in their path. The Butterfly recoiled and fired dozens of lasers from its wings.

Wind whistled as Miroslava launched her throwing knives. But neither the lasers nor the steel reached the Mole — the black flames melted everything before impact.

The emerging Coal Mole shook its head. Pitch black and the size of a baby elephant, it radiated pure instinctual terror.

I ordered the Butterfly to retreat. Meanwhile, I focused entirely on subjugating the Mole. The Mental Vortex inside its head was slowly disintegrating. If its DNA purity had been any higher, it would have easily dispelled my mental attack.

"What do we do?!" Miroslava's gaze darted between me and the monster.

"Follow me," I said through clenched teeth, backing away from the rock. But we didn't get far — I felt the Mental Vortex breaking through the Mole's mind. It obeyed the command I had been drilling into it — it buried its claws into its own head.

A howl rang out, followed by a hissing sound.

The Mental Vortex dissipated, but it had done its job — the Coal Mole collapsed, slain by its own claws.

"It worked," I muttered in disbelief. Then I snapped back to focus. "We'll leave this thing alone for now. Set your Magnetic Point at the rock's center, then we head to the Bird House. Move fast."

Miroslava nodded. She was pale, her lips trembling — she had been terrified. I reached out and brushed her hair with my hand.

"Don't be scared. Just a little more, and we'll be out of here."

"Yes," Miroslava said softly. She gave me a grateful nod and flew toward the rock. She landed on it carefully, sitting down to avoid disturbing her broken arm. It didn't work — she yelped, her eyes welling up with tears. Pressing her good hand against the rock, she closed her eyes. A blue light spread from her palm.

"I think it's done," Miroslava said as she stood and carefully touched her injured arm. A bright blue point had appeared at the rock's center.

"Yes, you did it right," I flew over. "How many Quarks did that take?"

"Twenty percent. I have fifty left, but flying drains a lot."

"That should be enough." I frowned. I had forgotten that Miroslava didn't have as much energy as I did. Each DNA spiral slightly increased Neutrino reserves. I needed to hurry and obtain my third spiral...

"Let's go. Your job is to pull the birds toward you. Remember how you did it last time?"

"Yes." Miroslava gave a pale smile, recalling the past.

"Do the same now. We need to lure them as close to the rock as possible. Then you'll activate the Magnetic Point and pour as many Quarks in as you can." I was curious to see how this would turn out. This strategy had been used many times before in my past life. But lately, my memory of that time had been failing me, and now I was worried about hidden pitfalls. What if there was a crucial detail that had never been publicly mentioned?

We reached the Bird House without any incidents, stopping half a mile away — if we went any farther, Miroslava's Magnetic Field would no longer register the Solid-Metal Sparrows.

"I'll begin," Miroslava closed her eyes. A faint blue glow enveloped her body. The manifestation of abilities in Fielders was always beautiful, unlike those of other Evolvers.

"It's working... but they're resisting. Hold on... Haha, did it just crash into the wall?"

I watched Miroslava murmuring to herself, struck by how beautiful she was. If I really thought about it, she was one of the most beautiful women I'd ever seen. But I was so used to her that I rarely noticed — only in moments like this.

"They're coming! Quick, back to the rock! Ouch, my wrist!"

I carefully scooped Miroslava into my arms and raced back with her.

"There's about thirty of them! Five are bright red, the rest aren't. Those five must be Sentients, right? They're speeding up, Vladislav."

I sped up as well. The rock came into view.

"On my mark!" I shouted as we flew over the massive black-and-blue boulder. The Butterfly fluttered nearby, waiting for commands.

I turned and saw the flock of crimson sparrows hurtling toward us. The creatures were breathtaking — like finely crafted metallic figurines. But five of them stood out — larger, their bodies gleaming like crimson steel, and their bright poppy-like eyes seemed to scan us like X-rays.

"Now!" I yelled as the birds neared the rock.

The blue point flared, and the flock suddenly changed trajectory.

There was a clangor. It sounded like a rain of coins clattering into a copper basin — the Sparrows smashed into the rock, their beaks crumpling, their bodies twisting on impact. The Magnetic Point had worked perfectly — not a single monster escaped the trap.

"Whoa!" Miroslava gasped in amazement.

"Butterfly, oh Butterfly. Will you kill them, please? I don't want to waste Neutrinos — I have too few left as it is."

I had to activate DNA Fusion again to issue the command. The Butterfly swooped down on the flailing monsters.

Solid-Metal Sparrows weren't just capable of shooting their feathers like projectiles — they could control them as well. A single one of these creatures was like a small army. But now, the five Sentients were completely powerless, unable to lift even their beaks from the rock, let alone launch feathers.

The Butterfly's eyes suddenly glowed. Two laser beams shot straight through the first Sentient's head, piercing it completely. The monster twitched several times, then went still. The Butterfly turned to the next target.

"She can fire from her eyes too?! This Butterfly is incredible!" Miroslava marveled. Then her expression darkened. "Vladislav, I'm sensing an impulse! I think more sparrows are headed this way!"

"Activate your tattoo and be ready to cancel your ability! Wait near the Mole's body!" I released Miroslava, and she took off. As the Butterfly systematically executed the Sentients, I finished off the Alphas.

"Cancel it now!"

The point on the rock vanished. In the distance, I could already see a crimson cloud approaching — we had to hurry.

I ordered the Butterfly to return to the slope, avoiding the Ant Nest. Then, with a gust of wind, I knocked the Sparrow corpses off the rock, sending them tumbling down to the Coal Mole.

"They're yours!"

Miroslava immediately started gathering the bodies. I descended and touched the dead Mole. Stretching out my free hand, I placed it against the translucent pyramid.

Just before I vanished, I heard an enraged avian screech.

Inside the pyramid, I yanked my hand back immediately. The Mole's corpse was lethal — even brief contact had burned straight through my glove, leaving my skin blackened and cracked, with darkened muscles underneath.

"I couldn't take all of them," Miroslava said in disappointment. "Only ten birds."

I cast her a quick glance and headed for the exit. The important thing was that she had retrieved all the Sentients.

On the way, I called my grandfather. To my surprise, he was out of reach.

"Should I call Miss Majewski?" Miroslava offered as she followed behind me.

"Yeah, go ahead," I replied absentmindedly, checking my phone. I opened my email and found a message from my grandfather:

I'm heading to the Asian Commonwealth. The Li clan has major problems. Find out what new potion the Brittas brewed — they're contractually obligated to tell either me or you. Stop by the lab, there's an issue with that box of yours. Felix is in Australia, but he's unreachable for now. Nikki Chan from your list needs help — this is your chance.

CHAPTER 25

PERSONAL SECRETARY

THE FIRST THING I DID was get some proper rest. I hadn't set an alarm, so I slept for twelve hours — maybe more. My Neutrino had almost fully recovered. The first thing I did after waking up was create two Mental Vortices. Each took twenty percent of my Neutrinos, so I decided to make the rest later.

After breakfast, I got down to business.

"Vladislav?" A plump face filled the screen — Georgie Brittas. "I barely recognize you. You're looking good."

"You're throwing compliments in the wrong place," I muttered. "What's this new potion? What does it do?"

"Vladislav," Georgie adjusted his tie with exaggerated importance. "I'm reaching out to discuss a partnership. We've developed a new formula, but its components are too costly for our family alone. We're looking for investors. Have you heard about our raid? It was a resounding success, I must say."

"I heard that half the participants had gotten killed, and the Brittas family is deep in debt." I had to hold back a chuckle. A resounding success, huh? I'd already checked their situation over breakfast. The news wasn't great — Blood Propane hadn't helped Weak Evolvers take down stronger monsters.

"Even half our raid's losses are still less than yours," Georgie waved a pudgy hand dismissively. "And those debts are nothing to us. So I can say with confidence — the raid was a success. I'd even call it a resounding success!"

"Sure, if you say so. What's the potion? Tell me how it works, and I'll think about your proposal."

The media in the United States of Europica had called the Brittas raid the "disaster of the century." No one in the entire Solar System considered it a success. The Evolvers hadn't even managed to retrieve the monsters' corpses — they'd just fled when the killing started. Some success.

"Our potion is a top-tier product, incredibly potent — divine, even! A true blessing from Poseidon himself. In fact, we named it Poseidon's Spit."

I barely stopped myself from grimacing. Awful name.

"Poseidon's Spit grants dominion over water," Georgie announced proudly.

"Lets you breathe underwater?" I asked after a moment's thought. In my past life, this potion had been known as Miller's Elixir.

"Yes…" Georgie deflated. "How did you know?"

"Send me the formula," I said, stifling my disappointment. I hadn't expected truly advanced and intriguing elixirs this soon, but there had been a flicker of hope.

"What about investments?" Georgie tensed at my expression. "I want to refine the formula with components from Sentient monsters. Let's make a deal. I need monsters, and you'll get potions in return. Poseidon's Spit is the best—" He trailed off. "Haven't figured out the slogan yet, but I will! The recipe will be delivered today. As you can imagine, this is top-secret information. I sent two hundred people to your grandfather's principality, but only one of them has the formula. If our enemies start picking them off, the chances—"

"I'll message you later. I have urgent matters to attend to." I cut the video call and closed my eyes for a few seconds. Georgie was exhausting to deal with.

My next destination was the lab. I spent five hours there — in complete secrecy. The moment I stepped out, a tall woman — easily six and a half feet in heels — rushed toward me. One look at her, and the word giantess popped into my head.

"Fladislaf!" she said with a thick accent. "I prought you a package!"

She handed me a folder. I took it, still unsure how this uninvited guest had even gotten in. The moment the package was in my hands, she clicked her heels and teleported away.

The facility's alarms blared. Armed guards poured out of the buildings.

Ignoring the commotion, I opened the folder. Inside was the formula for Poseidon's Spit — damn it. I wasn't mad at Georgie — he'd just exposed a glaring flaw in our security. Those who could teleport could infiltrate and escape undetected. Let Grandfather figure out how to fix that.

I scanned the formula and scoffed. One of the key ingredients was the saliva of a Silkworm monster. The Brittas were the foremost experts on those insects, but how had they managed to develop a formula like this?

"Vladislav." Oleg approached and gave a slight bow. "Apologies for the delay."

"It's fine. Is the plane to Hong Kong ready?"

"Yes."

"Then let's go." I tucked away the formula, and we headed for the waiting transport. "Time to pay Nikki Chan a visit."

During the flight, I maintained a cold, focused state, reviewing my grandfather's business affairs. Oleg had brought a briefcase stuffed with documents. Recently, leaks had become more frequent, forcing Grandfather to transition back to paper records.

It was clear — the Li family was on the brink of collapse. They'd already lost more than half their enterprises. Only their hold on the military-industrial sector and contracts with the army were keeping them afloat. But just a few days ago, several generals had turned against the Li family, shaking Ming Li's position. The new head of the family couldn't make decisions on his own, forcing Grandfather to travel personally to the Commonwealth.

There wasn't much he could do — it was a foreign country, after all. But he had aces up his sleeve — the formulas for the first elixir and Blood Propane. I was sure he'd find a way to ease the pressure on the Li family.

However, I didn't believe he'd succeed. Military-grade weapons — laser and electric blasters, plasma rifles, energy shields, and various cannons — were strictly off-limits to private armies and civilians. Owning such weaponry could wipe out an entire family — there were precedents for that. Government power was built on the monopoly of cutting-edge arms. Any family that tried to break into the weapons industry stood to gain immense profits, but also faced severe restrictions.

Yet plenty were willing to take that risk. The Zhou family — the one Mei Feng hailed from — was especially aggressive.

Major General Zhou was the one who had framed General Wu and his daughter, Yanling. I'd promised to help her take revenge. Now it looked like I needed to accelerate those plans.

Not everything was going badly. The Epsilon Syndicate was thriving. It now had branches in Beijing, Shanghai, Yekaterinburg, Moscow, Novgorod, Brussels, Kinshasa, and on the Moon. Beijing was particularly impressive — Lilit was doing an outstanding job. The Beijing branch of the Epsilon Syndicate had over seven thousand Evolvers. Among them, two hundred and sixty-three were Weak. No other branch had numbers like that. These people were scattered across various mountains, but the most important thing was that they were buying our virtual currency, Trigono. They were paid in Liquid Cores and purchased weapons, suits, intelligence, Blood Propane, and helium-3 cubes. They also ordered potions, though mass production was still a challenge. They were driving the growth of our organization, and that was a beautiful thing.

At the moment, Trigono was the most sought-after virtual currency among Evolvers. None of the others could compete — not even the Clowns' Evocoins.

Our reputation was also at an all-time high. After the recent events, many people had joined the Epsilon Syndicate, eager to be part of something greater. But the stronger we became, the harsher the attacks in the media. And there was no way to stop that. Even if I saved the world, they would still harp on about my Lunar connections, the countless casualties, and so on, and so on...

To my disappointment, Egghead wasn't in any rush to enter the Primordial World. Getting a hefty paycheck from my grandfather, Vadim had grown completely lazy — he didn't want to do anything himself. Was Evocom not going to appear in this life?

Grandfather's reports emphasized Lilit's achievements. Thanks to her time-slowing ability, she had become a key figure in the joint army of my mother and grandfather, and now her squad was the dominant force on their mountain. If they had some strategic assistance, I was sure they could take down a Sentient monster on their own.

There were also updates that weren't directly tied to me. Research into Crystallite technology was ongoing. The biggest question on everyone's mind was how to recharge them. Many of the "fingers" had already been drained, and no one knew what to do about it.

To my surprise, large-scale development had begun on the nearest large asteroid. Robots had already been sent to work on it, and soon, a trickle of much-needed natural resources would start flowing to Earth.

"Twenty minutes to arrival," Oleg interrupted my review of the Epsilon Syndicate's economic projections.

"Alright. Have the plane stay on standby — we won't be in Hong Kong for long."

"Next stop Paris?"

"Yes, to see Liang." I packed up the documents in my briefcase, pulling out a single sheet — the complete dossier on Nikki Chan.

There was nothing particularly remarkable about her background. She had grown up in a military family, served her term, and worked as a secretary. A year before the Eclipse, she had joined an international technology company with shares held by multiple major families.

And now, the moment I had been waiting for had arrived — Nikki Chan had crossed paths with the heir of the Meng family. She needed help, fast.

I had been keeping an eye on potential candidates for my personal secretary — someone to take on all the dullest, most tedious burdens. These were people who, in my past life, had never betrayed those they worked for, not even in the face of death.

Nikki Chan was a dogmatist to her very core. She adhered strictly to her principles and would never turn away from them.

"There's a problem," Oleg muttered, frowning at his phone. We were speeding along a newly built aqueduct — one of Hong Kong's major highways — the cityscape outside blurring into a single streak. "Our people report that Nikki is being dragged by force to the top floor. Most likely to Meng's office."

"Stop the car."

The sleek black Turbo slowed and pulled over to the side of the road.

"Inform the city authorities that I'm flying. And make sure they understand — if they don't want a tornado on their heads, they'd better stay out of my way. Head back to the airport — I'll meet you there."

"Understood. Take this headset — I'll guide you to the exact location." Oleg handed me a small case and began typing out a message.

I put on the earpiece, stepped out of the car, and soared into the sky. Hong Kong was the city of highways. Thrill-seekers flocked here just to experience the rush.

I knew where I was headed. The headquarters of Hsu Miao Corporation stood out even among Hong Kong's countless skyscrapers. A spiraling tower of glass and steel, it seemed to challenge anyone who dared to look at it.

I surrounded myself with wind and shot

straight for the skyscraper. The flight took only a few minutes.

"You need to circle around," Oleg's voice crackled in my ear.

I did as he said and soon found the right floor. I flew up to a window and shattered the armored glass with a transformed fist. Large shards crashed onto the plush carpet.

What I saw inside was a thoroughly disgusting tableau.

Two bodyguards were tearing the clothes off a struggling woman. Another man lay curled up on the floor, gripping his groin in agony — he had clearly taken a nasty hit. Meanwhile, a young man, no older than twenty, stood in his underwear, groping Nikki's chest and slapping her face, laughing.

Only the whimpering guard saw me. The others, their backs to the window, hadn't even noticed the sudden cold draft or the new presence in the room.

"Do you even realize who you just rejected, you bitch?" the Meng heir spat. "You think I'm a joke? You humiliated me in front of everyone, you worthless—"

He never finished. A blade of wind sliced through his shoulder, severing his arm at the joint. Blood sprayed across the room. Air bullets punched through the bodyguards' heads, and they crumpled to the floor. The director collapsed right after them — he had fainted.

"Get up." I stepped toward the sobbing Nikki. "I won't wait long."

Still sniffling, she got to her feet and pulled on her pants. Then she reached for her bra. I didn't stop her — I was busy tying off the stump of the would-be rapist's arm. Couldn't let him bleed out. The Li family had been deep enough in trouble as it was.

I heard footsteps — people were rushing this way.

"I'm ready," Nikki's voice was shaky.

"Then let's go." I cast one last glance at the guy lying in a pool of his own blood, scooped up the frail young woman, and jumped out the window.

Nikki was twenty-six and barely reached my chest. A short-haired Asian woman — not exactly a beauty, but pleasant-looking.

"You're Vladislav Li? Elder of the family? Head of the Syndicate? Delta?" She had calmed down and was now studying me.

"Yes. Want to work for me? I won't shortchange you on salary, and I'll help you become an Evolver."

"What kind of work?" she asked hesitantly.

"You'll be my personal secretary. The only thing I require is loyalty. If you agree, we start today."

She was silent for a few minutes. By then, I was already nearing the airport. Drones had spotted me, but they didn't interfere — just watched from a distance.

"I accept," she finally said. "I swear to serve you faithfully."

Relief washed over me. I knew I could trust her. I'd read the reports about how she had been tortured in vain for information about the Meng family. In my past life, she had worked for them.

"If you have any personal belongings or unfinished business, tell Oleg — he'll take care of it. Right now, we're flying to Paris. On the way, Oleg and I will bring you up to speed."

"Understood."

I landed near the airstrip just as a car pulled up to meet us. I knew I was breaking all sorts of laws — flying so brazenly here wasn't exactly legal. But we had to move fast before the Meng family recovered from the shock.

Oleg picked us up and drove straight to the plane. The entire flight to Paris, we talked with Nikki. I even told her about Muhiddin and handed her a phone — she'd be the one keeping in touch with him from now on.

At the moment, Muhiddin was in Warsaw, trying to recruit a new member for the group. But he seemed to be running into some complications.

"We're approaching," Oleg announced. "While you visit your friend, I'll take Nikki shopping. She needs to dress the part."

Nikki blushed and adjusted her blazer.

"Of course," I agreed easily. "And introduce her to Grandfather and Mother. From now on, all news goes through her first. By the way, Nikki, are you afraid of the Primordial World? You'll have to enter it and become an Evolver."

"I'm not," she said, paling a little.

"Good." I yawned. I hated flying in planes. But traveling through the air unaided wasn't an option — I wasn't strong enough to pull that off just yet.

I barely glanced at Paris — my car was waiting to take me straight to the hotel.

The team already knew I'd be in town today. Some, like Dumisa and Wang Bolai, had arrived in advance and were waiting at the hotel. Miroslava and Natsuko had taken off as soon as I messaged them.

Nitya, however, was stuck in India. Grandfather's people were trying to help, but she had run into trouble at the border. It was unlikely she'd be able to visit Liang.

The next morning, everyone who had made it to Paris gathered at the hospital where Liang was recovering.

When I arrived, Natsuko, Dumisa, and Wang Bolai were already waiting at the entrance. It was strange seeing them dressed like this. Natsuko wore a sleek black dress. Dumisa — of all people — was in a tuxedo. Wang Bolai had opted for a yellow hoodie and jeans.

"Vladislav, you haven't changed a bit!" Natsuko exclaimed. "But look at Dumisa! Without his gauntlets and combat suit, he looks like a congressman, don't you think?"

"A chief is a chief, no matter what he wears," Wang Bolai said respectfully.

"Are we late?!" I heard Miroslava's voice.

She wasn't alone — Yanling was with her. Both were dressed casually, in hoodies and sunglasses.

"No, you're on time," I said with a smile.

"You think we're as famous here as we are back home?" Natsuko eyed Miroslava and Yanling's outfits with curiosity.

"I'm just used to covering my face," Miroslava admitted, suddenly realizing we had walked in without disguises.

"Alright, let's go." I waved them forward.

Liang had been expecting us. His hospital room was one of the best — spacious, well-lit, with a comfortable bed and a workstation. Liang was sitting in a wheelchair, dressed in a hospital gown, smiling. A thin stern-looking woman with short hair sat at his desk, writing something. She looked about forty, maybe forty-five.

"You have no idea how happy I am to see your faces!" Liang beamed. "Everyone, meet my personal secretary — Camelia Giordano."

The woman stood, gave a polite bow, and left.

"Since when do you have a personal secretary?" Natsuko asked, the first to approach him, giving him a friendly pat on the shoulder.

"I'm an important man now," Liang boasted, wheeling himself toward the table. "I've founded a charity foundation, you know? We even designed some promotional flyers."

He grabbed a stack of papers and handed them out.

I took one — and couldn't hold back a laugh.

It featured Liang in his wheelchair, dressed in a yellow jacket and a green tie. A green blanket covered his lower half, where his legs should have been. On the floor in front of him sat a pair of red leather shoes with white laces. At the top was a cryptic acronym — SKL. And below it, the slogan: "Even the legless deserve shoes!"

"Here's another one," Liang handed out a second flyer.

This one showed a pair of tiny children's sandals on a sandy beach.

The same three letters — SKL — were at the top.

And beneath them: "Shoes for the little ones!"

"Well? What do you think?" Liang squinted smugly.

"So it's true you used to sell shoes at a market?" Natsuko eyed him sideways.

"Actually, no! But does it matter? If the whole world believes it, I might as well roll with it."

"What does SKL even mean?"

"Saaaandals for Kiiiids by Liiiang!" Liang declared theatrically, like a ring announcer hyping up a fight.

"...That's terrible."

"Sandals for Kids by Liang? What kind of nonsense is that?"

"I like it," Miroslava smiled.

"Liang, is it true they... you know... injured you down there?" Wang Bolai covered his groin with both hands.

"Yeah," Liang sighed, casting a glance at Yanling. She was busy examining the flyers. "But luckily, they've managed to fix it. Had to shrink things down to a third of the original size, but hey — it still works. Before, I could've given a Giant Gorilla a run for its money, but now... Ah, well. At least now it's human-sized."

While Liang spun his yarn with a straight face and the others laughed at his expense, I stepped away. A message from my mother had just arrived.

The One Who Changes the Future

I opened it — and couldn't help but smile.

> *Lily and I are in Novgorod. Come here after Paris — she wants to talk to you. And don't forget a gift!*

CHAPTER 26

MEETING WITH LILY

LILY WAS IN NOVGOROD? But how? The answer was obvious — the same way Adele had ended up in Yekaterinburg from the Primordial World in my past life. Crystallite technology.

After I became a Strong Human, Grandfather and I had talked a lot about the Crystal Fingers. He had mentioned that he could now trade for or purchase them and had asked me to identify artifacts from photographs.

I returned to the hospital room. Liang was passionately recounting his exploits to the others.

"...And then I created a Gravity Palm and crushed three Sentients at once! Just snapped them like twigs! Butterflies are so dumb, I'm telling you. Vladislav said they're the dumbest Sentients — but also extremely dangerous. When that thing started cloning itself, I didn't even have time to react. That's how I lost my legs. But it's fine — Nitya will fix it, right, Boss?"

Trying to ignore the reproachful look Mira was giving me, I nodded.

"She already has a Core prepared. As soon as we meet, she'll become Strong and take care of your treatment."

"Heh-heh. I can't wait to get back to the Primordial World. Let's meet there, yeah?" Liang grinned. "Have you seen what they call me online? The Legless King!"

"Pfft." Natsuko scoffed. "You think we don't know you're calling yourself that from anonymous accounts? Just accept your real nickname — Shoe Merchant."

"I'm the Invisible Fist, actually!" Liang protested. "And the Legless King!"

"More like the Legless Shoe Salesman."

"Hey, I'm a patient, remember? Why are you bullying a sick man?"

Natsuko didn't have a response for that.

"Yanling, how long are you staying in Paris? Want me to show you around the city?" Liang forced a smile. "I may be legless, but I can still fly."

"I need to go back to Beijing," she shook her head. She was unusually quiet today, withdrawn, her mind clearly elsewhere.

"You've decided, then?" I spoke up. "Come with me — I have something for you."

Yanling nodded.

"See you later," Liang waved awkwardly.

As we left, the last thing I heard was Wang Bo-lai giving Liang advice.

"You need to be bolder, brother. Practice on Dumisa first — just imagine he's a girl."

"Oh, up yours..."

Their voices faded as Yanling and I walked down the spacious corridor.

"The heart of the Triad is in Hong Kong," I began. "There's a group called the Devourers of Life. Heard of them?"

Yanling slowly nodded.

"I'm in contact with them. Their next target is the Triad — they plan to raid their armories and Core stockpiles."

"How does that help me get revenge?" Yanling frowned.

"First, weaken the Triad economically — make them panic. You won't be able to reach Major General Zhou in Beijing — he's untouchable there, even for me. But that old man is a lecher. He has countless mistresses. He has a private estate in Hong Kong — a harem where he plays god. And it's the Triad that protects it."

Memories flashed through my mind. In my past life, I had read reports about that mansion, and they were outrageous — Zhou had gathered over a hundred women there.

"All roads lead to Hong Kong," I continued. "That's where you'll get your revenge — not in Beijing."

"How do you know all this?" Yanling bit her lower lip.

"I know a lot of things." My lips curled into a bitter smirk. If only that knowledge didn't fail me so often...

"I have two pieces of advice for you. Want to hear them?"

Yanling nodded.

"First — ask Liang for help."

"Him?" Yanling frowned in confusion.

"Yes. Liang is the heir to the Fo family — the last survivor."

Her eyes widened, mouth slightly open.

"But he wants to clear his ancestors' name — that's why he started a charity. Liang doesn't want to be involved with the Triad. But he has connections — people from his family still follow him. Don't underestimate him. A pushover wouldn't have become a Strong Human so quickly. And he wasn't lying — he really did take out three Sentients in one attack. The Cores he gathered will help strengthen the Syndicate."

If only I were as confident in Liang as I made him sound... Hopefully, he wouldn't resent me for this. Yanling wouldn't betray his secret or hold him accountable for his family's sins. And who knows? Maybe something would come of it between them.

"My second piece of advice — don't rush into this until you're Strong. Whether you listen or not is up to you. I've sent you my secretary's number. Use it to contact the Life Eaters. They're complete lunatics, so be careful."

"Thank you," Yanling bowed deeply. "I won't

forget this."

"I promised, didn't I?" I didn't hold back my smile. "When the time comes, I'll help you kill that old man myself. And if you want to go further — I'll help you wipe out the entire Zhou family."

Yanling tilted her head slightly as if listening to something. Then she turned and walked back toward Liang's room.

I followed. It was time to say goodbye to the others and head to Novgorod.

I would have liked to visit Adele, but she had entered the Primordial World, and there was no telling when she'd return. I'd see her later.

"...I'm telling you, we took out the Butterflies, climbed inside the Sentient flower, and took a nap for a few hours! Then we woke up and went right back to hunting Sentients. Ask Vladislav — he'll confirm it."

When Yanling and I entered, the room fell silent.

"You really slept inside a Sentient flower?" Miroslava asked skeptically.

"We did," I nodded. "That flower was home to the Butterflies."

"See?" Liang beamed triumphantly. "And you didn't believe me!"

"I just came to say goodbye. I'm heading to Novgorod — to see my mother. I'll message you when I'm ready to enter the Primordial World."

"Can I come with you?" Miroslava asked unexpectedly. "I've heard a lot about that city, but I've never seen it."

"Of course," I nodded.

After a brief farewell, Miroslava and I left the room. We walked in silence for a while.

"...Why did you lie?" she muttered. "I believed you."

"I don't know what you're talking about."

"The Butterflies. You said they were really smart."

"Did I?"

"Yes!"

"You must have misheard."

"...You're mean."

*　*　*

Six hours later

The room was silent. I was already in Novgorod, in my mother's estate. But neither she nor Lily were here yet.

The door swung open. My mother entered — tall, red-haired, green-eyed. She had always been beautiful, but after becoming an Evolver, she had grown even younger and more radiant. She wore light-colored trousers, a blouse, and a blazer — she rarely dressed in anything else. A tablet was in her hands.

Beside her, Lily came running in, dragging Bumsy Senior by the leg — the once-white plush toy had turned into something gray and filthy. A live simian scurried along behind her, its head bobbing comically as it trotted.

"Vladislav!" Lily shouted. It was clear she hadn't spoken in a while — her voice was a bit strained. Her oversized clothes made her look ridiculous — a white sweater with rolled-up sleeves that reached her calves. Her face was smudged with dirt, and her bare feet were filthy.

She skidded to a stop in front of me and tilted her head up.

"Where's my present?"

I couldn't hold back a smile and patted her on the head. Lily had changed — no more dark circles under her eyes, and no more sickly pallor. The fact that she had even walked this far was proof of her recovery. Her light-colored hair stuck up in odd directions, making her head look like a little mushroom cap.

"Your gift... First, go get cleaned up and brush your hair. You look like a tiny and a very dirty mushroom, not a lady. Didn't you have proper clothes?"

"She's extremely picky," my mother said with a faint grimace.

"I'm not a mushroom!" Lily huffed. "Bumsy, tell him!"

The golden ape gave me a fierce look. It began to grow until it was my height.

I activated DNA Fusion, instantly linking two spirals. Two Mental Vortices shot from my head — but I didn't need them. The moment I started transforming, Bumsy Junior let out a squeak and scurried behind Lily.

But what was surprising — the two Mental

Vortices couldn't overpower Bumsy's mind. I had to retract them quickly before they dissipated inside this strange little ape's head.

Once again, I wondered — what exactly was this creature? Where had it even come from? The Titan Gorilla had asked me to take it to Earth, saying the baby was harmless. But she had lied — this monkey had unusual abilities. According to my mother, the only reason the other apes obeyed Lily was because of Bumsy.

"Bumsy Junior is afraid of you?" Lily looked bewildered. "He's never been scared of anyone... Even when a giant elephant with red ears attacked us, Bumsy drove it away."

"I'm not an elephant, little mushroom girl. And my ears aren't red."

"I'm not a mushroom!"

"Go wash up and put on proper clothes. Then we'll talk. And leave Bumsy Senior here. What did you even do to it? Wipe the floors with it?"

"I didn't wipe any floors..."

"You trampled the poor toy's dignity. Leave it here — I'll fix it."

Lily hesitated. I pressed her.

"Leave it. I gave it to you, so I'll fix it, and you'll have it back. Don't worry. But you need to clean up first — I don't want to talk to a mushroom girl."

"You're a mushroom yourself!" Lily spun to Bumsy Junior. "Tell him something!"

The little ape shook its head, eyeing me warily. Come to think of it, Bumsy Junior wasn't the first simian to act like this. The Titan Gorilla had run off the first time we met, too. It had to be because of the Titan Gorilla's Liquid Core — the one that had turned me into an Evolver.

"…Fine," Lily sighed. "Here, just don't hurt him!"

She held out the toy. I took it between two fingers, trying not to grimace. A maid approached. My mother, who had been watching us with interest the whole time, gestured toward Lily.

"Where's his leg?" I asked, inspecting Bumsy Senior with pity. "And his eyes? Why is his belly ripped open? Where are his insides?"

Lily stuck out her tongue and ran off after the maid. The monkey shrank back to its usual size and bounced after her.

"You're in an unusually good mood," my mother remarked with a smile once the door closed. "She's closer to you than I thought. She never listens to me. The only reason she agreed to come was because I told her you had a gift for her."

"Do you have someone who can fix this?" I held up Bumsy Senior. "No replacements — she'll notice. I need someone who can repair it properly. And use high-quality materials from the Primordial World."

"You just promised to fix it yourself," my mother teased but typed something into her phone.

A uniformed soldier in gloves entered, took Bumsy Senior, and carried him away.

"Did you actually prepare a gift for her?"

I pulled a string of wooden prayer beads from

my pocket. Round, smooth, and calming.

My mother raised an eyebrow.

"They're made of sandalwood," I explained. "I saw them and bought them. What else could I give a girl like Lily? Shoes? A hair clip?"

"Good point," she murmured. "Aren't you curious how I got her out?"

"Crystallite technology, how else?" I shrugged.

"So you figured it out... Who is Nikki Chan?"

"My personal secretary. I trust her completely. Send all documents through her."

"When did you start trusting total strangers so much?" My mother wasn't ready to drop the subject.

"That's a secret," I smirked.

She narrowed her eyes at me for a few seconds, then sighed.

"We've discovered a few more monsters with Sentient-level intelligence. Take a look." She handed me the tablet. "Let's sit down. It'll take a while to get that little one cleaned up — she's completely feral after living with the apes."

We took our seats. Mentally, I noted how much my mother had changed since the Eclipse. I remembered her visit to the hospital when a Gray-Eyed Bear had devoured my arm. Back then, it had taken serious effort to convince her that it wasn't time for me to leave Beijing — she had wanted to take me with her despite my protests.

But I knew why her attitude had changed. She had come to respect my strength. If I were still the weakling I had been before my rebirth, she wouldn't be treating me with such deference. She loved me, but in her own way.

"Stay away from that thing," I muttered, shuddering at the image on the screen. "Don't mess with it at all. That's a Honey Badger."

I didn't mention that the creature was an Alpha, not a Sentient. In my past life, it had been called the Mad Overlord. It belonged to the same class of unique Alphas as the Snow Leopard, Lord of Silver, or Bai Hu, Lord of the Wind.

"A Honey Badger?" My mother frowned.

"Yes. Even on Earth, honey badgers are considered the most gung-ho mammals of them all. And in the Primordial World, they're completely insane — they feel no fear. And their abilities are powerful. Even a pack of monster-hounds isn't as dangerous as a single Honey Badger."

I meant every word. Honey badgers were the lunatics of the monster world. Even now, with all my abilities, I wouldn't dare go near the Mad Overlord.

"I see," my mother nodded. "And the other monsters?"

She showed me four in total. Three of them were indeed Sentient, but each was far too dangerous.

"How about you become Strong first?" I suggested. "Fighting any of these could cost you your life. But if you were Strong, you could take them down. Especially that Rooster — his weakness is his eyes."

I handed the tablet back to my mother, thinking. Should I give her one of the Cores now? Or later?

I had seven Liquid Cores. Five were reserved for the Syndicate. Two were meant for Black, but I still had a couple of days before our meeting. I could gather more if I pushed myself.

My mother glanced at the tablet, about to say something, but I spoke first.

"Let's fly to Yekaterinburg. I have a Sentient Core for you there."

She narrowed her eyes, locking onto me with her gaze.

"And what about your debt to Black?"

"There's still time." I shrugged.

She turned away, her eyes clouded. Conflicted — her desire for strength clashed with her unwillingness to burden me.

At that moment, the door opened, and a soldier entered, holding the repaired toy.

Bumsy Senior had been completely transformed — clean white fur, and dressed in a violet outfit. His eyes gleamed black with silver specks at the center. A tiny golden crown perched on his head.

I took the toy hesitantly, noting the golden stitching on its paws. The outfit was clearly made from monster hide.

Once the soldier left, I asked, "Are you sure this is the same toy? Not a new one?"

"It is the same toy, don't you worry," my mother replied, shaking off her thoughts. "I had people ready in advance to repair it. But the girl was reluctant to give it up."

"That was fast work... And the crown?"

"The designers' whim," she chuckled.

The door creaked open again. The toy's owner had come to claim it — and she made quite the entrance, perched on the shoulders of a massive golden ape.

Lily had been washed, groomed, and dressed. She looked entirely different, but the stubborn expression on her face remained the same.

"Well, at least you're no longer a little mushroom girl," I noted.

Lily nimbly leapt off the monkey and ran up to me. She snatched Bumsy Senior, eyes wide.

"He's the King of the Monkeys now!" she declared, showing the toy to Junior.

The golden monkey respectfully bowed its head before its older "brother."

"And where's my gift?" Lily turned back to me expectantly.

"Here you go," I handed her the prayer beads.

She took them skeptically, rolling them between her fingers.

"...This is kind of lame," she muttered but still slipped them around her neck.

"Alright, we're heading to Yekaterinburg," I decided. "Lily, you're coming with us. Tell your monkey to shrink back down, or we're leaving him here."

"He's not a monkey!" Lily huffed.

"Oh? Then what is he?" I smirked, typing a message to Nika and Miroslava. "Do you know?"

"Uh... He's Bumsy Junior," she said, petting the now-shrunken ape.

"That's his name. But what kind of monkey is he? He's not a gorilla, right?"

"Monkeys can't grow big," she countered. "So Bumsy isn't a monkey."

"Who says they can't? They totally can. You just haven't seen it — monkeys keep that secret."

"Is the plane ready?" I glanced at my mother.

"Yes," she said with a slight smile.

"Then let's go."

It didn't take long to get ready. We were driven to the airport, where Nikki and Miroslava were already waiting.

"Adele Von Belga is at her branch right now," Nikki reported as we boarded. "You've asked me to track her movements."

I didn't change my plans. I'd reach out to Adele from Novgorod. It had been a while since I'd heard her voice.

Miroslava and Lily bonded quickly. The entire flight, Lily told stories about the Primordial World — some of which sent shivers down my spine. Like the time a fat snake crawled into her bed at night and started coiling around her. Bumsy Junior hadn't liked that. He had crushed the reptile's head. And there were plenty of stories like that...

When we landed and stepped off the plane, Nikki suddenly slowed.

"Vladislav, this is important," she said quietly.

I took her phone and read the message:

Meet me in Brussels, at Grand Place. Tomorrow

at 8 PM local time. Come alone. I'll be there in person. We have something important to discuss.

It was from Black.

* * *

United States of Europica
United Kingdom District

"You did well," Lady said, her cold gaze fixed on Allen as he bowed his head.

"As a reward, you'll receive a Sentient Core."

She snapped her fingers, and the Hatter approached. His face was as expressionless as a plaster mask, but his eyes simmered with resentment. None of Lady's inner circle had ever received as much in their entire lives as this little upstart had in a matter of days.

"A Sentient's Core...?" Allen's eyes bulged. "You have one? But how—"

"Don't ask unnecessary questions."

"...Yes. Forgive me." Allen's hands trembled as he pulled on his gloves.

While he fumbled with the cube, Lady examined her own reflection in the silver blade she held. Her face, her movements, her steady breathing — none of them betrayed the storm inside her. Only her eyes hinted at the chaos of emotions raging within.

"Are you done?" she asked, lifting her gaze.

"Y-y-yes," Allen stammered, wiping his sweaty forehead.

"Come closer and tell me what ability you got."

The Hatter and two other attendants subtly stepped away, already understanding.

Allen approached and whispered, "The ability is called… Hole."

"You're dismissed." Lady nodded. "Go to the Primordial World and wait for the Syndicate there."

"Yes, ma'am." Allen bowed deeply and backed away. He looked ridiculous, but no one laughed.

"Is the plane ready?" Lady asked.

"Yes," the Hatter replied, stepping closer.

"Then we're leaving."

Lady slid the knife into her sleeve and strode toward the exit. It was time to head to Brussels.

End of Book Three

Want to be the first to know about our latest LitRPG, sci fi and fantasy titles from your favorite authors?

Subscribe to our **New Releases** newsletter:
http://eepurl.com/b7niIL

Thank you for reading *The One Who Changes the Future!*

If you like what you've read, check out other sci fi, fantasy and LitRPG novels published by Magic Dome Books:

NEW RELEASES!

The Selected
A LitRPG Action Adventure Series
by Vasily Mahanenko & Yuri Vinokuroff

Nanomachines
A Progression Fantasy Adventure Series
by Nikolai Novikov

We Are Legion
A RealRPG Action Adventure Series
by Dmitry Dornichev & Evgeny Fox

The Dark Summoner
A Portal Progression Fantasy Series
by Andrei Tkachev

The Other Side
A Progression Fantasy Adventure Series
by Rodion Korablev

The Dark Healer
A Historical Progression Fantasy Series
by Alex Toxic & Nadya Lee

Me and My Demons
A Portal Progression Adventure Fantasy Series
by Oleg Sapphire & Alexey Kovtunov

The Coming of God of Death

A Portal Progression Fantasy Series

by Dmitry Dornichev

The Village

A LitRPG Progression Fantasy Series

by Dmitry Dornichev & Alexey Kovtunov

Condemned (Lord Valevsky: Last of the Line)

A Progression Fantasy LitRPG Series

by Vasily Mahanenko

Living Ice

A Portal Progression Fantasy Series

by Dmitry Sheleg

Ghost in the System

An Apocalypse LitRPG Series

by Alexey Kovtunov

The Goldenblood Heir

A Portal Progression Fantasy Series

by Boris Romanovsky

Law of the Jungle

A Wuxia Progression Fantasy Adventure Series

by Vasily Mahanenko

Crossroads of Oblivion

A Portal Progression Fantasy Adventure Series

by Dem Mikhailov

The Healer's Way

A Portal Progression Fantasy Series

by Oleg Sapphire & Alexey Kovtunov

In order to have new books of the series translated faster, we need your help and support! Please consider leaving a review or spread the word by recommending *The One Who Changes the Future* to your friends and posting the link on social media. The more people buy the book, the sooner we'll be able to make new translations available.

Thank you!

Till next time!